# The Voice of the Sea

*and other stories*

Also by Alberto Moravia

## FICTION

*The Woman of Rome*
*The Conformist*
*Two Adolescents (Agostino and Disobedience)*
*The Fancy Dress Party*
*The Time of Indifference*
*Conjugal Love*
*Roman Tales*
*A Ghost at Noon*
*Bitter Honeymoon*
*Two Women*
*The Wayward Wife*
*The Empty Canvas*
*More Roman Tales*
*The Fetish*
*The Lie*
*Command and I Will Obey You*
*Paradise*
*The Two of Us*
**Lady Godiva**

## GENERAL

*Man as an End*
*The Red Book and the Great Wall*
*Which Tribe Do You Belong To?*

## PLAY

**Beatrice Cenci**

# The Voice of the Sea

## *and other stories*

ALBERTO MORAVIA

translated from the Italian by
Angus Davidson

SECKER & WARBURG
LONDON

Published in Italian under the title of *Boh*
Copyright © 1976 by Casa ed. V. Bompiani

First published in England 1978 by
Martin Secker & Warburg Limited
54 Poland Street, London W1V 3DF

English translation copyright
© Martin Secker & Warburg Limited 1978

SBN: 436 28714 5

Printed in Great Britain by
Willmer Brothers Limited, Rock Ferry, Merseyside

# Contents

# Queen of Egypt

⁂

At lunch today, when my husband spoke with disapproval of a woman friend of ours who, so it seems, is being unfaithful to her spouse, I exploded with a heat that surprised me, since I myself did not know that I felt so passionately on the subject: 'Like all men,' I said, 'you're quite naive as regards women, that is, you believe they're what they appear to be. Women all have something childish about them, therefore something innocent – isn't that so, perhaps? No beards, faces that are round or of a delicate oval, great big eyes, tiny noses, very small mouths. They all look like little girls, even when they're fifty years old. And so you men are easily deceived by them. But don't let yourself be led astray by appearances. I'm a woman myself and I know women and I can tell you that there is not one of them, not a single one, that is not false, untruthful, treacherous, faithless and insincere. Only, from the woman's point of view, this falseness of theirs vanishes and takes on another name. That's the point. They're false only in relation to men, not in the absolute sense.'

My husband sniggered, his head bent over his plate. Finally he asked: 'And what is this falseness called, from the woman's point of view, as you express it?'

'It's called imagination, independence, power, freedom, adventure, life and so on.'

'All of them perfectly respectable things, without doubt. But give me an example.'

'An example? I could give you a thousand.'

'One's enough for me.'

Caught unawares, I became nervous, I bit my lips, I raked together the breadcrumbs on the tablecloth with my fingers.

'As for you, with your examples and your fussiness! Well, I don't know. For instance there's a woman I know, still young and very good-looking, who, owing to a burst of imagination, a mad desire for independence, a longing for power, a need for freedom, a taste for adventure, in fact a lust for life, is getting herself into the most incredible muddle.'

'What sort of a muddle?'

'After being courted for years by a rich, elderly man, she has finally become his mistress on condition that he gives her a certain sum of money every time they meet.'

'How does the muddle come in? It's a perfectly simple thing and only too common, anyhow.'

'Wait a moment. This sum of money she hands on, just as it is, to another man, a young man this time, with whom she's in love. And then the money goes to the benefit of a group of revolutionaries. The young man is in love with her, too; but she obstinately refuses herself to him. Their relationship is perfectly chaste.'

'So what – she's a woman who prostitutes herself for a so-called "cause"?'

'No, she's not, seeing that she loves the young man and is loved by him in return. If anything, she prostitutes herself for *him*.'

'By the way, you say that the falseness of women, seen from their point of view, takes on the name of independence. But independence from whom?'

'Independence from her husband. There can't be any other.'

'Oh, that's fine! But why?'

'For a very material reason : because one lives with one's husband, in his house. As everyone knows, one can do without anything, except a roof over one's head. Therefore one's only real dependence is on the owner of the roof.'

'That is, on one's husband.'

'Certainly.'

'So that women are desperate creatures who fear above all things to be thrown out into the street. And who compensate for this dependence by what you call getting into a muddle.'

'That's so, more or less.'

After lunch my husband went to have a rest. He is a man older than me; he might be my father. And he has, in fact, the protective benevolence of a father, the affectionate indulgence and – fortunately for me – the candid illusions. As for me, with all the affection that I have for him, I don't consider him either as a father or as a husband; but rather, just as I had explained to him, as the owner of the roof. True, it is a roof which covers the four hundred square metres of a *de luxe* apartment on the top floor of a small block of flats in the Parioli district. As for saying that I depend upon him, I haven't a penny of my own and, if he threw me out into the street, I should have to go back to my own people in the provinces.

With these thoughts in my mind I went to the other end of the flat and shut myself in my own room; then, lowering my voice to a subdued murmur, I made a couple of telephone calls. While I was telephoning I looked with delight through the french window open on to the terrace; it was a brilliant summer Sunday; my husband had business in town and so kept me with him at the time of the August holiday – to my secret joy because I detest country holidays and holiday-makers. The sun was shining with an intense light which, in contact with the green, motionless foliage of the virginia creeper, seemed transformed into silence. It was just the kind of Sunday I like.

When I had finished telephoning. I opened the wardrobe and selected a dress for the afternoon; something discreet, serious,

**A***

distinguished : a little silk frock that looked almost like a pina-
fore, with two pockets at the front and a belt. Then I held my
face close to the looking-glass in order to touch up my eyes. So
many people have told me that I look like that queen of Egypt,
one of the Pharaohs, the subject of a famous piece of sculpture,
that, when I look at myself in such moments as this, I myself feel
the fascination of my thin, eager face, with its bright, slightly
prominent eyes, its narrow, delicately modelled nose, its sensual,
bitter mouth. I couldn't help it : I gave myself a kiss in the glass.

I went down to the ground floor in the lift, then across the
hall and out into the street. I was met by a cool, light breeze
which made the silk of my dress cling to my legs and stomach.
The car was there, parked all by itself in the sunlit street – a
luxurious, enormous car. My husband says that I look more than
ever like the queen of Egypt when I am at the wheel of the car,
with my enigmatic face thrust forward above my long, thin neck.
He says I really look like an ancient queen in her royal chariot.

I switched on the engine, producing a rich, powerful metallic
hum; meanwhile I was looking up at our apartment building.
Everything there seemed to be asleep, including, no doubt, my
husband. On the third floor two big, orange-coloured curtains
slowly swelled out and then, helped by the wind, fell back again.

Dan-dan-dan-dan-dan, the car glided from the side road into
a long, straight avenue, with plane-trees, tramlines and houses
with closed windows. All was silent and deserted. At the traffic
lights I waited, all alone, for red to change to green. I waited
patiently even though in a sort of way I was impatient : the thing
that was making me impatient became fundamentally more
fascinating if I knew how to be patient.

Dan-dan-dan-dan-dan, the car travelled at a moderate speed
along the suburban avenue, from one deserted set of traffic lights
to the next. I drove calmly, both hands on the wheel, almost
without moving. Then I took a tape – of Stravinsky's *Rite of
Spring* – and inserted it in the radio. It was what I needed to
accompany and express articulately my progress across the town.
I regulated the volume; then I lit a cigarette with the lighter from

the instrument panel.

Dan-dan-dan-dan-dan, we passed over the Tiber, crossed the Piazzale di Ponte Milvio, climbed up along the Via Cassia, reached the fork in the Via Camilluccia, turned off to the left. Then up towards Monte Mario, past densely-planted gardens of invisible villas. One turning, a second turning, a third turning. I threw away my cigarette and moistened my dry lips with my tongue.

When I came near the gate, I stopped the car in a shady place, got out, slipped between the half-closed leaves of the gate, then walked in a leisurely way across the wide gravelled space, my hands in the pockets of my dress, my eyes lowered. On the far side of the open space the villa, with its three rows of closed windows, watched me as I approached. A Great Dane, pink and grey and white, came and sniffed at me in a friendly way, recognizing me, then went off slowly in the direction of a glasshouse full of tropical plants.

Suddenly someone appeared on the threshold of the front door of the villa, between two big terracotta jars overflowing with geraniums: it was a manservant. When I reached the door, he stood aside and allowed me to enter.

How long did I remain in the villa? Let us say, an hour and a half. I came out again by the front door, walked across the gravelled open space with my hands in my pockets and my head bent, as when I arrived. The Great Dane came and sniffed at me in a friendly way, recognized me, and went off slowly in the direction of the glasshouse. As I pushed open the heavy iron gate, I noticed that the sun which, a short time before, had lit up the top part of the villa, had now completely disappeared, leaving the front of the house in shadow. I went out into the road and the light breeze blowing upon me made the silk of my dress cling to my legs and stomach. I got into the car, started it up and drove off.

Dan-dan-dan-dan-dan, how good one feels after having felt bad. Now again I should have liked the journey by car to go on indefinitely – if only to feel myself once more queen of Egypt, my head in profile crowning my thin neck, my two hands resting on the wheel, my mouth wearing an expression of bitter experience. I slipped another tape into the radio, this time Ravel's *Bolero*. The car moved down towards the Via Cassia, from one turning to another. What a marvellous day, what a stupendous day! I was driving with one hand only; with the other I did other things : I lit a cigarette; I passed the palm of my hand over my smooth black hair, gathered, at the back of my neck, into a small, glossy bun; I slipped the last button of my skirt, unaccountably left undone, into its buttonhole; I fumbled blindly to count the banknotes in a large, heavy envelope in the bag at my side. What an incredibly light-hearted, attractive day!

Passing through the Piazzale di Ponte Milvio, I turned along the Tiber Embankment, having on my right the marble buildings of the Foro Italico. I turned on to the bridge at the point where the obelisk stands, passing a couple of traffic lights, then glided at a moderate speed into the cheerful shade of plane-trees in an avenue. At a certain point in this avenue, a dark, shapely young woman in a green sweater and black trousers almost threw herself under the car to make it stop. I braked sharply; the girl came up and spoke to me; I took the envelope with the money in it and handed it to her; she in turn put it into the bag slung over her shoulder and saluted me as she drew back. I started off again.

Dan-dan-dan-dan-dan, as the car sped along beneath the plane-trees and then came to a halt at another chance spot. I turned off the *Bolero,* lit a cigarette and smoked without moving, as though I were meditating. My face expressed no feeling; I knew this and was glad that it should be so. Having finished my cigarette, I started the car again and drove it up the road leading to my own home, on the Parioli hill.

Later, after taking a shower and putting on a dressing-gown, I sat out on the terrace, in the silence and calm of the summer evening. My husband also came and sat on the terrace, before dinner. Again we talked about women; the story of that friend of mine with the two men, one rich and elderly, the other poor and young, who made love with the former in order to finance the political party of the latter with whom, on the other hand, she did not make love, intrigued him. Then I gave him the last news that had reached me about this unusual character: the young man had not put in an appearance at the usual appointment; he had sent a girl, possibly his new girl friend, to fetch the money. My friend, faced with this alteration of plan which upset a difficult equilibrium, felt it her duty to reconsider the whole situation thoroughly before deciding on what she ought to do.

# The Rotund Monster

I read Plato twenty years ago when I was a student and preparing to take a degree in medicine. Of this reading I have retained, more than anything else, the fable of the androgyne, according to which there was, at the origin of the human race, a rotund monster with two heads, four arms, four legs, two backsides and two sexes. Zeus, worried by the vitality of the monster, decided to weaken it and split it into two exact halves, in the same way (as Plato says) as one splits a hard-boiled egg by cutting it with a single horsehair. Ever since then these halves, whether of the female or the male sex, go frenziedly about the world, seeking the half, of opposite sex, that will make them complete and thus permit them to reinstate the rotund monster of their origins. Why did this fable linger on in my memory? Because – at least as far as I myself am concerned – it is not a fable but a truth. In spite of my profession, my culture, my intelligence and my experience, I am perpetually engaged in an anxious and consuming search for my male half. This continuous, desperate search makes me commit follies, such as, for instance, at this moment, when I climb the stairs of a block of working-class flats in search of a certain Mario, a young waiter at a seaside resort, in whose arms I felt myself to be complete barely ten days ago, when I was on holiday in an hotel in the Circeo neighbourhood.

The lift, naturally, was out of order; and so, when I arrived at the sixth floor, after running up twelve flights of stairs, I stood still for at least a minute in front of the door, trying to regain my breath. On a brass plate was written, in italic letters, 'Elda – Milliner', perhaps to create an impression of elegance. Elda was the name of Mario's mother; and this ostentatious, naive plate contrasted with the modesty of the wooden door, badly painted in grey, of the narrow landing flooded with cruel sunshine, of the cramped, dirty staircase, of the entire building. Soon I was no longer out of breath, so I put out my hand and pressed the bell.

The door was opened immediately, as if to demonstrate the smallness of the flat; a woman wearing a dressmaker's black apron, with a yard of yellow waterproof material over her shoulder and several white threads scattered over her chest, no doubt Mario's mother, appeared in the doorway. She was a good-looking woman but with a haggard, sullen sort of beauty; she had become misshapen and overweight as a result of mother-hood and of her work and her food; she must have been of my own age or possibly a few years less; but, of the two of us, I certainly looked the younger, partly because my hair was dyed whereas hers was grey.

She looked at me diffidently and asked what I wanted. I answered with a lie which nevertheless contained an element of truth. 'Your son is a patient of mine; he telephoned me yesterday evening to say he didn't feel at all well and wanted me to visit him. So here I am.' Why do I say that this was a lie that contained some truth? Because that was how our love affair began : in a suffocating little staff bedroom in the hotel where I was staying, with Mario, who was suffering from a colic, lying on an untidy camp bed. I sat on the edge of the camp bed and held his hand; he twisted and turned as little as he could and in the meantime his anguished eyes were all the time seeking mine.

9

His mother showed no surprise either at my presence or at my pretext; she appeared to be accustomed to this kind of situation. In a resigned voice, she said : 'I'll go and see if my son's at home.' She turned her back on me without inviting me to come in, and disappeared behind a piece of material which, serving as a curtain, separated the entrance from the rest of the flat. Left alone, I hesitated; then I drew aside the curtain and looked in. There was a small passage, with a glass door at the end of it, no doubt the bathroom; and three other doors. I calculated : one door for the kitchen, one for the trying-on room, one for Mario's bedroom. But where did his mother sleep? Probably in the trying-on room, on a divan bed. During these, so to speak, topographical deliberations, I was listening carefully.

The door which, according to my calculation, led into Mario's bedroom, had been left ajar and I distinctly heard his voice arguing, in a subdued tone, with his mother. Then his mother suddenly reappeared; and I did not have time to fall back towards the entrance. She announced, in her usual gloomy, maternal tone of voice : 'I'm sorry, but my son isn't there.' I looked her straight in the eyes; and she withstood my look. Quivering with anger, I exclaimed : 'You're lying, your son is there, I heard his voice.' As I said this, I started to make a dash towards the door of Mario's bedroom. At that same moment Mario came out of the room and stood in front of me.

His black, glossy hair was all rumpled; he was wearing briefs and a sleeveless vest; he appeared to have just got up from his bed. I noticed that he had a folded towel under his arm; I thought, stupidly, that I did not remember he was so small, so well proportioned and so hairy. At the same time, however, I felt a kind of urge forward, frenzied and compelling, which, if I had not controlled myself, would have made me run to him, embrace him, clasp my body to his; clearly this was the Half spoken of by Plato which, after long searching, had at last found its other Half. I opened my mouth and exclaimed : 'Mario . . .' and then stopped, paralysed by the sudden realization that Mario, for some reason unknown to me, did not wish to have anything more to do with me and that, in consequence, I had made a mistake in venturing right to his own home on the crazy pretext of a doctor's visit. And so it was. Mario looked at me, frowning, for a moment; then, from that mouth that had been so beloved by me, there burst forth, humiliating, brutal, what may be described as the traditional invective of the young man against his mature mistress. But with, in addition, the differences of class and of culture which, in my Platonic imagination, I had considered as elements destined to join us closer together. Finally, in addition, there was the heavy local accent, so well adapted to dissolve, in the twinkling of an eye, even the most tenacious love relationship, with remarks of a coarse, slangy nature such as : 'What the hell d'you want?', 'Who d'you think you are?', 'Haven't you ever looked at yourself in the glass?', 'Look at this old girl, how she gives herself airs !' – and so on.

These remarks pursued me and beset me as I beat a bewildered retreat – rather like a ruffled, terrified hen trying to escape the blows of an infuriated housewife with a broom. Mario's mother, standing in the entrance, looked at me and looked at him, in a calm but undecided way; one might almost have thought that she had a special experienced sympathy for me. I went past her and out on to the landing; but not hurriedly enough not to see – the final outrage – Mario slipping into the bathroom, pulling the glass door behind him with a clatter.

After this scene, something precise and unusual happened to me. Every morning about five o'clock I would wake up with a start and begin thinking of Mario – or rather, I did not think of him in the sense that one says 'I think of you all the time', which means, in effect, not thinking but abandoning oneself to feeling; but, in my imagination, I repeated the humiliating scene of my being chased out of his house. I saw myself ringing the bell, telling a lie to his mother, going into the flat; I saw Mario appear, look me up and down from head to foot, rail at me and then shut himself in the bathroom, banging the door. You may think that at this point I would turn over on my side and go to sleep again. If you think this, it means that you do not know the difference between remembering and re-living an experience. Remembering means extracting a person, an event, from one's memory, looking at them as one might look at an old trinket that has been shut up in a drawer, then replacing them in the drawer, that is, in one's memory, and no longer thinking about them; re-living, on the other hand, means feeling and re-feeling, endlessly, the sensations which that person or that event had aroused in us while we were experiencing them. And, in fact, one remembers only once; but one re-lives infinite times. But it does not occur to anyone to re-live disagreeable sensations. Only pleasant sensations are re-lived; the others one tries to forget. How is it to be explained, then, that I, every morning, again and again, go back in memory to the scene of my expulsion from Mario's flat, dwelling particularly on the most humiliating, the cruellest details? Why do I dwell upon them, with a kind of obtuse fascination, relishing again and again the acute pain as though it were a disturbing pleasure? I thought it over for a long time and finally said to myself that, in reality, during those early morning recollections, by some mysterious psychological alchemy, the pain was changed into pleasure. Masochism, it will be said. That may be so. But how can masochism be reconciled with the yearning to find the other half of oneself, to re-form the mythical rotund monster, complete in every respect, as spoken of by Plato? Can a person be complete who is divided into two parts, one of which humiliates, outrages and degrades the other?

It appears that he can. The voluptuous grief that I felt began, after a couple of months, to become insipid, enfeebled. The scene of my expulsion from Mario's flat became pallid and half obliterated, like an old film become worn through age and use. However I had by now, alas, become accustomed to this gloomy enjoyment; I had an absolute need to feel again, each morning, the suffering of those few cruel minutes. And so I took a decision that may perhaps seem incredible but that, in my situation, was quite logical : I would present myself again at Mario's home, I would again provide the same improper pretext of a visit from a doctor; I would get myself thrown out again in the same insulting manner. Perhaps Mario might even catch hold of me by my hair, throw me down on the floor at the entrance to the flat, literally kick me out on to the landing. Like a drug addict who has acquired a fresh supply of his favourite narcotic, I would come back home with a good supply of humiliation, so that I should be able to get along without any further fresh supplies, for a long period of time.

Without hesitating, I put my plan into action. I presented myself early one morning at the block of working-class flats, walked up six floors (the lift was out of order again) and rang at the door; Mario's mother came and opened it and I repeated my lie about a doctor's visit. I was expecting her to drive me away, even if it were with her usual gloominess tinged with sympathy; I was expecting Mario to appear and rail at me. Not at all. The mother, though still gloomy, invited me in. 'You can go straight to him,' she said. 'He's in bed. Last door on the right.' Then she went away. More dead than alive, I went forward and knocked at the door. I was bidden, from inside, to come in, and there was his bedroom, small and plastered with illustrations of film actresses and footballers cut out of magazines. Mario was lying on the bed, in briefs and sleeveless vest as before, flat on his back with his hands clasped at the back of his neck. He did not get up, he did not move; all he did was to say to me in a voice at the same time rough and kindly : 'I should like to know why you haven't turned up before? Is it because I was a bit harsh that morning? But, you know, you're a strange sort of person.'

All of a sudden the impulse to throw myself upon him, to embrace him, to clasp my body to his – all this left me as though by enchantment. It was succeeded by something automatic, mechanical. I sat down on the edge of the bed, took hold of his wrist and felt his pulse. He protested, at first hesitatingly, then with greater and greater decision; but I did not listen to him. With professional coldness I repulsed an attempt on his part to embrace me; I rose to my feet, warned him that he was not well, took my notebook, scribbled a prescription and handed it to him. Then, without giving him time to recover from his surprise, I left the room, walked out of the flat and on down the stairs.

As I got into my car to start on my usual round of visits, all at once I began almost to laugh. I remembered, in fact, that Plato's rotund monster, so it seems, walked in a comic way, turning like a wheel on its four arms and its four legs, in the manner of an acrobat or of certain Indian divinities. Precisely! What else can so strange a being do, a being who owes his unity to disunion, his strength to weakness and his joys to sorrow?

# Madness

⟊

A woman can have many men in her life; but only one father. Perhaps that is the reason why the person whom, in my heart, I call 'the man in my life' was, in the end, when all was said and done, for me, above all, a father. Yes indeed, a worthy father in place of the unworthy father who had brought me into the world; a father – in fact, a 'papa' – who would have allowed me to live my whole life as if it were a very long, well-protected, happy childhood. This was the real, genuine basis of our relationship. What then did it matter that he was older than me by almost thirty years; and that I was a kind of intellectual (I took a degree in physics and do research for a university professor) and he a financier, probably uncultivated, immersed up to the eyes in money? What mattered was that, with him, I felt myself going forward all my life, precisely because there was between us, apart from the love relationship – which lasts as long as may be – the paternal-filial relationship which, obviously, can never cease to exist.

One day, after almost two years of a secret, in fact a clandestine, relationship (he had to hide when he saw me, because he had a wife and children), I went on some errand or other to a, for me unaccustomed, quarter and, coming out of a shop, I noticed, not far off, standing on the pavement as though waiting for someone, a very smartly dressed woman, tall, very dark and shapely, with something of the mulatto about her. I had barely time to observe her when a car appeared, a car well known to me, with my financier-papa at the wheel. The car stopped, he opened the door, the woman got in; the car started again, the woman threw her arms round the neck of 'the man in my life' and kissed him full on the ear. Then they both vanished.

I rushed home in great haste, sat down in my study and looked round. Then, all of a sudden, I underwent what I may call a crisis in which I rejected the things that lay around me, that is to say, the whole of reality. Yes indeed, these pieces of furniture, these books, these curtains, these carpets, everything — it seemed to me, literally, that I had just vomited them up and that I was looking at them with precisely the mixed feeling of disgust and astonishment with which, after vomiting, one looks at the repulsive heap of variegated mess that one has poured out of one's mouth a moment before. It was a winter evening; I stayed there, contemplating my rejected life for I don't know how long, until it grew dark.

Then I felt my way into my bedroom, threw myself on the bed and began thinking about what line I should take, henceforward, with my lover. I thought of different solutions, but none of them convinced me. Certainly I ought to go away until I had got rid of this feeling of disgust for existence; but where should I go?

Then I considered, very logically: 'It is not a case of leaving one place and going to another. It's a case of leaving *all* places'; and, without hesitating, I turned on the light, poured myself out a glass of water and swallowed, two at a time, all the tablets from a tube of sleeping-pills. I was possessed, however, not so much by the idea of death as by that of escaping from my senses and my mind, so that I would no longer either see or think of anything and, above all, would no longer have before my eyes the image of the car driving away, with my lover-papa at the

wheel and that woman, that love-thief, with her mouth glued to
his ear. I fell into a black hole; I emerged from it twelve hours
later, in a room at a nursing-home. I had been taken there actually by him, by my financier who, having an appointment with
me and failing to see me arrive, had had a presentiment that
something had happened to me. In this nursing-home they
treated the milder type of mental illness, not lunatic-asylum cases;
but my ex-papa had not thought that I had gone mad; he had
taken me there merely because the doctor in charge was a friend
of his.

Had my lover guessed that I had tried to kill myself on his
account? I never understood this; but it might have been thought
that he suspected something because afterwards, through all the
long years that followed, there was always, in his attitude towards
me, a touch of embarrassment and as it were the stimulus of a
sense of guilt. As for me, I stayed in the nursing-home for about
a week; and I made the doctor say that I was still in a state of
shock from my attempted suicide and that therefore, at least for
the time being, I preferred not to see anybody. Meanwhile, however, those seven days spent in the solitude and silence of the
nursing-home were very useful to me, because I at last came to
understand how I should behave towards the man who had been
unfaithful to me. Therefore I would neither break off relations
with him nor would I continue them; instead, I would 'suspend'
them.

Naturally I did not want him to grow tired of me, I wanted
him to go on paying court to me, even if in vain. It may be
thought that I had worked out a form of vengeance of refined
cruelty; but this was not so. In reality I should have liked to see
him again because I still loved him; yet at the same time, just
because I loved him so much and my love had been insulted, I
no longer wanted to see him. Between these two opposing re-
quirements, the mental illness from which one can recover but
from which one can also *not* recover, and which, if one does not
recover, prevents any relationship with other people – this mental
illness fulfilled the function of 'suspension' that I had assigned to

it marvellously well.

My stay in the nursing-home was useful to me, furthermore, because, after observing the large number of sick people living there, I was able all the better to determine the imaginary illness by which I had decided to be, from that moment, chronically affected. This, then, was a mild but tenacious and possibly incurable form of depressive melancholy, with phases of greater acuteness characterized by a rich variety of hallucinations. I was gloomy, depressed, misanthropic; at the same time I saw and felt things that were not there and that definitely could not be there.

I explained all this on the telephone to my ex-papa a few days after I returned home. I told him, while I was speaking to him, that I was in the dark; that I was alone, completely alone; whereas it seemed to me that there was a man living in the house. I did in fact hear this man walking about in the room next door, opening and closing doors, humming under his breath. My ex-lover was astonished : wasn't I frightened of these noises? No, not in the least, I heard them, that was all. And didn't I want him to come and see me, to come even at once; his presence would certainly stop the hallucinations. No, for Heaven's sake, no, I couldn't see him, I couldn't see anyone. But when were we going to meet, then? Soon, very soon, the moment I was restored to health, in a month's time, for instance. The sincerity of my tone, suffused as it was with a melancholy which was not feigned, convinced him. So, after making me swear that I still loved him – an oath which I willingly gave because it was the truth – he made an agreement with me that we should telephone to one another, from then onwards, at least once a week.

In swearing to him that I loved him, I had told him the truth; but with regard to my hallucination of the presence of a man in the house, I had lied to him. I was a young, good-looking woman, and there was no lack of suitors; as soon as I came out of the nursing-home I had immediately picked up again with the least unpromising of them, a student called Manlio, and had promptly gone to bed with him. I did not love this Manlio, I loved my financier; I was not seeking to avenge myself; I did not wish to take any precise step : it was merely a continuance of life, but with the addition of this strange fiction that I denied such a continuance with my ex-lover. Mental illness, in fact, stood between him and me like that special kind of glass which allows one to see out but prevents one from seeing in. I saw my financier and his love for me; but he did not see me and, behind me, Manlio who was waiting impatiently for me to finish telephoning.

And so there began, for me, a double life, or rather, a life divided into two parts, one of which was real with its reality denied, the other unreal but claimed to be the only real one. I lived like everyone else in this world, in a normal, day-to-day fashion; but to my ex-papa I continued to say on the telephone that my life was interrupted on account of my psychic troubles and that it would resume its existence only on the day when we met again. It may be pointed out here that it would have been easy for him to ascertain the truth, to discover that I was not ill, that I had a man, and all the rest of it. My answer to that is that we belonged to different social circles; that in modern towns even years may sometimes go by without one's running into people whom one knew quite well in former times.

It may also be objected that no man would go on for years telephoning to a woman who refuses to see him. To this objection also there is an answer. And that is, that my financier, conscious of his own guilt, wanted at all costs to regain possession of me.

Five years had passed since my return from the nursing-home, and many things had happened in my life. What things, you may ask? Here they are, in brief. In my bed, gradually, Manlio's place had been taken by Alessandro, Alessandro's by Raniero and Raniero's by Livio. I went on various journeys to distant countries, each time with a different man, to Brazil, to India, to Morocco, to South Africa. After South Africa I became pregnant by Livio and had a son, and for three years I accompanied Livio on his travels : he was special correspondent to a daily newspaper. Then I broke with Livio and had another son by the man I was then living with, Federico. In the meantime I had moved house three times and had changed my job twice : I did scientific research; I became secretary to the editor of a town-planning review. Et cetera, et cetera. But my ex-papa and lover continued to telephone me regularly.

Just as regularly, I refused to see him, alleging ups and downs in my illness. In a special voice that I used only when speaking to him, a voice that was sad, vague, subdued, patient and reticent, I would tell him that I was unwell, very unwell, that I was seeing nobody, that I was always alone, that I had strange illusions, hallucinations : at one moment I was convinced that I had two children; then that I had three men, all three of them in love with me; then again that I had just returned from a distant journey, to a tropical country; and then that I had moved house. I told him the truth, in fact; but presenting it to him as an illusion, as a waking dream. And always, in tones sincere even though gloomy, I assure him that I love him, that I have never loved anyone but him, that some day we shall see one another. This promise is a bait, strange to say, which he always swallows.

I must now admit, however, that these monthly telephone calls with the only man I have ever loved made the perfectly real existence that I led from day to day seem curiously imaginary and hallucinatory. From the fiction of a mental illness (but is it indeed a fiction? Is it not actually an illness, to pretend that one is ill?) the persons and the events of my life came to be endowed with an unreal, a phantom-like quality like things in a dream which, by repetition and even by actual development, did not succeed entirely in persuading me of their effective existence. So much so that sometimes, while I was talking on the telephone to my old lover, I would contrive that the man I was living with should be close beside me, should embrace and caress me – as if to assure me that he was there, that he was not a creature of my imagination.

The last telephone conversation that I had during those days went like this; and I transcribe it because it was typical : 'How are you?' 'So-so.' 'Unwell, then.' 'Yes, let's call it unwell.' 'You know what you need to cure you? A family, a husband, children.

Unfortunately I can't give you these things; but I should be happy if you had them.' 'You're right, what I need is a family. It's perfectly true that when I'm worse, my hallucinations are all – how shall I say? – of a family, a conjugal kind. I seem to hear the sound of running and laughing in the children's room next door; I wake up in the night and it seems to me that I have a sleeping man beside me. But, you see, I do actually hear the quarrels and cries of the children; I do actually touch the back of the sleeping man.' 'Do you suffer much?' 'Well, yes, sometimes it seems to me that I have gone mad in earnest. That is, that I have got worse, that I am imprisoned irreparably in a particular kind of madness.' 'What kind of madness?' 'It seems clear to me, don't you see? It's the kind of madness that makes you think you're normal, just like everyone else.' 'My poor dear, how well I understand you. But wouldn't you like – wouldn't you really like me to come and see you? I am real, very real, and my realness would drive away these phantoms of yours.' 'No, no, it's not possible, I can't see you, I'm unwell, too unwell.' At this point we said good-bye and I went off in a great hurry to dress. My unreal husband was waiting to take me out to an unreal dinner at the house of some unreal friends. Ah well, it takes little to turn reality into dream and much to turn dream into reality.

# Thunder and Lightning

⚬⚬⚬

Every now and then there come upon me what, in my private slang, I call thunderstorms. And what, for me, is a thunderstorm? It is a slow accumulation inside me, over months and years, of hatred for something or other: but I don't know what. This hatred becomes more and more threatening and sinister, like a thunderstorm gathering on the horizon on a fine summer day. Then, all of a sudden, on some pretext or other, the hatred explodes; and then, and only then, do I discover what the object of the hatred was – and this through the torrent of words, words just and precise even if furious, by means of which, in a state almost of trance, I express and unburden myself. It is a kind of cyclone and no one resists it, least of all myself. What, you ask, was my most important and memorable thunderstorm? Certainly it was the one which, when I was eighteen, set me off against my father, a veterinary surgeon at G., a small and sleepy little provincial town. On that occasion I screamed for three hours on end, without ever stopping, in the presence of my mother, of my sisters and brothers, all of them terrified. What was I screaming at? At everything, at my father, at the family, at the town, at the whole world. I screamed that I was fed up with this mean provincial life; that I wanted to live and not to languish in idleness; that, if things went on like this, I would run away with a passing lorry-driver, I would go on the streets. I screamed also that I couldn't stand respectability any longer, that bourgeois morality did not suit me, that I felt I had a vocation to be a first-class cosmopolitan adventuress. I went on screaming, alas, that even my parents disgusted me, and I enumerated, one after the other, all their defects, both physical and moral. What did I *not* say during that thunderstorm of mine? It was just like a waterspout which sucks up all kinds of dirty rubbish from the ground and then spews it out again miles away.

Incidentally, how did that eighteen-year-old thunderstorm come to an end? It ended extremely badly, for, what with the mortification of having treated my parents like that and the complete impossibility of continuing to live in that way, I married the first man who came along; and now here I am tied to this first-comer and with a thunderstorm brewing which, in my opinion, is concerned with *him* and which I feel has been intensifying almost since the day when I said 'yes' to him in church.

But here he is, my first-comer. At the far end of the immense living-room of our super-luxury super-penthouse, there he was, coming forward amongst the groups of armchairs and sofas, mean, anonymous and insignificant, in a dark-grey suit like that of any ordinary lower-rank civil servant or minor lawyer or other worm of the same kind, bespectacled, bald and, of course, with a long beard, and with the badges of mourning, naturally, for some remote relation or other – the black band on his arm, a black tie, a handkerchief with a black border. He walked forward slowly and as though disconcerted – or was this an impression created by his bowed, crooked legs? And in his hand he clasped, in a single bunch, a bundle of crumpled newspapers. When I saw these papers, all of a sudden something was released inside me, a fit of fury like a too-long-compressed spring; and indeed I immediately exploded: 'Ah, so there we are, the news-

papers, you and your newspapers! How many of them d'you
read, eh? Five, ten, fifteen? The Roman papers, the ones from
Milan, the ones from your own dirty town? I should like to know
what you're looking for, what you find in your stupid papers.
Don't worry, neither you nor I will ever get into the papers. Anyhow I never even look at the papers. The people who read the
papers are those who are alive, who have a share in life, who
have a life of their own; but you and I – are we alive? No, my
dear, we vegetate, so why all these papers? Do the flourishing
plants on my terrace read the papers?'

Now he was standing in front of me, ugly and miserable, staring at me through his enormous spectacles; perhaps he wanted to
speak, but I did not give him time. 'Besides,' I said, 'the moment
has come to say it, I'm fed up with you, with our marriage, with
the whole intolerable hovel we live in. Yes, I know we have a
super-penthouse which cost several million lire, decorated by a
famous architect, in which every piece of furniture weighs a
hundredweight and is worth millions; but what do we do in this
apartment? Nothing, absolutely nothing. Or rather, we do, we
lead a "family life". Oh, family, let us talk about "family" for a
little, let's talk about it once and for all. You have the cult of the
family, and much good may it do you; but you make a mistake
when you try to impose it on me. D'you know, or d'you not
know, that I myself, in this multi-million apartment, have never
up to now seen anybody except members of your family? Certainly there are plenty of them. The family! *I* know what it
means to lead a family life; there's nothing I don't know about
that. It means to have a whole tribe of brothers, sisters, brothers-
in-law, sisters-in-law, uncles, grandparents, nephews and nieces
to feed at lunch and dinner every day. It means spending the
evenings in front of the television, with that shaggy old ape of a
mother of yours and that equally shaggy monkey, your old maid
of a sister. It means trailing mother-in-law and sister-in-law
round in the afternoons, going from one shop window to another,
into one shop after another, without buying anything. And anyhow, why should I buy clothes and jewellery and furs like so

many other women? To flaunt them in front of the tribe, to cut a dash in the family?'

He looked at me, dropped the newspapers on the floor, fumbled in his pocket, lit a cigarette with a trembling hand. I knew that no one had ever spoken to him in this way about his family; but I was well away by now and his displeasure, instead of moderating my rage, re-kindled it. 'Yes,' I shouted, 'yes, I have a family, a family that can be called perfect; but where it surpasses even perfection is in religion. Oh yes, religion, it can't be denied that you people are religious, religious to the point where it might be said that you have a God all of your own, a Jesus all of your own, a Madonna all of your own and, above all, a crowd of saints all of your own. Pilgrimages to sanctuaries; prayers, one after the other, from morning to night; no fear for religion in *this* house. This is not a flat in the Parioli quarter, it's a convent, it's a church. And images into the bargain, and holy pictures and statuettes and rosaries brought from Lourdes and bottles of Jordan water imported from Jerusalem! Not to mention photographs of bishops and cardinals with signed dedications and benedictions. But *I'm* not religious, not in the least, d'you see? And in my native town I used to go to Mass only on Sundays, to please my parents, not as we do here, every morning.'

He smoked and looked at me; he looked at me and smoked. I had never seen him like this, and he almost frightened me; but there it was, the storm was still raging and had to work itself out. 'But d'you know,' I asked, 'what it is that I especially cannot endure in this lovely family life that we lead? It's your way of talking. I'm an Italian, I speak Italian and I don't understand a thing of what you say. I should like to know what your confabulations are about, what is the subject of your chatter, what the devil you're whispering among yourselves. So-called investments, is it? Bank accounts in Italy and Switzerland, eh? Shares, bonds, securities, gold in bars and in coin, eh? Yes, you're a businessman, you earn a lot of money, so it seems; but that is no reason for talking in your incomprehensible dialect in my presence. What are you afraid of? That I shall go and blurt out that

you have deposit accounts abroad? That I shall take away the
key of your safe? But with me there's no need of so many myst-
eries, of so much dialect. I was born poor; but I'm proud and,
as for your money, I don't know what to do with it. I despise
your money. So speak Italian in front of me, even about your
affairs, talk Italian. Otherwise I don't see you and I don't hear
you.'

Then he went over to a distant table, stubbed out his just-lit
cigarette in an ashtray, and came back slowly towards me with
his two hands thrust deep into his jacket pockets. Then came
the final thunderclap of my storm. 'Finally,' I said, 'I've got to
tell you : you're too bourgeois, too traditional, too serious for me.
Only look at how you dress. You look like an undertaker's man.
Can't you see what young men's fashions are like, in the streets?
Full trousers, common shirts, long hair and beards, sandals and
a guitar. You and your family, from your boobies of sisters to
your good-for-nothing brothers – you're all too conventional for
me. And now I want to tell you something I've never told anybody : today is a day of confidences, you see. D'you know who is
my ideal man – d'you know that? Well then, it's Alain Delon,
when he's playing a gangster, a thief, committing robbery with
violence, a criminal, in fact. Yes, that's my ideal, the handsome,
intrepid man who has no fear of anything or anyone, quick on
the draw, leading a legendary life. Alain Delon who plays it up
in night-clubs, in expensive hotels, who rushes from Paris to New
York, from New York to Rio de Janeiro and from Rio to Paris.
Yes, that's the magnificent result you've obtained with your cult
of the family, your religion, your morality, your respectability :
that your wife dreams, with her eyes open, of being the wife of a
gangster.'

So there we were, the thunderstorm was over. I had unburd-
ened myself; and now, all of a sudden, I was a little frightened.
Partly because he was eyeing me with a look that I did not know,
a new look, fixed, deliberate and in some way inhuman. He came
over to me with short, stiff steps; when he was close to me he took
one hand out of his pocket and then – slap, slap, slap – he

smacked my face several times with an outrageous force which was also new to me. I staggered as he hit me, then regained my equilibrium; I looked at him and then uttered a strange cry as though I were seeing him for the first time; then I ran away. Through the anteroom, headlong down the stairs and out into the street. I slackened my pace and walked away towards a public garden that lay not far from our house.

There was a big lawn on which some children were playing and a number of seats round it. I found an empty one, sat down and tried to reflect. But the blows had been so violent that I could not manage to remain calm; and so, in spite of myself, I began to cry. People were passing, and I was ashamed of being seen weeping; someone had left a newspaper on the seat; I took it up and pretended to be absorbed in reading it. The tears fell from my eyes on to the page and confused my vision.

Then, gradually, my tears lessened, and I saw better. And suddenly, right on the first page of the newspaper, still veiled by tears but recognizable, I saw the photograph of a man whom I seemed to know. I looked at it and was convinced : it was he, it was positively *his* face, the face of the man whom, when I married him, I had privately baptized with the not very flattering nickname of 'first-comer'.

I unfolded the paper and saw that there were two columns devoted to him; and all at once I recalled that I had shouted at him that neither he nor I would ever appear in the papers. But I had to see what it was all about.

I started to read and could not believe my eyes. In those two columns there was everything, literally everything that I had never known about him and that he had hitherto concealed from me : robbery, homicide, conspiracy for unlawful purposes, drug-trafficking, prostitution. Yes, even prostitution. There was also an interview of his with a journalist, in which, of course, he denied everything. And with a final declaration in which I recognized him : 'Why, you're joking. I don't know anything about all this. I'm the father of a family.'

Now I understood why, that mornng, he had appeared so disconcerted and wretched, with those newspapers dangling from his hand. For the first time, he had got into the papers; he felt himself unmasked, as they say, before the world and especially before me. And to think that I had shouted into his face that my ideal type of man was a gangster! Serve me right.

There had been a thunderstorm; but there had also been lightning. And I had been struck – a direct hit. Burnt to a cinder!

And now let me ask your advice. I married a conventional man of the first water; and discovered that he was a criminal. What ought I to have done, then? Marry a criminal, to discover afterwards that he was a noble soul, a superior type? Or search elsewhere, Heaven knows where, for something new and unknown that will let me avoid this dilemma which I feel, fundamentally, does not exist? Alas, it is my own fault; I made a mistake, but where was the mistake?

# Life on Top of Me

⌒⌖⌒

Slaps, punches, kicks. Suburb, drain, rubbish. Hut, bed, chairs.
Mother, father, sister. School, cave, basement. Shop, bank, jewellery. Prison, prison, prison . . . I could have said that I was born
and brought up in a suburb where the drains were open and the
piles of rubbish reached to the roofs. That I lived in a hut where
there were only two chairs and a big bed in which I slept together with my father, my mother and my sister. That one day,
instead of going to school, I ran away with a boy called Mauro
and we made love in a tufa cave and used to meet there for a
year and then went to live in a basement. That, after carrying on
with bag-snatching and minor robberies, we attempted a coup
at a jeweller's shop but it went wrong. Mauro escaped and I
ended up inside . . . I could have told the story of my life in this
way; but I have preferred to tell it in plain words, nothing but
things and facts, to convey the feeling of a life precisely like mine,
which has always been, so to speak, on top of me, just as the other
passengers in a tram are on top of you and you want to get out
in order to breathe and you can't. It wouldn't matter if I were
one of those women who attack life for it is they who are on top

of life and who don't allow it to survive. But I, alas, am as it were flayed alive : I am timid, apprehensive, everything offends me, wounds me, does me harm.

I came out of prison after almost four years and immediately joined Mauro again : he was now the man whom I loved. We set up together again and, perhaps out of a desire for revenge, again attempted a raid on the same jeweller's shop, trying, this time, to force the roller-shutter at night. But once again it went wrong; the police arrived, I ran away and Mauro finished up inside. He was found guilty; and so I, while I waited for him to come out, took a place as a maid with a family who had put an advertisement in the paper.

This family consisted of a husband and wife and – strange to say – they were a couple very similar to our own families, mine and Mauro's. Like Mauro, the husband was very dark, red-faced, not so very tall but robust; like me, the wife was fair, with a delicate face but with a figure, exuberant but shapely, that did not match her face. However the resemblance stopped there. The husband was a professor and the wife did translations from a foreign language; whereas Mauro and I were practically illiterate. And then the books! In their flat, on the top of an old palazzo, the books began in the entrance hall, covered the walls of the sitting-room, continued into the passage, invaded the bedroom, stood in rows even in the bathroom, even in the kitchen. The real difference between Mauro and me and this couple lay in these books and in the book-words that the two of them used when they spoke together or with their friends. Words, as I noted at once, which, instead of bringing things closer, of blending with things, put them at a distance, cancelled them out. Life, in short, was not on top of these two as it was with Mauro and myself, for they kept at a distance all the things of which life is made, using words that could be mistaken for each other and those that are to be read in books, all of them words that were in the first place words and then – sometimes, possibly – things, also. Yes, protected themselves from the injuries of life by means of words, just as they protected themselves from rain and wind by means of the thick walls of their dwelling-place. But Mauro and I were exposed; and when we spoke, we spoke only of things. As for books, how do you manage to read them unless, like these employers of mine, you believe that words are not things?

At last Mauro came out of prison; and I left this couple who were so like and yet so unlike us and went to live with him in an old villa with crumbling plaster, with round balconies formed like the stern of a ship, close under the railway embankment. Mauro was now in league with a gang of thieves whom he had got to know in prison, and he went to work with them; and I had to stay at home to guard the stolen property, to cook for them, to be always ready, in fact, to serve them. The days were long and generally I lay on the bed, listening to the din of the trains that went past. Under the bed was a suitcase in which Mauro, as time went on, would hide the most precious of the things he had stolen, and from this suitcase it was evident that there arose some sort of intoxicating vapours, coming up to me through the mattress, for I indulged in fancies all the time. In my fancies I imagined nearly always the same things, more or less : Mauro and myself sitting at a table covered with books, in a house full of books. Calmly, serenely, quietly, relaxed, we would talk. And how we talked! And our serenity, as I realized, came from the words that we spoke, all of them vague, indirect, imprecise, weightless, made out of nothing. Words, words, words. Finally the blaze of sunset flared behind the glass of the big window near which we were sitting. The room was plunged in darkness. And we, serene, distant, quiet, went on talking.

One evening Mauro came running in all breathless, with the expression on his face of one who is overwhelmed by, at the same time, a great joy and a great fear. He showed me two imitation-leather bags, crammed full, and told me that inside these bags there was enough for us to live quietly for the rest of our days. Quietly! I thought of my dreams full of words and asked what there was in the bags.

My heart sank when I heard him reply that there were valuables just stolen from a shopkeeper : jeweller's shops, as you will remember, had always brought us bad luck. Mauro then explained that this time, for a change, he had been unwilling to share with the others; he would keep the whole lot for himself. But the others had realized this and would be looking for him and therefore we must get away in the greatest possible haste. But where? Mauro showed me two air tickets: we would go abroad. In the meantime, however, I must conceal the two bags on me and go and await him in a certain bar, not far off. He would come along later and pick me up.

I retained only one point of this explanation: the fact that I had to conceal the bags on me. I started slowly to indicate, by shaking my head, that I refused, at the same time backing towards the bed. By now he was already in a rage, and he asked me: 'Why, what's wrong with you?'

'It's that I don't want to burden myself with anything.'

'What?'

'Don't look at me like that: you frighten me.'

'What?'

He did not wait for my answer; he seized me by the hair and threw me down on the bed. Then, as I struggled with him and he was alternately slapping me and undressing me, I thought that life was now truly on top of me, pitilessly. For it was life and not Mauro that was snatching away my blouse and my skirt, seizing me by the throat, giving me one blow after another, then taking me by the arm and, naked as I was, dragging me into the middle of the room and arranging the bags on top of me, one below my stomach and one on my chest, much as they arrange the harness on a recalcitrant mule. Mauro helped me to dress again, then pushed me out of the house, saying: 'Walk without stopping straight to the bar and wait for me there.' I went off downstairs with my head lowered; my cheeks were still burning from the slaps he had given me; the bags weighed heavy upon me, one on my legs and the other on my breast, just as though they had been made of lead; and I said to myself that life had never oppressed me to such an extent as it did at that moment. But at the second flight of stairs, in a dark spot, two men suddenly seized me by the arms. Two others rushed up the stairs in the direction of our flat.

I closed my eyes, I waited. The two who were holding me were talking together; but I did not hear them because I was listening intently to another sound : the cry that a man may utter when he is being killed. So I heard nothing of what they said; and the time of waiting was prolonged. Finally there was the sound of footsteps; the other two had come back. I kept my eyes closed all the time. I heard a voice say : 'However they must be some-where or other. Let's see what this one will have to tell us. Come on, let's go.'

We went downstairs; the two men were still gripping me by the arms and the bags were banging against my chest and legs more than ever. A car was waiting for us in front of the main door; they made me get in and I understood from their remarks that they were taking me to some place where, by fair means or foul, they would make me tell where the valuables were. So, in a faint voice, I murmured : 'I have the two bags on me.'

The car immediately swerved as though it had ears and had acted on its own. We stopped; it must have been in the country, to judge by the darkness. The four of them leapt on top of me, like dogs on a dying deer. With frenzied hands they tore off my blouse, pulled up my skirt, almost strangling me when they dragged away the bag I had on my chest and almost sawing into my belly when they snatched away the one I had in my lap. My eyes closed, I made no resistance : I knew for certain that Mauro was dead and hoped that they would kill me too. One of them wanted to kill me; but another answered that it would be a pity, since I was young and attractive and might be quite useful and he felt inclined to make me work. Thus I understood that, in-stead of killing me, they would start me off on that profession which, as long as Mauro was alive, I had never been willing to practise for any reason. They threw my blouse and skirt at me, the car went off, and I dressed myself again as best I could. Then I closed my eyes and reflected that now I could no longer even say that life was on top of me. Reduced to a body which no longer belonged to me and which would soon be put up for sale, I should henceforth be wholly identified with life and should be, so to speak, oppressed by my own self. Who, in fact, has ever succeeded in freeing himself of his own body and continuing, nevertheless, to live?

# Speaking in Order to Live

❧

Does the word come before the thing or the thing before the word? Does one live because one speaks or does one speak because one lives? For myself there can be no doubts: one lives because one speaks, because the word and the thought (which are the same) come before the thing. Anyhow, judge for yourselves: if I had not discovered the word, brand-new to me – the word 'love' – do you think I should have married a humble secondary-schoolmaster, my fellow-townsman, who, once we had moved to Rome, was to reveal himself, in the much wider and more complex world of the capital, as an irreparable nonentity? And if I had not discovered successively the words – they too perfectly new to me – 'error', 'disillusionment', 'boredom' – do you think that I should have realized my husband was a nonentity? And with regard to the word 'nonentity', it was only when I discovered it, when it exploded like a bomb in my modest little Roman flat of two rooms and a kitchen, destroying and pulverizing everything in the place which until recently had seemed to me a perfect love-nest, it was only then that I became aware that, instead of my husband, bent over the homework of his pupils,

there was nothing, positively nothing, not even the teasing noth-
ingness represented by a question mark.

After this outburst of words never before uttered or thought
of, all of them concerned with my domestic situation, I plunged
into a sort of lethargy. I no longer discovered new words; all I
did was to vegetate. And then, behold, all of a sudden, this torpor
was illuminated, in an unforeseen, brilliant flash, by the word
'hope'. It happened at an exhibition by a woman painter of little
artistic talent but who moved constantly in 'society' circles. Olga,
the wife of an extremely rich building contractor, agreed to be
photographed with me in front of one of the pictures. Afterwards
we talked, and then the mysterious mechanism which permitted
me every now and then to discover words capable of changing
my life, started to work again. One after another, indeed, there
floated to the top of my consciousness – my verbal consciousness,
so to speak – four words which truly I should never have dreamt
of considering or of uttering even a year earlier, four frank, brutal
words, entirely new to a person like me, delicate, timid, well-
mannered : 'idiot', 'to break out', 'to exploit', 'suburban'. These
four words may seem to be unconnected, but it is not so. With
disconcerting naturalness, they almost immediately lined themselves up in the following remark : 'This idiot can help you to
break out. If you don't know how to exploit the opportunity,
you'll prove yourself to be the usual suburban character.' Do I
have to say that such a manifestation of verbal cynicism frightened me at first? But already another word, this one entirely
insignificant, the word 'done', in the context of a rather vulgar
phrase : 'Come on, you've done it!' supervened to confirm that
I was no longer the naive person I had once been. Olga and I
exchanged telephone numbers; then I went back home, my heart
swelling with 'hope', the key-word which had that day re-opened
the horizons of the future for me.

I saw Olga again; we became friends, or rather she became a
friend to me and I pretended to be the same to her, waiting for
the occasion which would allow me to 'break out'. A couple of
months passed and the occasion came about through the dis-

covery of a word at first sight entirely neutral : 'invitation'. This was how it came about. Olga and her husband had built themselves an enormous villa on the Via Cassia about which the whole of Rome was now gossiping; and they had decided to inaugurate it with a party which would certainly be the principal social event of that spring. What was it that suggested, that even insisted upon the word 'invitation', which suddenly flashed out to light up the twilight of my life? It suggested to me, it insisted upon my contriving, at all costs, to be invited to this party. And why? Because yet another word, the word, 'everyone', made my presence at the party indispensable. 'Everyone', in fact would be going to the party, everyone, absolutely everyone. How could I be left out?

Olga was no beauty. Tall and bony, with square shoulders from which her clothes hung as though from a coat-hanger, and hard, awkward hips which suggested the idea of a skeleton, with a flat, pale face lit by the dubious light of two neurotic eyes, she gave always the impression of expecting something from other people, in fact of exacting it with authority and arrogance. But, finally, *what* thing? The first time I said to her, casually and without thinking : 'You who are so beautiful', I realized, from her face which had suddenly become demure, as of a woman looking at herself in a glass, that at that moment she was looking at herself in my remark as though in a glass and was very pleased with what she saw. Then a barrage of unknown words reverberated in my astonished mind : 'vanity', 'stupidity', 'weakness', 'adulation'. And this was the sentence in which these words lined themselves up, so to speak, of their own accord : 'In Olga vanity is equalled only by stupidity; you must exploit this weakness of hers by means of adulation.' Very long, isn't it? But the way that the words, like moles seeking the light, had travelled through my mind, had also been long.

And so : adulation ! From that day onwards I snatched every opportunity, or actually provoked it, to praise the imaginary qualities of this person without qualities. I praised her taste which was execrable, her intelligence which was embryonic, her elegance which was vulgar, her culture which was elementary, her generosity which was microscopic, her tact which was elephantine, her beauty which was non-existent. Do you remember the king without any clothes in Hans Andersen's tale? Well, I became, systematically, the courtier who assures the king that he is clothed in every respect. Indeed, with regard to this tale, I should like to say, incidentally, that the word 'adulation' led me at that time to discover another word of harsher significance: 'lickspittle'. But nothing happened, by which I mean nothing to contradict my theory that the word comes before the thing. In point of fact, I discovered the word lickspittle and, immediately, felt myself to be a lickspittle and behaved like a lickspittle.

At that period Olga was intensifying her preparations for the inauguration of the villa; and I became practically her inseparable companion, for by this time she could no longer do without me, or rather, without my flattery. Every day we went in her enormous motor-car, driven by a uniformed chauffeur, to make the last purchases in the shops; and while the great car advanced imperceptibly in the congested Roman traffic, I took care to keep the fire of praise alight in such a way as shrewdly and gradually to roast my conceited rich friend. She sat stiff and upright, her voluminous, pointed bosom thrust forward, without looking at me, her face in profile; but her ear – her very large, ape-like ear, curiously naked and cartilaginous – was wide open and straining to receive the sugary flow of adulation. Then, once we reached the retailers', her gratitude expressed itself in a kind of authoritative dependence upon me, whereby she asked me my opinion on every sort of decision, listened to me with attention and then, very often, chose according to my suggestion. I had wanted to become indispensable to her. In that I had succeeded.

One morning Olga ordered the chauffeur to drive us to her new abode, on the Via Cassia. She had never shown it to me and I was drawn to this plan because it would be a further step forward in the direction of an invitation to the party. We came out almost into the country; and I saw, on the top of an isolated hill, a great red building with three floors. Lickspittle as usual, I immediately cried out that it was extremely beautiful and that it had, in particular, the merit of resembling her, Olga : unexpected, strange, original, surprising. It was, in reality, the usual Roman farmhouse immensely magnified and rendered insipid precisely by this exaggeration, so as to be really and truly commonplace; but I was a lickspittle and the word 'worked'; and so I responded to the situation for all I was worth, without any scruples.

The car came to a stop in a vast open space, bare and windswept; Olga and I went into the villa; we found ourselves faced by a large room with scattered symmetrical groups of armchairs and divans : an hotel 'lounge' and not all that luxurious. I uttered appropriate exclamations; Olga, flattered, opened a door, telling me to shut my eyes; she pushed me forward, bidding me open my eyes again. I then saw a horrid sort of pantry got up like a Bavarian beer-cellar : wooden wainscot, beer-barrels and big beer-mugs, a large table with felt table-mats, massive shelves, stained-glass windows. I felt that I must, as they say, excel myself, so I murmured in a very low voice, in a tone of bewilderment : 'No, no, this is a dream, it's really a dream, I can't believe my own eyes.' This shameless flattery went beyond all I had foreseen : Olga furtively squeezed my hand in sign of gratitude. Suddenly there exploded in my mind the brand-new word 'imitation'. Yes indeed, it is right that a strong mind should subjugate a weak mind. Yes indeed, it was my duty to 'imitate' Olga, to 'plagiarize' her. Putting immediately into action the programme indicated in the new word, I demanded with authority : 'All that remains to be done now is to see who we're going to invite to the party. You must prepare the lists of guests for me. I'll come tomorrow and we'll examine them together.' Docile, submissive, 'plagiarized' in fact, Olga answered : 'I was going to propose that to you.'

Next day, when I came in, Olga embraced me saying : 'What should I do without you?' Then she sat down with me at the desk and displayed to me some sheets of paper full of names and of cancellations. I said that in the first place I would have to read them all, so as to get a comprehensive idea; then we could go on to discuss the list name by name. Olga agreed and I started reading greedily. Everyone was there, that same 'everyone' which I had formerly discovered as a word, before discovering them as a thing; but I myself was not there. I came to the bottom of the list and then re-read it carefully : nothing. Olga had made use of me; the better to employ my services, she had allowed me to be on intimate terms with her; but she had not invited me.

My vision was dimmed and the world went black. In this darkness there exploded one after the other, like fireworks, various new, utterly new words whose existence I had never hitherto suspected : 'servant', 'pariah', 'inferior' and so on. The meaning, then, was clear : 'you are a servant, a pariah, an inferior. It is right that Olga should not invite you.'

It was at this point that there occurred inside me a complete inversion of the mental process which had hitherto led me to discover the word before the thing. Suddenly, without any relation to those docile and passive words 'servant', 'pariah', 'inferior', the thing that normally goes by the name of violence burst forth inside me. I grasped a sharp-pointed paper-cutter, threw myself upon Olga who by a narrow margin evaded the blow and fled away screaming. The rest, made up entirely of things which happened without words, derives logically from that first contradiction of my theory. I was shut up in the living-room; the police were called; from the police-station I was forcibly transported to a clinic for mental patients. And now here I am, in a padded cell, of the kind in which raving lunatics are usually confined.

Naturally I have a lot of time to reflect upon what happened and to draw conclusions. In the end I at least understood this : as long as I was discovering first the word and then the thing, everything went more or less well. On the other hand, as soon as I discovered first the thing and then the word, everything went wrong. I had found the word 'inferior'; I should have behaved as an inferior. Instead of which I behaved as a 'rebel', for the first time placing the thing before the word. But the thing was interpreted by others in a different manner. Where I saw revolt, they saw madness. And they shut me up in an asylum.

# Inside and Outside

I have success with men and I myself am surprised at this because I am far from beautiful. In fact, with my harassed face,
dark and slightly twisted, my green, rather prominent eyes, my
big mouth full of over-white teeth, my thin, leggy figure but with
a great bosom coming down almost to my waist – with all this I
consider myself to be genuinely ugly. But men say that I have an
irresistible voice; and if they say so, one must believe them. And
what is my voice like, you may ask? Some say it is deep, guttural,
grave, harsh. Others that it is a masculine voice. Others, again,
that it is seductive. Someone, however, gave the most correct
description : it is a voice that comes from 'inside'.

However, you must know that, apart from my voice, nothing
in me comes from 'inside', everything comes from 'outside'. For
example, my head literally does not work. I am ignorant of what
it means to be lucid, clear, rational; for twenty-four hours out of
twenty-four I am completely stupefied, as though I had a perpetual, violent cold. But I do not mind; on the contrary. This
stupefaction protects me, so to speak; it is like a wall behind
which I can stay in safety, lying in wait. But its principal effect

is to divide me between a mysterious 'inside', from which comes my voice, and an 'outside', not in the least mysterious, from which everything else comes to me. Let me explain. Stupefied as I am, I never think of anything, I never decide anything, I never choose anything. On the contrary, it is what there is 'outside' me – both things and people – that thinks, decides and chooses for me.

In the morning, for instance, when I get up, I am so bewildered that I don't know whether I am awake or still sleeping. Tottering, vague, obtuse, I turn towards the minute little bathroom and stare feebly at the chaos of shelves and brackets, of various little tables, bottles and jars, looking-glasses and toilet articles. By chance my eye rests casually on the tumbler in which are placed my toothbrush and tube of toothpaste; otherwise I should not wash my teeth because, bewildered as I am, I should not reach the point of thinking that I *ought* to wash them. But the brush and the tube 'demand' that I should do so. And I obey. The same thing happens, after I have washed, with my clothes which, in my greatly disordered bedroom, command me, from a chair, to put them on : if the clothes did not behave arrogantly towards me, I believe I should remain undressed all day, trying to remember what I ought to do and not succeeding; and then with all the other little everyday jobs such as getting my breakfast (this is suggested to me by the teapot which had been placed somewhere or other); going and doing the shopping (commanded by the shopping-bag, hanging on the coat-stand in the entrance to the flat); buying the newspaper or the illustrated magazine (insistently demanded of me by the kiosks on the pavement); and so on. If, once I have done the shopping, I start walking aimlessly, with my shopping-bag full, from one street to another, between the Campo dei Fiori and Piazza Navona, this is not due to any precise act of will on my part but to the continual interference of the 'outside' in the otherwise somnolent and inert course of my life. And in any case the same thing happens with the more important things. In love, for instance, I am – how shall I say? – promiscuous, not by temperament however, but because I don't know how to say no. To illustrate this passivity on my part all that is needed is the following conversation, over- heard by me in a bar, between two young men of my acquaint- ance. 'What, *her*? Ines? Where you put her, there she stays. You give her the first shove and then everything works by itself.'

All this, as I have remarked, concerns my 'outside'. And what of my 'inside'? Certainly it exists; but I cannot speak about it: indeed how could one manage to speak about something of which one knows nothing precise? It may be that my passion for paint- ing must be attributed to my 'inside'. I know that I have no talent; but this does not prevent me from spending every after- noon painting. I live in a small flat of only one room, very cramped; thus I am forced to paint small pictures standing up in the corner by the window, where I have arranged my easel in such a way that the dim light coming in from the courtyard – which is dark and deep as a well – strikes directly on to the canvas. And what do I paint? Why, I paint my 'inside', letting myself be guided by it. Some professional – and I mean a pro- fessional painter – saw my pictures and told me I ought to ex- hibit them. But I, although I agreed with him (it was a sugges- tion that came from 'outside', and so I cannot disregard it), for some reason keep on putting off the affair to some distant and vague future. To tell the truth, how can one bring oneself to ex- hibit one's own 'inside', placing it under the eyes of everybody, like the dissected, bloodstained pieces of meat to be seen on the slabs of butchers' shops?

My 'inside' does not merely translate itself into painting; some- times it plays jokes upon me that leave me perplexed. Something that happened to me a few days ago can give an idea of this. For some time, then, I had been persecuted by the attentions of a perfect type of bourgeois man. (Incidentally, by bourgeois I do not mean anything political: I take no notice of politics, under- standing nothing about the subject; nor yet social: I have nothing against society; merely I take no part in it. I mean, rather, quite simply someone who is not stupefied like me and who uses his head in order to think. But what does he think about? This is the point: in my opinion, about commonplaces, about rubbish, about stupidities, all of them things, in fact, which come from 'outside'.) Well then, this bourgeois man used to take up a position in the streets of the quarter where he had noticed that I habitually wandered about aimlessly and he would follow me wherever I went, without speaking to me, keeping at a distance of one or two paces, as though he had been my shadow. A shadow very different from me, however: small and stocky, with something wild-boar-like about him, both in his muscular, prominent-chested figure and in his face in which the pronounced protrusion of his nose was counterbalanced by a complete absence of chin. He was always dressed in grey, with a white shirt, a thin, twisted tie, short socks and laced-up shoes. Someone at this point may say that I pay regard to appearances. Of course, seeing that I am so passive and that my 'outside' – that is, precisely, appearances – makes me do whatever it wishes.

In the case of this bourgeois man, my 'inside' at first did not wish to have anything to do with him. Then, one way and another, the look of a small wild boar, the grey suit, the short socks, 'acted' upon me; and one day, after he had followed me right to the door of my house, I turned round and, with my face at its most dazed and inexpressive, said to him: 'If you like, come up and I can make you a cup of coffee.' And would you believe it? He bowed, his feet together, holding out his hand and saying: 'Allow me to introduce myself: Eugenio, to you; by profession a gymnastics instructor.' I said nothing and went in at my dark little doorway, at the same time throwing him a furtive glance, to see if he was following me. He did follow me.

Once we were in my one-roomed flat he, naturally, threw himself upon me immediately, and so what happened, happened. I shall not pause to describe our – let us call it – love-making because I should not know what to say about it: things of this kind come to me from 'outside' and leave no trace 'inside', not even as memories. Then, when it was all over, we found ourselves lying on the bed, he flat on his back and I lying on my side, behind him, leaning on one elbow, my eyes gazing over the top of him at the room, and myself more dazed than ever. Then he began to talk. My God, how that man could talk! He talked about himself and his life (he had always done something concerning the human body: gymnastics instructor, wrestling manager, masseur, male nurse, sports trainer); about his love affairs (he liked girl students and had thought that I was one such); about his travels (he had been, with groups of athletes, everywhere; he recalled Japan, especially, with its geishas and tea-houses); about his musical tastes (he preferred popular songs and light music); about his political ideas (he was for the military Junta in Chile, he wanted law and order; yet he also wanted sport for the masses, games and well-being, otherwise 'they go in for politics'); about his ideas on religion (he did not believe in it but wished to do so); about the books he read (thrillers but also history books); and, of course, about sport (he knew everything, he knew everybody: footballers, boxers, racing cyclists and car-drivers, swimmers, canoeists).

I stayed listening to him for some time, in a state of complete obtuseness, aware that my eyes were wandering idiotically over the untidiness of the room. Then he made some sort of a gesture; he sat up and turned his back to me while he reached over me to fetch the packet of cigarettes from the pocket of his coat which was hanging on a chair beside the bed. Then something came to me from 'inside'; and, as I looked at his bare back, with its glossy whiteness, I suddenly said, to my own astonishment as I said it: 'If you don't go away at once, I'll stick a knife in your back.' The proof that this threat did not come to me from 'outside' — for instance from catching sight of a knife – but from 'inside', was that, apart from the fact that there was no knife within reach, there was no knife at all: I do not possess any knives. But my famous harsh, guttural voice worked instantaneously. He stared at me for a moment with wide-open eyes, then jumped off the bed, dressed in a mad hurry and went away. From the doorway, however, he made a sign at me, pointing a finger at his temple, as much as to say I was mad.

Once I was alone, I lay for some time without moving, more

dazed than ever, gazing into vacancy. Then I got up, dressed myself and, still dazed and bereft of thought, went over to my easel. I took up a brush and painted a big red spot, circular and rough-edged, with a number of sharp projections all round it that made it look like a head with disordered hair. Then I remembered that once, in a book on astronomy, I had seen an illustration of the spurt of flame from an explosion of the sun, so large that the earth appeared like a tiny black point lost in a sea of fire. Without intending it, but clearly inspired by my 'inside', I had painted this spurt of flame or something very similar. And so, after working on it the whole afternoon, I wrote underneath, in black, 'Solar Explosion'. Then I lay down on the bed and went on looking at the picture for five hours on end, from seven until midnight. Finally I fell asleep.

# The Virgin and the Drug

❦

I grew up with the incubus of a mother who was a heavy drinker, an erotomaniac, dissipated in her life and, in particular, a feeble and unsuccessful painter. My mother parted very soon from my father, an honest engineer and constructor of dams (perhaps his profession was symbolic!), and went to live with her lover of the moment in a penthouse at the top of an ancient palazzo. My father and I remained in our flat in the Parioli district. I said that I had an incubus of a mother. Besides this incubus, I had also the incubus of myself and of my wish to be in all respects different from her. My mother had permitted herself everything in life: men, alcohol, painting and a great many other impossible or illicit things. I myself, ever since childhood, had trained myself to create taboos, having decided to deny myself everything, beginning with toys and sweets (I was educated by the nuns and renounced what was appetizing to me by making small acts of sacrifice to the Madonna) and even renouncing love, when I grew up. Renunciation, prohibition, impediment, denial: this was my life. At twenty-four I was still a virgin; to make up for this, I had taken a degree in philosophy, a degree which I did

not know what to do with and which I had taken simply in order
to be the opposite of my mother, who was half illiterate even
though a pseudo-artist. Immediately after obtaining my degree
I started as an interior decorator – my true vocation. But
imagine where I set up my workroom! In the same building in
which was my mother's penthouse, but on the ground floor. It
was as though I wished to demonstrate to her that the Art with
a capital 'A' in which she believed was finished; and that, in
contrast, it was necessary to turn artistic creativity to practical,
commercial purposes.

At that period anyone who saw me might well have exclaimed : 'Why, she's come straight out of a fashion magazine!'
And indeed it was so. Do you remember the photographic ad-
vertisements in the fashion magazines in which the models 'present' the so-called 'line' of the so-called 'season'? Those terribly
thin girls, with crazy eyes and dazzling smiles, their bodies twisted
in violent, puppet-like attitudes, their legs thrown out in one
direction and their busts in the other and their arms stretching
forward, and, in the expression of their faces, something sterile
and hysterical – and all this to show off, dramatically, a coat or
a dress? Well, I myself, at the time when I began to have a
success as a decorator of the flats of the middle-class inhabitants
of the Parioli district, was exactly like that. One single word can
be used to describe me : repressed. I was so repressed that I had
almost forgotten I was a virgin. This was partly because I could
not help seeing a relationship between repression and success;
and there is nothing like success to make us forget the price we
have paid to achieve it.

I undertook the interior decoration for a young diplomat who
lived alone. He invited me to lunch and to dinner, sent me
flowers, took me to the cinema and the theatre, telephoned me
every day. Finally we became engaged; my father, who liked
him, approved; my mother, who detested him because she found
him 'bourgeois', did not. We were married in church, we invited
a hundred people to the wedding breakfast, we went off to
Greece. Everything right and proper, in fact, except the first

night in the Athens hotel where my husband, after a few vain attempts, threw himself on his knees and, tearfully embracing my legs, confessed to me that he was impotent. We went back to Rome in two separate planes; he still impotent; I myself, as usual, what is termed 'unsullied'.

The failure of my marriage should have been for me an alarm bell. I ought in fact to have realized that I had married an impotent man 'on purpose' : in order not to give anything to anyone, in order to remain a virgin. Instead of which, I understood nothing, even though a gloomy, secret rage overcame me. I was looking for something, I was no longer very sure of myself, I felt that I was making a mess of my life. Finally, after thinking it over, I seemed to understand : my mistake lay in the fact that I was living the life of an egoist, devoting myself exclusively to myself, and to what further purpose? In order to forbid myself practically everything. I ought, on the other hand, to let myself go, to devote myself to others or to one other, to love. More than anything, virginity had by now, in my eyes, lost its quality of purity, and had become mere coldness and aridity. Yes indeed, I ought to fall in love so as to cease to be a virgin; I ought to love a man and devote myself to him.

One evening the harsh, low voice of my mother – the voice of an alcoholic – told me on the telephone that there was a little party in her flat; and why didn't I come, I would be amused, and it would also do me good, for recently I had given her the impression that I was tired and nervous. I was on the point of answering her that I was not interested in being amused, when I said to myself 'but is it really true that it doesn't interest you?'; and so I accepted.

My mother's little party was a melancholy assembly of a certain number of people like herself : painters without a market, writers without talent, intellectuals without prestige, all of them, however – according to my mother – destined unfailingly for recognition in the near future. Faced with these people, I had the same feeling of repugnance as I had in face of the picturesque rags and scraps picked up at the second-hand dealers' with which my mother had furnished her flat. I myself, on the other hand, was in favour of successful people as I was of enormous sofas, massive tables, rich and expensive furnishings.

I was already seeking an excuse to leave when my mother threw her arms round the neck of a new arrival, a young man of extraordinary beauty. My mother then introduced him all round. He was not an Italian but an American and was called Robert, otherwise Bob. When she came to me, my mother positively threw him on top of me, saying with a knowing wink that we were made for one another. The young man squatted at my feet, glass in hand, but he did not speak to me. So I looked at him; and when the moment came when good breeding would have demanded that I should turn away my eyes, I continued to look. My God, how handsome he was! Rudely, shamelessly, greedily I was absorbed in examining his astonishing blue-green, liquid eyes, his noble, straight, perfect nose, his marvellous, haughty, proud mouth. He allowed himself to be gazed at with a good grace, even though in silence : he must have been accustomed to it. Then, suddenly, he rose to his feet and, without saying good-bye, left the room.

I sat still, more from astonishment than from hesitation, for perhaps one or two minutes; then I rushed after him. The first thing I saw, when I came out into the open in front of the palazzo, was the young man standing motionless and as if perplexed amongst the cars in the parking-place. Instinctively I went to my own car and sat down at the wheel, leaving the door open, as I had so often seen done by motorized prostitutes in the places where they waited. I had not long to wait; the young man understood, came straight to the car, sat down beside me and told me without delay the address to which he wanted to be taken, just as one does with a taxi-driver.

I pretended not to understand and did not move, and then the situation was explained. In short, he had no money and wished me to drive him to a certain bar, a very long way away, where he would meet someone whom he called a 'connection', that is, as he explained to me without embarrassment, a retailer of drugs. Of course, as well as driving him, I would have to pay for the drug. He expressed himself in good Italian, even with a few Roman words and inflexions which sounded comic on his lips. Now I understood his silence and his indifference. I admit that I did not expect such a proposition: moralist as I was, it seemed to me that certain things should be said in a more gradual and hesitating way. He therefore interpreted my astonished silence as the beginning of a refusal; and with strange, desperate determination suggested a bargain to me: if I went with him and paid for the drug he, afterwards, would be prepared to pay off his debt with what may be called a 'sentimental service'. At first I thought: 'So I must really have the face of a mature old maid, starving for love, that he should propose such a thing to me'; but then I realized that it was merely due to the frantic, spasmodic impatience of a drug addict. A fierce decision then sprang up within me. Brutally I told him that I would do everything he wanted but after love-making, not before. I must have spoken with an impatience even more peremptory and desperate than his; for he looked at me in astonishment for just one moment and then, as though realizing that I would not relent, nodded his consent. We hurriedly got out of the car, I took his arm as though fearing he might escape me, and we went back into the house.

Would you believe it? Once we were in my studio, and when, after undressing, I went over to him as he sat waiting on the divan, smoking in a thoughtful way, and I warned him: 'Mind, I'm a virgin', he – in his own childish and gracious way – made quite a scene. I still seem to hear his voice, dismayed and exasperated, protesting in that comic Anglo-Roman accent. What d'you mean? I was a virgin? And I told him so, just like that? And wasn't I ashamed of myself? And why had I waited so long? And didn't I realize that this would mean a double effort for him? And, in short, why hadn't I told him at once, in the car outside, and then he wouldn't have come in, he would have looked for somebody else, etc. etc.

I made no answer; I was too mortified and at the same time,

nevertheless, was now sure of my hold over him because I was aware, in his voice, of more, even if angry, resignation, than of revolt. And indeed all of a sudden, and with expeditious, eager violence, he threw himself upon me; and everything happened much more easily, rapidly and even affectionately than I could have imagined. And then came the great, the true, the marvellous surprise of that unforgettable night : instead of reminding me of my promise to take him to meet his 'connection', he went to sleep in my arms. We remained like that for a couple of hours, I lying on my back and he with his arms round me, his head on my breast. Then I very gently freed myself and went to fetch a blanket and wrapped him in it and lay down again beside him; and I started thinking again and finally understood : Providence was sending me a man who seemed cut out to fit my moralism : I must save him from drug-taking through my great love. I had, in fact, found someone to whom to devote myself and, in saving him, I should also save myself.

I shall not stop to recount the details of our love affair. Love affairs are all alike and anyone who reads what I write can imagine our affair by thinking of one of his own. Furthermore, there is nothing to be said about love; it is an unutterable thing; when one speaks of love, in reality one is speaking of the lateral circumstances that accompany it. In my case the circumstance was called drugs. Which is as much as to say that probably I loved him mainly because I wanted to save him and did not want to save him because I loved him. Is it necessary to say that my victory over the drugs was rapid and complete? All my terrifying capacity for repression, like an army attacking the enemy at the weakest point of formation, flung itself against the deadly habit of a young man who was at the same time affectionately docile and artfully rebellious. I achieved victory partly thanks to a piece of astuteness which was also of a repressive kind : by associating Robert with my decorating business, substituting work for drugs. He was not stupid, he had taste, he was only lazy because he was lacking in self-respect. I appointed him officially as my secretary, with a salary and precise duties. As always, he submitted with apparent goodwill to his new position. Even though I was careful not to show it, I was mad with joy : at last I loved and was loved in return. And I was loved in return by one of the most beautiful young men in the world. Then, suddenly, came the catastrophe. One day he failed to arrive at the studio. Instead of him, I found a note from him that was positively offensive, in which he told me that I was too bourgeois, that he was fed up with my sofas and armchairs, that even if I were no longer a virgin, I had remained so in my mental outlook. So he was leaving me, thanking me for everything and begging me not to look for him.

I was terrified, bewildered. So I had failed at the very moment when I was deceived into thinking I had succeeded. I had thought I was being useful; instead of which I had been able only to do harm. And so, even in questions of love, I tended irresistibly to deny, to prohibit, to create taboos. In the case of the young man, in fact, I had sought to create the taboo against drugs, even though I had done it out of love. But now, logically – partly with the insane logic of passion – I had to reverse the direction of my vitality. Hitherto I had prohibited; now I must permit, must throw off restraint, must break out.

I went up to the penthouse in which my mother lived. I had met him with her; surely she would know where he had gone. My mother was painting one of her horrible pictures. She left her painting and came to meet me; and I, for a moment, as I looked at this little woman in a colour-stained overall, with her vaguely Mongol face like a withered red apple, had a precise feeling that I was facing a victorious, pitiless rival. In my madness I almost thought it had been she who had taken the young man away from me. But my mother reassured me. The young man had gone to live in a villa in the country with a rich, mature woman. Had he perhaps also gone back to drug-taking? Never again, replied my mother ingenuously; no drugs, for this was a great love, the first great love of his life, without drugs being either permitted or prohibited. Precisely the love, I could not help thinking, of which he had need and which, it seemed, I had not been capable of giving him.

Passion suggested a decision which was extreme and, ultimately, criminal. I knew a doctor who had been in love with me and, in fact, still was. I went to see him, told him my story and said that he must procure me a syringe and a certain quantity of heroin. I noticed him looking at me with an expression at the same time both desperate and furious and I feared for a moment that he would throw me violently out of his consulting-room. But suddenly he calmed down; and, with a cynicism even greater than mine, told me that he would give me all I wanted if, just once, I would make love with him. I did not even say yes; or rather, I said it by directly lying down on his white waterproof couch, as though to undergo an operation that was indispensable even though unpleasant. Next day I received a small package; it contained the syringe and the phial of the drug. I put the whole thing into my bag and drove off in the direction of Sacrofano, where the villa was in which the young man was living with my rival.

I arrived about midday. Just at the moment when I was about to turn into the drive leading to the villa, a car came out of it, with the young man at the wheel. He disappeared round a bend in the road; I backed the car and followed him. I caught up with him easily, for he was going slowly, like somebody who wishes to be approached. When I was close to him, I sounded my horn and he at once went and stopped beside the ditch. I drew up with my car beside his and, without greeting him or saying anything but looking him straight in the eyes, I showed him the syringe. I saw him turn pale and appear troubled, and his lower lip began to tremble. Then he made a gesture as though he understood and jumped out of the car. I got out too. But he was already preceding me through a gap in the hedge and then across a field, where the long, luxuriant grass of May came up to one's knees.

It was clear that my silent offer had revived his love or, at least, his cruelty: or perhaps, ingenuously, he saw in it the final collapse of my moralistic attitude. Certainly we made love with unaccustomed violence, plunged in that thick, deep grass. Then I stayed lying on my back, my eyes turned to the blue, luminous sky in which, at that moment, two birds were fluttering, chasing one another and as it were showing off in a saraband of joyous swoops. He was now sitting beside me and, if I wished, I could see his bare arm and the hand that was fingering the vein before plunging the needle of the syringe into it. I closed my eyes and then, after a very long pause, feeling him slip down at my side, I re-opened them and looked at him. He was lying with his eyelids lowered, very pale, motionless, his fair hair sunk deep in the green tangle of grass. I thought, stupidly, that the drug was filling him with a death-like serenity. Then, seeing that he did not move, I called to him, I shook him, and then I understood that he was truly dead.

# Stupendous!

I shouted at my mother: 'You don't know who I am. You haven't the slightest idea of the person who lives with you, under the same roof'; and then I went out, banging the door violently. Once I was in my shabby little car, driving slowly so as not to strain the engine which was in need of a complete overhaul, I asked myself, just for fun, who, basically, I was. And then I realized that I merely had an embarrassment of choice. Who am I? I am the great poetess in the course of writing an immortal poem: I live in a penthouse on top of a New York skyscraper, and from the window I see other skyscrapers rising in competition towards the heavens. I am the brilliant scientist discovering the cancer bacillus: in the silence and solitude of my laboratory, in Paris, I know the intense joy of the greatest discovery of the century. I am the heroic Latin-American revolutionary who, at early dawn, goes to attack government headquarters: I walk through an ancient Spanish street, past gratings over windows; my pockets are full of bombs and I have a pistol tucked into my bosom. But why, though I am nothing at all, am I nevertheless the great poetess, the great scientist, the great revolutionary? For

57

the good reason that I 'know' that I am. And why do I 'know'
it? That is the point: where can the idea of one's own greatness
come from, if not from reality? There is no getting away from
it: if there is the thought, there is the thing, and vice versa; and
that's that.

This reflection brought back my good humour which had been
jeopardized shortly before by a remark of my mother's: 'You're
twenty-eight, you're a good-for-nothing, an idler, spending your
time smoking, listening to records, biting your nails, squashing
your lice.' When I remembered the allusion to lice, for a moment
my exaltation subsided as the level of boiling water subsides if
you pour cold water into it. Yes, it's true, the lice give me no
peace: one goes away and another comes and I, for some reason,
take pleasure in squashing them in front of the mirror, for hours
on end – so much so that, if I don't find any, I invent them, so
to speak, squeezing my healthy skin until I make the blood come.
But this depression did not last long. Almost at once the water
in the saucepan of my head began to boil again. Exaltation again
got the better of my thoughts. Forward! Advance! ... Bang!

I pulled up the handbrake, opened the door and jumped out.
Jammed into the wing of my little car was the bonnet, intact and
glossy, of a big, expensive car, of the 'convertible' type, cham-
pagne-colour. A middle-aged person, tall and narrow, in a grey
suit and with an ugly cloth cap over his eyes, was facing me in a
twinkling, with a biro pen and a notebook in his gloved hands.
Round us there was already the inevitable crowd of idlers, greedy
for some cheap entertainment. The person said to me, in a nasal
voice: 'Signorina, you were coming from the right and you
blocked my road. It doesn't matter. Give me the terms of your
insurance.'

I looked at my wing, all crumpled up, and shouted: 'What
d'you mean, my terms? What d'you mean? Now I shall be without a car for goodness knows how long. Perhaps you can tell me
how to manage.'

'You will have to walk. The terms of your insurance, please.'

'It's you who can walk, you ugly bastard. What d'you think –

that I'm afraid of you because you've got money while I, from my appearance, might be mistaken for a poverty-stricken wretch? But you're wrong; even though you've got gold-rimmed spectacles, you don't see properly. I'm somebody that you'd never even think of, somebody you ought to kneel down in front of.'

'Here is my visiting card. Please give me your name and address.'

'To hell with my name and address. Write down: Genius. Yes, I'm a genius, that's the truth of it, and you can put down "genius" in your notebook.'

The crowd round us guffawed, filled with joy; they had hoped for a scene and now they had it. The man with the big car waited, frowning, his notebook and pen in his gloved hands. Suddenly a policeman popped out from somewhere or other and then, perforce, I had to give my so-called 'personal particulars': Zoe Proetti, twenty-eight years old, daughter of Giovanni and Rosa De Santis, unmarried, typist. As I gradually provided these pieces of information I had exactly the same feeling that a wolf or a leopard doubtless has on seeing itself shut up in a cage, after a long struggle. I was the wolf, the leopard, that is, the genius; and the bars of the cage were my name, surname, parentage, civil status, profession, address.

But see what spirit can do! As soon as the incident was over, I drove off again and then my exaltation flared up once more: my brain was again in flames. Almost without being aware of it, I parked in the usual little street, stopped to examine a pair of rather nice trousers in a shop window, paid back in their own coin a couple of youths who stopped to accost me; I did, in fact, a number of things and, at the same time, in my not very lyrical state of mind, did not realize I was doing them. Then, all of a sudden, I discovered that I was in front of Geremia's front door. How did I get there? A mystery.

Geremia is my boy friend, and he too is a genius even though of a different kind from me. The difference between him and me is that I am a genius who might develop in any direction: science, art, politics; whereas he is, let us say, a specialized genius.

The special character of his specialization is to write scripts for
the cinema. These scripts of his are stupendous – there is no other
word for it – true, genuine masterpieces. Naturally, since Geremia
is a genius, people do all they can not to recognize his originality.
And so the scripts pile up, one on top of another, on his shelf;
and a genius like him is forced to live by expedients, almost in
poverty.

I ran upstairs, two at a time, with these thoughts in my head
(but many others were piling on top of each other : my mind
was a sea in a continuous storm) – up the steep, damp stairs, and
on the fifth floor knocked at an obscure door. Geremia came
and opened it. He is tall and robust, with a big head of curly
hair, a low forehead, small eyes, a big nose and a big mouth. It
is a simple face, of a uniform colour like under-baked bread, the
face of a peasant : and in fact his father *is* a peasant, living in a
farm in the country and digging the soil. But I 'know' that he is
a genius, just as I 'know' that I myself am a genius. Yes, he is a
genius and there are few equal to him; and I must needs hang
on to him tightly, otherwise, if I lose him, where shall I find
another similar genius?

I went in and sat down on the only armchair, which in any
case was broken and lacking one of its feet, in the chaos which
was the only room in which he lived. I asked him : 'Have you
telephoned the producer?'

He sat down on the edge of the bed. He answered in a sulky
tone : 'Yes, I telephoned him.'

'So what?'

'He refused to speak to me.'

'Blackguard and idiot !'

'Yes, idiot, because this time I had really made the script to
fit his actress like a glove. But what does he want? I should like
to know what it is he wants. With this script he could have been
certain of more than a thousand million lire.'

'A thousand million? Say rather two or three thousand.'

From an almost empty packet of cigarettes I took a very small cigarette-end and lit it, scorching my lips. Then I said : 'Read me the script.'

'But you know it; I've read it to you before.'

'Read it again. It's stupendous. I want to enjoy it again.'

He resigned himself at once, because, between us two, I am the genius who commands and he is the genius who obeys. He rose, went to his desk, fished out the folder of the script from amongst the confusion of papers, went back and sat down on the bed again, coughed two or three times and then started reading in the embarrassed, reflective voice of a peasant who does everything with slowness and careful application. The script recounted the adventures of a boy and girl who robbed a jeweller's shop and then, with the money, bought a holding of land in the country, built a house and started to cultivate the soil. Geremia read the script and I listened to him, smoking and approving with nods of the head at the finest points. As soon as he had finished, I said, with deep conviction : 'Once again – stupendous ! A real masterpiece. Geremia, you're a true, genuine genius.'

He said nothing but sat with his head lowered, like an ox that has received a stunning blow between the horns. Then he replied : 'I may be a genius. In the meantime, however, I can't manage to place it, and there's no money here; neither I nor you have any.'

He was silent for a moment, then he resumed in a slow, mournful voice : 'I'm sick of living like this. I've made up my mind to go back to my village, to my parents. For the present I'll help my father in his work on the land. Later on, I'll see.'

'But this means we shall have to part. Or am I wrong?'

'No, you're not wrong; we shall have to part.'

'Geremia, tell me the truth; you want to leave me.'

'It's not I who want to; it's the situation.'

Then, all at once, I realized that I had to make a great effort to prevent his leaving me and, above all, to restore his confidence in himself. My head, as usual, was like a firework display of ideas : a whole explosion of initiatives. In a determined manner I threw away the cigarette-end which was by now reduced to a few filaments of tobacco and said : 'Geremia, I have an idea.'

'What is it?'

'Geremia, they don't want your script. And so, seeing that they don't want it, we'll make them accept it forcibly.'

'What d'you mean? How can you compel a producer to make a film, if he doesn't want to?'

'The film has nothing to do with it! No more has the producer. We'll make the script come to life and we'll palm it off on the world. Instead of making a film about a boy and girl who go into a jeweller's shop, stick a gun in his mug and make off with his jewellery, it'll be we who really do go into a shop, who really do make use of the gun, who really do carry off the jewellery.'

'But that would be a burglary.'

'Practically – yes.'

# A Smell in the Nose

೨൮൨

I was sixteen years old when a man with a benign, paternal aspect but a mind authoritarian, violent, hypocritical, a man in his forties with a round clerical bald patch on the top of his head, like a priest, a prominent stomach, gluttonous, breathless and lame, discovered me in the little Central Italian town where I lived with my modest family and carried me off to Rome, forcing me to become the poetical attachment to his hopelessly vulgar personality. Why did I marry him? Possibly because he had been so obstinately insistent. And then, I was a silly girl: and I wanted to leave home and see the world. I did see the world, for three years; but it was the world of my extremely busy, extremely dubious husband. Go-between in political-financial arrangements, broker in contraband and fraudulent exchange, procurer in black market dealings, my husband, during those three years, exhibited me in a whirlwind of cunningly planned luncheons, of significant dinners, of purposeful expeditions, of ambiguous parties, of equivocal meetings. I was the beautiful, elegant, spiritual, dreamy wife (do you remember Botticelli's Venus? That was me, identical: the same violet eyes, the same figure with flowing, pale, undulating lines) but also idiotic, the wife who 'promotes' her husband by her simple presence, like an expensive make of car or a swimming-pool in the garden. I was also an enchanting bait on a hook in many affairs in which the hope of an improbable adventure facilitated the outcome – a bait never devoured, it is true, yet always exhibited and offered.

In this life, complicated and enigmatic as it was, there was one word floating in the air, so to speak, a word like a very slight but persistent smell: *mafia*. Nevertheless, during those three years which I spent glued, so to speak, to my husband, I never heard this word mentioned either by him or by his friends, not even once. It was just like a faint, diffused smell which is noticeable mainly when one is paying no attention to it and which vanishes as soon as one directs one's regard to the source of the smell in order to focus and identify it. I had it in my nose, this smell of the mafia, I sniffed it with my transparent, delicate nostrils in everything that my husband did and said and in those he associated with and in what these people said and did; and yet it was always merely an odour, that is, a suspicion; and today I still know nothing precise about it. It may have been mafia just as it may, on the other hand, have been lawful, tumultuous business activity – who knows? Besides, how can one bring oneself to ask one's own husband: 'Tell me, my love, are you a mafioso?' Impossible. For I was also sure that he would answer by shrugging his shoulders and saying: 'Mafia? What d'you mean by that? But the mafia doesn't exist. It's the journalists who've invented it. It's an old story, it belongs to another age. Today there's no mafia and there are no mafiosi.'

The smell, moreover, did not merely persist but became even stronger on occasions not connected with business, by which I mean at parties and festive and religious gatherings: weddings, first communions, funerals, patron saints' days, birthdays, Christmas, Easter, and so on. People would gather in one house or another, all of them very spacious dwellings furnished with a crude and hesitant luxury that was both ostentatious and provincial; or again in the so-called banqueting rooms of restaurants.

## A Smell in the Nose

The usual friends would arrive with their wives and perhaps even their children, and then also the friends of the friends, also with their wives and children; and after a general exchange of kisses, embraces, caresses, tender exclamations, admiring remarks about good health, compliments and good wishes, they would start eating. My goodness, what a lot they ate, my husband, my husband's friends, and my husband's friends' friends! Personally, I scarcely touched the food, excellent as it was; and meanwhile, looking with bewildered eyes at all these people with their red, congested faces, and mechanically, with my long, white ethereal hand, making little balls of breadcrumbs, I would ask myself, as usual, whence came this tenacious stink of mafia, mingling with the odour of victuals, from which I could not manage to rid myself. Sometimes I told myself that I was unjust; that such a smell could not emanate from people who were so good and so cordial, so simple and kindly; that it was I who had the smell in my own nose. But what power have thoughts against a sensation? Absolutely none.

It was, in fact, in connection with one of these banquets that the first and only quarrel broke out between my husband and me. When he, driving home in the car, commented with satisfaction on the dinner, I suddenly rebelled, astonished, almost, at doing such a thing, and shouted at him: 'Now listen, don't mention this dinner to me.'

'But, my precious one, everything went so well.'

'Yes, everything went well, but at the same time, everything was disgusting.'

'My darling – why disgusting?'

'Why, I don't know; but everything was disgusting. Yes, the bridegroom was disgusting, the bride was disgusting, the priest was disgusting, the witnesses were disgusting, the parents of the bride and bridegroom were disgusting. And I myself, in the midst of all this disgustingness, felt that I was disgusting too, in fact the most disgusting of all.'

'You don't know them, you can't understand them; and then, you're so different: different upbringing, different habits. But some day you will learn to know them and then you'll see that they're all good people, all honest people.'

Then I had a desire to be offensive to him, so that he would throw off the mask of fatherliness and show his true face. I knew how to do this, and with what precise words; and, with the rage that was shaking me, I did not hesitate : 'I don't know them, I've no wish to know them. I don't want to know anything about them. I know only that I'm fed up with acting as a snare for the unwary in order to forward the shady dealings of a husband who would really deserve, one of these days, that I should make him a cuckold.' I had said the magic word, the 'Open Sesame'; and indeed the mask at once fell from his face. My husband gave a swerve and went and stopped gently beside the pavement. He put on the handbrake and, speaking between his teeth, without looking at me said, with extraordinary calm : 'Did you say cuckold or am I wrong? Tell me if I'm wrong.' I confess I was afraid, and I answered : 'I didn't say that word; what are you thinking about? You heard wrong.' It was a lie of the mafia type, a barefaced, absolute, total lie which contradicted the evidence; but he accepted it immediately, without batting an eyelid. Stooping to restart the engine, he said : 'Ah, well, well, I thought you did. Evidently I heard wrong.'

There were, as I have said, three years of this life, between business gatherings and family parties. Then, one morning, I awoke with a feeling of nausea and with a strange flow of saliva in my mouth. I connected this sickliness with a certain irregularity in my physical being, and suspected that I was pregnant. A visit from the doctor, shortly afterwards, turned the suspicion into a certainty.

My first impulse was to run happily to my husband to make him, in turn, happy. The impulse, however, was neither strong nor truly joyful; fundamentally it was conventional, one of the conventions from which it is difficult to escape because, from time immemorial, they have been those of the whole of humanity. Then, immediately afterwards, a second impulse, incomparably more profound and more sincere even though sad and despairing, repelled and obliterated the first. No, this child of mine must not be born, seeing that it would be born with this father and among these people. And to become, later, inevitably, a man like its father, like the friends of its father, like the friends of its father's friends.

I did not pause or delay. I went to see a middle-aged widow, a fellow-citizen of mine, to whom I was bound by trusting and faithful friendship; I told her a lie, which was that I was going to have a child by a man who was not my husband; she gave me the address of an obliging doctor who would rid me of my unwanted child; I went to a pawnshop and pawned a ring, then telephoned the doctor and made an appointment for two days later. Finally, serene and comforted, like one who has accomplished a bounden duty, I returned home.

That same evening, pursuing a plan of my own, I took my husband and some of his usual friends to see a famous film, *The Godfather,* which was being shown in a cinema in our district. As a worthy ex-student of Letters, I wished to imitate Hamlet when he makes the players act the scene of his father's death in front of the uncle who murdered him. I wanted, in fact, to see what effect this film about the mafia would have on a group of people whom, rightly or wrongly, I considered to be mafiosi. Hamlet, nothing! And it was far from being a performance that aroused confusion, remorse, fear. After the film was over, I invited the company home to a cold supper; and then all these crude, uncultivated men started seriously and solemnly discussing the 'artistic merits and defects' of the production! It would have been a laughing matter if it hadn't rather been something to weep over. Filled with a sort of impotent rage, I deserted all these unqualified film critics and went into the kitchen with the excuse of helping my husband get the bottles of champagne out of the refrigerator.

The bottles were on the table, black against the dazzling whiteness of the shining majolica. Black as the bottles, my husband was conspicuous in the brilliant whiteness as he lay on his back on the floor, his legs wide apart. The orthopaedic shoe of his shorter leg, with its enormous, glossy heel, aroused a feeling of pity in me, for the first time since I had been living with him. Then I stooped down and saw that his eyes were open but had no sight in them; and I realized he was dead: a stroke.

My duty now was to inform his friends and to improvise a scene of conjugal grief according to their taste, that is, histrionic, heart-rending. But I wished first of all to express, in my own way, my immense, joyful relief. Holding with both hands my little belly which already seemed to me to be more convex than usual, flinging my legs hither and thither and keeping a dreamy, fixed look in my eyes, I danced round the table quietly humming a little song of my own which went more or less like this: 'My child, my child — you'll grow up big and beautiful — with neither a father nor a godfather — my child, my child.'

# The Idea of a Goddess

❦

I left the house to go and see the man whom I have loved during the last two years and whom I ceased to love twelve hours ago. My love lasted for the same length of time as the success of this man, a very well-known film director; and it finished yesterday evening when, in the private theatre in which his last film was being shown, the lights went on and the spectators, most of them film critics, looked into each others' faces in silence and then, one after another, went out a few at a time, without even shaking hands with the director, as the custom is. Sitting in my seat in the darkness, I had followed the slow but inevitable descent of the film towards disaster and, at the same time, that of our love affair towards coldness and detachment. Bonifazio, my director, was sitting beside me; I held his hand in mine, a habit that had lasted since the beginning of our relationship; a short time before the finale I withdrew my hand and, when he sought to take it again, I rebuffed him, whispering to him – I hardly knew why – this remark which was unforeseen not only for him but also for myself: 'Leave me alone. Everything is over between us.' He immediately bent himself double, as though I had struck him in the heart with a poisoned arrow. Then he accompanied me home in silence and took his leave on the doorstep, saying : 'I beg you to spare me any further comment. Now, especially, we must preserve our love. Good-bye, we'll meet tomorrow morning.'

Preserve our love ! As I was driving my car very slowly, in an automatic way, through the gay, crowded noonday streets, I looked down at my personal appearance and realized that the end of our love affair was already visible in my clothes. You must know that from the very beginning Bonifazio had formed an idea of me with which, willy-nilly, I had finally had to comply. He said that I had the body of a goddess and the soul of a child; and that he did not know what to do about the child and only loved the goddess. Bonifazio was, in fact, a genuine masochist; and to please him I had to falsify my real character, which fundamentally is infantile, capricious, fickle and naive, and behave instead like an authoritative, unemotional, pitiless virago. In the same way, in my manner of dressing, I had to renounce the free, ragged, 'hippy' style towards which I was naturally drawn, and adopt, instead, a very 'dressed-up' style, that is, to go about adorned like a statue on an altar. But now, thanks to the failure of the film, I was at last able to rebel against the absurd idea that I was a goddess. Looking at myself, I realized that this morning, almost without noticing it, instead of the usual trappings from expensive dressmakers, I had put on a shapeless sweater and a pair of ugly old faded trousers. Bonifazio did not wish to have anything to do with the child there is in me because in reality he himself wanted to be the child between us two – he who always required to be caressed and dandled and yes, even to be punished. But this sort of game cannot go on for ever : the child was now freeing herself of the goddess and finding her own self.

Nevertheless there was no doubt but that Bonifazio's fiasco created, for me, a quantity of new problems. I was not so foolish nor so ungrateful as not to recognize that I owed a great deal, on the material level, to Bonifazio. He had found a job for my unemployed father; he maintained my brother at his school in

Switzerland; every now and then he gave my sister work as a film extra; he allowed us to live in a flat owned by him without paying any rent. It may perhaps be thought that Bonifazio did all this and continued to do it because I asked him. Nothing is less true. It was he who imposed his benefits upon me; and fundamentally they only concerned my family, with the more or less obvious purpose of binding me to him by making himself useful, in fact indispensable. Indeed, to put it briefly and brutally, it was his successes and not his favours which made me remain with Bonifazio, because of my almost physiological need of success, which for me is, at the same time, the substitute, the symbol and the proof of sexual potency. But now Bonifazio was no longer successful; and I discovered that, correspondingly, it was not so very easy to leave him, because he had entered into my life, or rather into that of my family; and that this cunning calculation on his part of binding me to him by means of helping my family revealed itself in the mysteriously clinging manner typical of things that grow upon one, and when one becomes aware of them it is then too late to get rid of them. And so, whether I wished it or not, I found myself faced with a depressing dilemma : either to leave Bonifazio, sacrificing my family; or to stay with him, sacrificing myself.

Luckily, when I reached this dead end in my reflections, my eye suddenly fell upon a large green folder lying on the dashboard, between a small bag of sweets and a box of paper handkerchiefs. It was the final draft of a film script, and it had been there for a month; it had been given me by Girolamo, a young director who had had a great and genuine success that winter with his first film. He had given it to me, asking me – absurdly, to my mind, since I am well known for my crass ignorance – to read it and then telephone my opinion of it to him, and he had indeed even written his telephone number in red pencil on the cover : as good a way as any for telling me that he liked me and making me say that I liked him. The folder, as I said, had been there for more than a month and, of course, I had not read it; but during those thirty days the underlying message of this strange request for advice had acted upon me, slowly but profoundly. I had the proof of it : that morning I had dressed like a ragamuffin – not so much, perhaps, to annoy Bonifazio, who likes me as a goddess, as in order to please Girolamo who, to judge from his own way of dressing, wants me to be a 'hippy'. This shapeless sweater, these tattered trousers *were* my favourable opinion of the script; just as his request to me to read the script *was* a declaration of love of the clearest kind. But what should I do now to communicate the message suggested by my clothes? It was simple : by telephoning to him and fixing an appointment, in fact by letting myself be seen.

I braked suddenly in the avenue along which I was advancing at walking pace, then took my car out of the row of cars and went and stopped in front of a big, crowded bar. I got out, went into the bar, purchased a telephone token at the pay-desk and went and shut myself up in the telephone box. I felt very timid; I noticed that, while I was dialling the number, my heart was thumping in my chest and my breath almost failed me. When Girolamo's voice saying 'Hello' came from the receiver, for a moment, before giving my name in a faint voice, I had to struggle against the agitation that oppressed me. But you see what success means! Immediately afterwards, his ringing voice, self-confident, aggressive, like a strong drink of immediate effect, raised me from the depression induced in me by Bonifazio's fiasco of the evening before, brought me to life, made me almost rise in the air physically so that I seemed suddenly to be closely confined in the narrow telephone box. We said a great number of things to one another in a confused, tumultuous way, as though we were both exploding at the same moment. In the end he asked me, with a lingering touch of uncertainty, whether he could see me during the week. Shamelessly I answered him that I would come to him that same afternoon.

When I left the telephone booth I had a precise impression that the people crowding the bar turned round as I passed, as though my conversation with Girolamo had made me suddenly visible, in an expanded, provoking manner. Then, almost to my surprise, I discovered that, without being aware of it, I had solved my dilemma : I would stay with Bonifazio and thus would not harm my family, now dependent on him; but the success which, it seemed, I could not do without, I would henceforth demand from Girolamo. I was so pleased with this solution that, once I was in my car, before starting it I looked at myself in the mirror above the windscreen and, childishly, winked at myself and put out my tongue. Then, instead of going straight to Bonifazio's, I went quickly home, tore off my sweater and trousers and dressed myself up again in the solemn clothes that transformed me into a statue.

Later I went up in the lift to Bonifazio's penthouse. The lift was an enchanted chariot in which stood a goddess, serene, unemotional, inhuman. And indeed, when Bonifazio opened the door to me and saw me on the threshold looking at him, silent and motionless, he was almost on the point of throwing himself at my feet. But he restrained himself and led me in, going to sit at his work table. I stood facing him, in silence, offering myself to his gaze. Finally, with sincerity, but humbly, he said : 'How beautiful you are! At least as beautiful as my film is ugly.'

# The Apartment

What, in truth, has happened to me? What has happened is that I am stuck, irremediably, and not from days or months ago or even years, but permanently, perhaps actually from the time before I was born. I have no enjoyment in anything and continually change everything : my studies (four branches of study in five years); the learning of languages (successively, and without result, Spanish, French, Russian and English); social groups (from the so-called 'jet set', through the hippies, and right down to contacts with certain shady gangs, almost of the underworld); and men (half a dozen of them, the important ones; of the others, many more).

I change, however, not because I exhaust my experiences but because, essentially, I don't have them. Just as someone who suffers from insomnia continually changes position in bed but does not therefore manage to sleep. Once again, what has happened to me? What has happened to put it briefly, is that 'I have no destiny'.

I was thinking of these things while I was going up in the lift to the fourth floor of an unknown house, with two enormous suitcases full of all sorts of things at my feet. The lift was going up and I was weeping, with sobs that redoubled at every floor I passed. I was weeping because I knew for certain that I was engaged in doing a thing that was both mistaken and tasteless and that would once more confirm the failure of my life. Driven on by despair and perhaps at the same time slightly drunk, in some house or other, I let myself go the other evening like a madwoman and confided in a woman called Viva of whom I knew nothing but who, to judge by her cold, vulgar beauty and her concise, expert language, evidently carried on the trade of a prostitute – and if she didn't, then it means that I no longer know what a prostitute is. I told her that I was 'stuck'; I told her that I was thirty years old and that the last ten years were like a black hole and I did not know how they had passed; I told her that the blame for everything resulted from my family, with whom I was forced to live, together with my parents and two sisters, without a room where I could study and be on my own. Viva, naturally, disregarded what I may call the existential side of my outpourings; and, as a practical woman, concerned herself solely with the question of the room. With a sudden show of affection (but why, seeing that we scarcely knew one another?) she told me that she was going away for two months; that if I liked she would give me the keys of her apartment and I could go there to study, and even, perhaps, live there : it would be convenient for her, with so many thieves about, to have somebody living there during her absence. With one of my bursts of enthusiasm, as sudden as they are short-lived, I accepted. And so there I was, in the lift, with these two suitcases full of clothes and books, the worn and crumpled books which I needed to prepare for my university exams and, finally, to learn English or French.

The lift stopped at the top floor; I got out, with an effort pulled out the two suitcases and pushed them, by kicking them, as far as the door which I opened after unlocking, one after the other, at least three locks. I went in and had my first surprise : the flat was not in darkness as, for some reason, I expected; but full of a strong, dazzling, unpleasant light. Second surprise : Viva had scattered notes all over the place with warnings, pieces of advice, cautions. I went all round the flat, which turned out to consist of a big living-room and a small bedroom, and everywhere I found these notes, at the same time so sensible and so authoritative. In the bathroom : 'Do not throw sanitary towels down the lavatory', 'Do not turn on the water-heater and the air conditioner at the same time', 'Do not not use towels to clean off make-up'. In the kitchen : 'Put only fireproof dishes into the oven', 'Turn off the gas before going out', 'Use only the right detergent for washing the pots and pans'. In the living-room : 'Do not place lighted cigarettes and full glasses on the arms of armchairs and sofas', 'Brush the gramophone records after listening to them', 'Do not leave the television, the air conditioning, the radio, the gramophone turned on, after using them'. Finally, in the bedroom, there was one single note, perhaps the most curious : 'Telephone at will. Answer if necessary'.

But apart from these notes, which testified to the almost obsessive worries of a perfect housewife, Viva's apartment had no character, did not in any way reveal her personality, was, in fact, absolutely anonymous. White predominated, almost without any other colours; the living-room was white, with white sofas, white rugs, white curtains; the bedroom was white, with an entirely white, broad, low bed, a white carpet, white wall-cupboards. White of course prevailed, in glittering tiles, in the bathroom and the kitchen also. Everything, in fact, was white, in the white light of the clouded sky coming in through the living-room windows; and yet, strangely, this whiteness did not suggest an idea of purity as, by ancient convention, it usually does. Rather, it suggested a highly coloured life, a life in intimate, forbidden colours, a dissolute life of mercenary rites against the background of all this immaculate whiteness. The quietness of the house, in turn, suggested the same thought : it was not a *silent* house, it was a house in which one would think that people had just stopped talking so that echoes of unbelievable voices, of words unheard, might linger on.

Anxiously I searched for further indications, for other messages, apart from those in the notes. I opened drawers, I lifted the cushions of the sofas, I looked inside the wall-cupboards. I found nothing; or rather, I found the usual clothes, the usual household objects; but nothing that spoke to me, nothing that ordered me to do something. I myself, on the other hand, was in need of orders; is not destiny perhaps an order which it would be in vain to oppose with a refusal? Finally, in despair, I stopped in the middle of the living-room. Should I then have to unpack my bags, put my clothes in the cupboards, my books on the shelves, my exercise-books on the table, and return to the empty aspirations of a life without a destiny?

From the centre of the living-room I turned my eyes into the bedroom, of which the door was wide open, to a sight that suddenly made me giddy. For I saw, all at once, something black sticking out from underneath the pillow, at the far end of the bed. Slowly I walked across the room, went and stooped over the bed, put out my hand towards the bed-head. With a vague feeling of wonder I pulled out, gradually, an openwork undergarment, a pair of black stockings with seams at the back, a black suspender-belt, a pair of black gloves and finally, by thrusting my hand more deeply in under the pillow, a whip, also black.

Then I stood upright again and looked. All these black objects were now lying on the white bed-cover, arranged with a certain orderliness in which, almost without noticing it, I had placed them as I drew them out, like a diligent maid laying out clothes for her mistress who is going out. The undergarment was spread, so to speak, flat on its back; the suspender-belt was under the edge of the undergarment; and the stockings were below the suspender-belt. The gloves, one on either side, suggested the idea of arms; one of the gloves had the whip within easy reach. I looked downwards, following the line of the dangling stockings; and then, on the white bedside rug, I saw a pair of black, glossy shoes with pointed toes and very high stiletto heels. All at once I wondered why Viva had left all this stuff under the pillow. I told myself that the fact of her having left it so that I should find it was the equivalent to her having left a note saying: 'Put on these garments, grasp the whip.' Meanwhile, as I thought of all this, I had begun to undress.

I did this without haste, with docile professional scrupulousness, and with a dull, dreamy suspension of all thought. Viva is a big woman with broad shoulders, a prominent bosom, narrow hips and long legs. I have the same sort of figure. The only difference is that Viva is fair and I am dark. But possibly Viva dyes her hair.

I slipped on the undergarment, then sat down on the bed and pulled on the stockings up above my knees. Then I rose to my feet and buckled up the suspender-belt. Finally I put on the gloves which I pulled up above my elbows, and the shoes, bending down to fasten the straps. Then I had finished. With slow steps, feeling myself to be unusually tall and aggressive, I walked over to the looking-glass.

How the female body changes according to the clothes it puts on! My own body, after I had attired it in the manner suggested and intended by Viva, now stood before me and I could hardly recognize it. Beneath the provoking transparency of the open-work undergarment, my breasts had broad, dark nipples like a couple of big copper coins; my groin stood out with hairy, aggressive prominence; my thighs, veiled in black, looked whiter and larger, my calves more fleshy. I stooped down to pick up the whip and then, all of a sudden, the telephone on the night table started ringing.

It rang once, twice, three times, four times; I looked at it, brandishing the whip in the air; it went on and on, shrill, arrogant, insistent, authoritative, urgent. There was no doubt but that it was ringing for me; it was another message, with another order, following on those that were written in the notes and the message of the clothes hidden under the pillow. Then, while the ringing seemed intending to go on for ever, I went to my bag which I had placed near the telephone, put out my hand, careful not to touch the receiver, and unfastened the clip. The little bundle of banknotes that I had brought with me for the necessities of two months' stay in Viva's flat was in it. Now I had to 'pay myself'. With the tips of my fingers I extracted two notes and was about to place them on the night table; then I changed my mind: the character that I had accepted to be demanded a different place; I slipped them in under my right-hand stocking, in the manner of prostitutes in brothels.

The telephone started ringing again, obviously again for me. In that shrill sound, in fact, one could surmise astonishment, anger, even a threat. I let it wear itself out; and unhurriedly, walking majestically balanced on the high stiletto heels and slapping the whip against my leg, I went over to the window. I pulled the cord and the curtains opened, then, withdrawing into a corner so as not to be seen, I looked out through the glass.

The flat was in the Parioli district; in front of me there was the usual panorama of that quarter: house after house rising up the slope from all directions, dense and close together, and, amongst all this cement, like a tuft of hair under an armpit, a clump of trees in some narrow garden.

I gazed with a strange intensity at this panorama. Strange, because nothing had happened; whereas I gazed as though everything had happened. And what feeling did I have as I opened my eyes wide in an astonished, dreamy stare? The feeling of life in action as it is contemplated in the very moment when it is being lived. Then, suddenly, I realized that I had come here and had done what I had done so as to be able, finally, to look out of the window in this way, at the cloudy sky, at the roofs, at the façades of the Parioli houses, at the trees in that garden. Now all that remained for me to do was to dress myself again, pick up my suitcases and go away.

# Judith in Madrid

There is nothing more squalid than a pair of holed and torn tights right in the most intimate part of one's body. As I was explaining to my boy friend that the moment had come for us to part, I looked at my body as it lay on the ragged divan bed and perceived that my tights, the only sound pair that I had left, must now be thrown away. The strange mermaid-like air that tights confer on the female body, blunting its shape and veiling its colours, was disfigured by an irregular tear starting from the hip and ending in the groin, disclosing a large stretch of white skin, as though the mermaid had lost part of her scales. Meanwhile, at the other end of the line, I heard his voice asking me, in distress, why I wanted us to part.

I answered at once: 'Because there's a new man in my life'; and I was very nearly tempted to add: 'thanks to whom I shall have all the tights I want and many other things as well.' My boy friend then raised his voice to ask me whether I loved this new man.

I replied, with scrupulous respect for the truth: 'I don't love him, but I like him, and besides he's rich and that's enough for

me.' I should never have done this. At that sincere remark of
mine, the barrier of respect collapsed and I was plunged into a
hitherto contained tumultuous flood of insults. I listened in a
rather absent-minded way to the angry voice, enlarging meanwhile the tear in the tights with the tip of my finger, and with,
as it were, a childish pleasure in destruction. But when he told
me that a street-walker, standing in front of her little fire in a
suburban avenue, was a hundred times better than me, because
at least she did not disguise the sale of her body with the excuse
of 'liking' somebody, I decided privately, in a cold but firm
manner, that I had had enough of it; and I had recourse to a
telephone-trick which I had adopted before with other suitors
who were over-insistent : I pretended that the line had been cut
off and started crying : 'Hello, hello' as though I no longer heard
my boy friend's voice, although I heard it perfectly well.

He, for a short time, went on insulting me, then he too began
shouting : 'Hello, hello', convinced that communication between
us had ceased. We went on like this, shouting at one another, he
more and more desperate and I more and more indifferent :
'Hello, hello'; then, very gently but with deliberate pitilessness,
I put down the receiver and broke off the call. Ugh ! So that was
all over. I got up from the sofa and prepared to pack my bags.
The new man in my life was to await me at the airport. He was
a businessman; he was going to Spain about some question of
exports and wanted me to go with him.

But when I began to transfer the things from the drawers to
the suitcase, I realized that the whole of my wardrobe was more
or less in the same state as my tights : discoloured brassières,
panties with holes in them, mended stockings, singed blouses,
skirts out of shape, torn trousers : all my clothes, underclothes
as well as top-clothes, testified to the disadvantage of having a
proud, disinterested mind. It was true, I had already had many
love affairs; but all of them in the role of an honest, passionate
ragamuffin who was not concerned with self-interest and thought
only of feeling. And so this would now be the first time that
interest was combined with feeling; a new life, then, even if,

apart from being new, it was unconstrained and cynical. With regard to this lack of constraint, after a rapid examination of the deplorable state of my wardrobe, I took a decision that was entirely in accord with the situation : in my little poor-student flat I would leave all my rags; I would wear nothing but a light overcoat and would present myself at the airport, to the new man in my life, naked as I came into the world. If he were not stupid, he would understand the symbolic significance of my nudity. And once we were in Madrid, he would provide for re-clothing me from head to foot.

So, a few hours later, while the aeroplane was staggering towards the runway, I said to my companion who was sitting beside me : 'I came not only without any suitcase but also without any clothes : look !' and, notwithstanding his scandalized gesture, I opened my coat so that he might see that I had nothing on, absolutely nothing. 'At Madrid,' I added, 'you'll buy me what I need, won't you ?' 'We'll buy everything,' he said. At the same time he took my hand, because he is affectionate, very much so, and is determined that I should be too. We held hands : then the plane, with a powerful thrust, hurled itself forward, rushed along for a short distance, left the ground and rose obliquely towards the clouds.

In Madrid we went to an expensive hotel; then spent the whole afternoon of the first day going from shop to shop to reconstitute my wardrobe. It was like playing with one of those modern dolls that are sold naked with their clothes separately, and little girls amuse themselves by dressing them, beginning with the slip and going on to the blouse and skirt. I myself was the doll, naked under my coat; and, for my companion, dressing me was an erotic game because he was in love and it amused him to spend money on me and it gave me pleasure that he should be amused in this way. Brassière, tights, panties, trousers, skirt, blouse, stockings, suspender-belt, shoes, handkerchiefs, handbag, gloves, dressing-gown and, finally, a large, lightweight suitcase to put all these things in : the afternoon flew past, easily, gaily, tenderly, playfully, just as though we were both playing with this doll to be dressed from head to foot – my body.

Every now and then he stopped in the street, opened my coat and said : 'Let's see, let's have a look and see what's still lacking'; and I could not help bursting out into happy laughter. In the end, we went back to the hotel, tired and content, with my big suitcase full of new things. My companion went out again on his business; and I, once I was alone, gave way to a naive feeling of satisfaction with the luxury into which I had been plunged for the first time in my life. How smooth and soft under one's feet was the fitted carpet in the bedroom ! How flattering were the many looking-glasses which, in shadow, reflected my image ! How light, how cool, how smooth were the sheets between which, finally, I slipped, delighted, for a brief rest ! Yes, decidedly the man whom I did not love but whom I liked was gaining ground more and more. Certainly, if things continued in this way between us, I should end by truly loving him.

Next day he again had his business to see to; and so, finding myself alone, I went off to visit the Prado museum. Not that painting interests me much but anyhow, once dressed and, I may add, very well dressed, what can a solitary, beautiful, elegant woman do in a foreign city where she knows no one, except go and visit a museum? So there I was, then, going round the Prado, from room to room, letting my eyes wander over the masterpieces of painting. I thought I ought to stop in front of some picture and examine it with care; but, somehow or other, I felt distracted and remote. Then, all of a sudden I stopped, fascinated. There was a big picture representing a famous subject : the slaying of Holofernes at the hand of Judith. But it was not the subject which fascinated me; it was rather the extraordinary resemblance between myself and Judith. The same robust, almost athletic figure; the same shapely bosom; the same vigorous back; the same capacious hips; the same delicate back to the neck, the same small head; the same face with its large, black, limpid eyes, its finely modelled nose, its mouth red and fleshy as a cherry.

It was I, there was no doubt about it, it was I myself; and what

I was doing was mysteriously to my taste. What was I doing? Holding up the head of Holofernes, bleeding, with hair dangling and eyelids lowered, at that very moment detached from the body which, indeed, lay there in front of me, decapitated. But why this terrible gesture appealed to me, I did not know. I thought about it for some time; then, coming to no conclusion, I left the museum and went back to the hotel.

I found my companion there; so we went together to visit the Escorial, not far from Madrid. During our visit and then in the restaurant belonging to the place, where we ate, he showed himself extremely affectionate, extremely in love. At the Escorial, during our visit to the private apartment of Philip II, in spite of the fact that the little room looked out into the grey, icy abyss of the church, he wanted to embrace me at all costs; in the restaurant he ate with only one hand, clasping mine with the other, thrusting his fingers between mine as if to suggest a similar embrace of our bodies. So much passion, I was conscious, began to have an effect upon me. Supposing I made up my mind to love him? I was not a pure spirit : I was a person made of flesh and blood; a man's desire and all the things that go to testify to that same desire – that is, presents, luxury, new clothes and, in fact, money, yes indeed, simple, brutal money in banknotes and in small change – all of this did not leave me indifferent. Who said that love is a pure, disinterested feeling? Whoever said that did not know that in reality love is a plant with beautiful, scented flowers and roots sunk in manure.

In the evening we went to a characteristic night-spot and sat at a table to drink wine and watch traditional dances. All the time my companion murmured passionate remarks to me and I cannot deny that from time to time I gave him a more or less ardent look. He, naturally, noticed the excitement in my look and redoubled his attentions and his passion. On a small platform quite close to us a woman wearing a mantilla was dancing in flamenco style; and I, excited by the inspiring, crackling sound of the castanets and the clicking of heels in the dance, all at once, yielding to some sort of impulse, put my mouth to his ear and murmured to him in a warm, vibrant voice : 'I adore you.' And he, in return : 'So do I, you.'

It was very late when we got back to the hotel and, our arms round one another, like a boy and girl, crossed the hall beneath the impassive eyes of the night porter. In the bedroom we made love and then went to sleep just as we were, both of us naked. I slept for perhaps a couple of hours and then woke up with a start. Darkness enveloped me, I was quite naked, I realized that I was kneeling up on the bed and that I was grasping in my fist a long, sharp-pointed hunting knife which we had bought the day before during our excursions round the shops. I felt tense and violently disturbed; truly in the state of mind of somebody about to commit a crime. Terrified, frantic, I searched for and found the lamp on the night table, turned it on and saw to my horror that the point of the knife was turned towards the bare back of my companion who, owing to his bent position, gave the impression of being without a head. Then suddenly there came back to me the memory of the picture in the Prado, in which Judith can be seen rising, revengeful, beside the decapitated body of Holofernes. Automatically I threw down the knife, slipped on my coat and left the room on tiptoe.

I went down into the hall, ran and shut myself in the telephone box and dialled the number of my ex-boy friend in Rome. Then something sinister occurred. I heard almost at once, on the telephone, his voice saying : 'Hello'; I hastened to answer : 'It's me, I'm telephoning from Madrid – hello, hello'; but he, whether out of revenge or because of a fault on the telephone, did just what I did with him in Rome and merely went on shouting 'Hello, hello', as though something had come between us which prevented our communicating. We went on saying 'Hello, hello' in turn, he in a quiet voice and myself getting more and more desperate; finally, with a click, the connection was really broken off. I left the telephone box and went up to the bedroom again.

In the dark I took off my coat and slipped in under the bed-covers. I was Judith, not yet a murderess lying beside a still living Holofernes. I reflected that, for the moment, it was better for me not to go beyond this initial phase of the Biblical episode; later on, we should see. Very soon I fell asleep.

# The Superbody

For some time my husband might be said to be dividing my person into two quite distinct parts, one of them irritating, superfluous, negative, the other alluring, necessary, positive. It did not take me long to understand that the first begins from the neck upwards, the second from the neck downwards. When I speak, my husband interrupts me, snubs me, mimics me, calls me an idiot. When, on the other hand, I am lying on the bed or walking in front of him without speaking, his eye dwells on my body with a strange approval strongly mixed with regret. This attitude on his part naturally produces in me an analogous tendency towards dissociation. More and more, when I speak, my ideas become confused, my words become timid, vague and muddled; I feel that all the time my husband is thinking: 'But what an idiot! Is it possible to be more of an idiot than that?' On the contrary, more and more, when I am lying down or walking and he is looking at me, I find myself adopting a pose, as though to be watched and gazed upon more lovingly. And all the time I feel my husband is thinking: 'But look what a splendid body she has, this idiotic wife of mine!'

# The Voice of the Sea

In order to understand my husband's attitude, you must know that he is a film producer of the 'risen from the ranks' type, as they say, entirely devoid of artistic ambitions, specializing in consumer films mainly of the licentious kind. In fact it was precisely on the occasion of one of these films that I, a very well-known star of the erotic cinema, first met him. He fell in love with me; I saw him as he was, in truth rather vulgar but good-natured and affectionate; and in the end, chiefly perhaps because he insisted so much, I married him. But after the wedding, tired of exhibiting the provoking forms of my famous body on the screen, in enormous close shots, I faced him, brutally, with the alternative: either he must give me the part of protagonist in a serious film, an 'art' film; or else I should choose to stay at home and play the part of housewife. He promised me, there and then, everything I wanted. But later, when his passion had cooled off, it was obvious that he again began to think of me as protagonist in an erotic film, one of his usual ones. He did not tell me so, he hadn't the courage; but he allowed me to understand it from that special way he had of looking at me, of which I have already spoken, somewhere between admiration and regret.

My husband's admiration and vexation had recently been accentuated because a film upon which he had set particular store had made a decided sensation ever since its first evening. He had now become unreasonable, always, it might be said, on the point of exploding into uncontrollable, blind rages. And his glances, between disappointment and pleasure, had by now become so frequent and so pronounced that they aroused in me an embarrassing consciousness of my body, to such an extent that I was continually thinking: 'My right breast – what is it doing? Is it exploding out of my blouse, or is it behaving properly, enclosed inside the cup of its brassière? And my belly – is it protruding naked above my trousers, or is it hiding, calm and serious, with its belt fastened over my navel? And what is happening to my right buttock? Is it rising up or falling down, is it rotating more than the left one?'

One evening, while the two of us were alone in our living-

room, he sitting at one end of the sofa and I at the other, in front
of the television, suddenly, urged on by an irresistible impulse, I
leapt to my feet, not worrying about the behaviour either of my
right breast, my belly or my left buttock, and rushed over to turn
off the set. Then I went back and sat down again and faced my
husband. 'Tell me,' I said, 'your last film is going badly to a
serious extent, isn't it?' At once he growled at me: 'Don't say
such half-witted things. It's going extremely well. It's a great
success.'

'But at its first showing it didn't last even a week!'

'You're being an idiot, as usual. Don't you know that cinemas
have their commitments? But you'll see, later, at the second
showing, how it will take up again.'

'The critics said it's a film that is not merely ugly and vulgar
but also extremely boring. One might think that this time, anyhow, the critics are right.'

'The critics understand nothing. This is a film that will make
a heap of money.'

We remained silent, both of us, looking at one another, like
two duellists before the attack. Then I made the first move. 'I
am your wife,' I said, 'and I love you and it grieves me to see you
so nervous, so unhappy. Now answer me sincerely. If I said to
you: all right, for love of you I'll give up the idea of a serious,
original film and agree to be the protagonist, more or less undressed, in one of those erotic films in which I – or rather, my
body, and even more my breasts, my belly, my bottom – have
had such a success, what would you say?'

Would you believe it? Although he is fat and short of breath,
he threw himself on the floor in front of me, grasped my foot,
took off the shoe, bent down and kissed my toes and then cried:
'Hurrah! hurrah! Three cheers! At last I recognize my dear,
my beloved Lucilla.'

So it was really true: there was only one hope in his head now
– to get me to return to the exhibitionism that had made me
famous. And that look of mixed pleasure and annoyance which
he threw at me more and more often was that of the businessman

who sees his capital lying unused and unprofitable. I jerked up my foot which he was smothering with kisses, like a lunatic; my heel struck him full in the face; then I rose to my full height and hissed at him : 'For some time now you have been looking at me like one of those traders in human flesh, in the times of slavery, looking at a female slave belonging to him and calculating what price he could put on her to sell her. Well, I say no. You shall not put me up for sale either today or tomorrow or at any time, ever. To your great fury and consternation, these breasts will fall down and become a pair of wrinkled pockets, this belly will lose its shape like an old shopping-bag, these hips will become as broad as the sides of a barge without your being able to get a single picture of them. And now I am saying good-bye to you.'

He had fallen back and was looking at me, touching his mouth with his fingers where I had struck him with my foot. Then I saw his lips form the word 'idiot'; and I warned him, crying : 'No, I'm not an idiot, remember that and get it well into your head : I'm not an idiot in any sort of way, and soon, very soon I'll prove it to you.' Having said these words, I turned my back on him and hurried out, almost at a run. But how badly she moves, in a manner at the same time both awkward and pro-vocative – a woman like me, when she does not control the changes of position of her body to the last millimetre !

My challenging remark to my husband was neither casual nor improvised. For some time I had been feeling more sure of my-self because a couple of months earlier Gildo, the director of a rival film-producing company to that of my husband, had made me a proposal of work to my own taste. 'A serious, original film?' had exclaimed this cultured, civilized, modern, up-to-date young man, taking off his glasses and gazing at me with intensely ex-pressive eyes, as if to search inside *my* eyes and to create a human, intimate, confidential relationship with me from the very start. 'My dear Lucilla,' he said, 'for you I can't imagine anything except a serious, original film, only that; you must think about it and take your time. The day you decide, come and see me here in the office. And if the decision happens to be taken outside working hours, come and see me at home. At any time. I'll be there, expecting you.'

I had accepted in a general way, as they say; but I knew in my heart that I should have to have some pretext for leaving my husband who, certainly, would not endure that I should return to the screen in a production different from his own. My husband had now provided me with the pretext, and I, just as I was, in trousers and sweater, went out into the hall and then down to the street. Gildo lived at no great distance from us; I went on foot through two or three of the quiet, elegant, minor streets in my district, past the rows of cars parked close together beside the deserted pavements. I ran; and all the time I was feeling that my body was shaking in a disordered sort of way; and I cursed my husband for having caused me this self-consciousness; and I said to myself that all this feeling of shame was coming to an end and that I should be making my début in a film worthy of me and would be forgetting my body, once and for all. I reached the main door of the house, rang the bell, spoke into the inter-com. When his well-educated voice asked who it was, I answered all in one breath: 'It's Lucilla, open the door, I've run away from home, I've left my husband, I *must* speak to you.' What was there between myself and Gildo for me to announce myself in this way? Nothing, to tell the truth, nothing beyond that promise he had made to let me appear in a serious film. And yet everything, since the hope of expressing myself was, by now, everything to me.

The door opened with a discreet murmur very similar to his voice; I went in, ran upstairs with the whole of my body still writhing in a violent, uncontrolled way; without waiting to re-gain my breath, I rang Gildo's bell; and, when he answered, I threw myself sobbing into his arms. Have you ever had the im-pression that you were inflicting a role on someone for which he was not prepared? So it was with Gildo. Clasping me affection-ately, he closed the door and led me towards the living-room, but I felt all at once, quite clearly, that he did not feel like assuming the role of a lover. His hand barely touched my shoulder; his body was curved outwards in such a way as not to encounter mine; his chin pressed on my head as though to prevent my throwing it back with my mouth close to his. He piloted me to a sofa; then went and sat down opposite me, at a considerable distance. Then, suddenly, I stopped crying and said to him: 'I'm sorry, but it doesn't happen every day that one leaves one's husband.'

Taking off his glasses and gazing at me with his strangely magnetic eyes, he replied: 'Never mind. I understand you and I respect your sorrow.'

I looked at him, at this point, with a new attention, to see what it was that was wrong with him, apart from his over-refined voice. And then I understood. His eyes, which were beautiful, dark, profound and always unchangingly fixed and intense, like those of a hypnotist, made a disagreeable contrast with his nose and mouth, the former being slightly crooked and flattened, the latter shapeless even though fully-formed. He had, so to speak, been born with those eyes; whereas one could not help feeling that his nose and mouth had been artificially moulded, as well as possible, as in the case of someone who had been the victim of a serious accident. Gildo smiled at me and then resumed: 'Now I'll tell you how I see you in the film you'll make for us. Now listen carefully, for there's nothing written down, nothing definite. Simply I see you as I should see you on the screen, myself sitting in an armchair in the studio theatre when the film is finished.'

He was silent for a moment, then he resumed: 'I see a very beautiful woman tormented by a typically existential drama. This woman has a mind, has a soul; but everyone is determined to allow no importance except to her body. And so she, to avenge herself, decides to be as everyone wishes her to be, nothing more than a stupendous, marvellous, fascinating piece of flesh. Further to avenge herself, she overdoes things, she goes too far, she behaves, to put it briefly, like a nymphomaniac. I see her going with a man, immediately afterwards with another, and then another and another and another. I see her abandoning herself among all these lovers; her body is indefatigable; her nudity is unsparing. I see her going up staircases, entering rooms, throwing herself on beds, walking through apartments, looking out of windows, going out on to balconies. And this, all the time, clothed only in her own beauty, in a continual exhibition of her body. But listen carefully, once again. This woman does not behave like this because it gives her pleasure; she suffers in doing all these things, and does them merely to avenge herself on men's lack of understanding. As much as to say: you wanted me to be a body and nothing more. Very good. I will be as you want me to be. In fact, I will be a superbody. What d'you think of it? Indeed the title of the film could be: "The Superbody".'

I had had plenty of time to prepare my answer because he had been speaking slowly, almost in the rhythm of the imaginary film in which he affirmed that he could see me. So I replied, promptly: 'I'll tell you in turn what *I* see. I see a cunning film director who, knowing very well that my nude body is worth money, wishes to make me make one of the usual erotic, consumer films under the pretext of an existential drama. I see this same cunning man reciting his long string of balderdash, thinking that I am an idiot and that he can lead me by the nose as much as he likes. Finally I see this same idiot woman telling him "not on your life!" and going back to her husband who at any rate knows nothing of existential dramas and is only interested in making money.'

So I went away. I went back home, to sleep beside my merchant of human flesh. Ever since that night I have given up the idea of a serious film. But my husband, on his side, has never again asked me to go back into the films.

# The Self-Taught Man

Why am I made like this? Yesterday, at eight o'clock in the evening, I repeated once again to the Self-Taught Man (I call him that because of his passion for culture; in reality his name is Gaspare and he is a businessman) that I loved him to the point of madness; today, barely twenty-four hours later, I wait for him, thinking bitterly of the best way — that is, the cruellest and most offensive way — of throwing him out of the house. What has then happened between yesterday and today to make the wind of my feeling blow in so contrary a direction? That is what I ask myself, huddled up in the bed in which I spend practically the whole of my life, surrounded by a chaos of newspapers and illustrated magazines, the telephone and telephone directories, my breakfast tray and my lunch tray, the turned-on radio and the books glanced at and lying open.

I search for the reason of this incredible instability on my part and the more I search the less I find. Perhaps it is because there is, between the Self-Taught Man and me, a difference of age, he being fifty and I twenty-eight? Or because he is a married man with three grown-up children and not the slightest intention of

94

leaving his wife for me? Or because he is a tradesman, with a
not altogether prosperous business, a shirt-and-tie shop, whereas
I myself am, as they say, 'of good family', that is, of noble descent, and comfortably off into the bargain though not really
rich? Or because with me he shows off his culture – the culture,
precisely, of a self-taught man – in a wizard-like manner, taking
on an air of omniscience, and I, after being for some time fascinated, begin, perhaps unconsciously, to rebel? Or is it because
in love-making he is so undeniably virile, and virility, as is known,
especially if it is self-satisfied, can be irritating? In reality these
are all insufficient reasons, whether taken singly or all together.
And so, in the long run, the only valid reason seems, paradoxic-
ally, to be lack of reasons. As when one says about somebody:
'I've no fault to find with him, but there's something about him
that just doesn't do'; and this something that 'doesn't do' leads
in the end to hostility and the breaking off of relations.

When was it, incidentally, that the surging tide of my love, so
high and so impetuous for more than a year, started to ebb?
That, at least, I know for certain: it was, precisely, last night at
a quarter past eleven, in the restaurant on the Via Cassia where
we had gone to dine. He was facing me and he never stopped
looking at me, with those curiously magnetic, stupid eyes, like
the eyes of a stage hypnotist. Then he stretched his hand across
the table to take mine and asked me, in a low voice: 'D'you
love me?' I looked at his hand and saw that his wrist-watch
registered a quarter past eleven. At the same time there came
upon me, rapidly and irresistibly, a kind of spasmodic contraction
in the lower part of my stomach and I felt my whole body pain-
fully taut with anger, like a spring about to be released. Lowering my eyes which I felt to be sparkling with hatred, I nevertheless answered in a flash: 'And you ask me that?' It was, in fact,
an entirely physical, indeed a physiological, impulse: one
moment before a quarter past eleven I was predisposed, aband-
oned, open to his love; a moment later, paralysed, trembling,
closed.

But now, there he was at the door. Even the very brief ring of the bell, as of someone so very sure of himself as actually to be discreet, aroused in me a feeling of bitter aversion. Perhaps it was due to the hostile feeling that intoxicated and confused me that I forgot to put on my dressing-gown and went, quite naked as I was, to open the door to him. No sooner was the door open than I found myself with my breasts plunged into an enormous, fresh, delicious-smelling bunch of red roses which he held out to me from the landing outside. In a slow, spiteful voice I said to him : 'Thank you, thank you, they're really magnificent' : I gave him a kiss over the top of the bunch of flowers, led him inside and then turned my back on him and went straight into the bathroom. I turned the key, lifted the lavatory seat, threw in the roses, then sat down and urinated on them. Slightly relieved but not pacified, I turned on the shower and stood under the jet of steaming hot water. When I left the bathroom, in my dressing-gown, refreshed and with my hair combed, my hatred was no longer the sullen poison it had been shortly before, it was a whetted blade, ready to wound.

I am quite a good cook and often, in the past, I had prepared more or less elaborate meals for him. But this time I did not wish to do anything; all I had done was to telephone the snack bar and get them to send me up a complete dinner. He was sitting at the already laid little table in the kitchen. Without looking at him, I opened the fridge and took out smoked salmon, eggs *à la russe,* roast beef, salad, cheese, strawberries and cream. Then as I sat facing him, he immediately began eating with a good appetite, chewing in an excited sort of way which once upon a time touched my heart but now irritated me. I watched him without touching the small amount of food that I had put on my plate, and meanwhile asked myself coldly what pretext I could bring forward to provoke the decisive quarrel.

It was he himself who, shortly afterwards, provided the pretext. It was by no means without reason that I called him the Self-Taught Man; as I have already said, he not merely had a passion for culture but also a passion for talking about it and popularizing it. It went in periods : at one time it would be existentialism, at another, Zen; or some particular writer, Proust or Kafka; or again, some book or other on ecology. That evening it was the turn of cybernetics, one of his favourite themes, perhaps because of that touch of wizardry which this science, so full of philosophical implications, confers upon him (in his opinion) in my eyes. While continuing to eat with a good appetite, he explained to me the marvels of retroaction or 'feedback'. Having given me a summary definition ('it is a question of a self-correction device which allows a machine to regulate its action by means of the rejection of that same action'), seeing that I said nothing and did nothing but look up at him from downcast eyes, he went on in an enthusiastic and didactic way : 'Don't you understand? All right, I'll give you an example. You know, don't you, about oil-fired boilers? There is a thermometer immersed in the water of the boiler. When the water exceeds a certain temperature, for example seventy degrees, the thermometer dilates and interrupts an electric contact and as a consequence stops the flow of the fuel oil. The temperature immediately starts to be lowered, finally causing a new electric contact which in turn again starts the action of the oil-pump. Now isn't it marvellous that a machine should regulate itself – that is, should communicate information to itself in an automatic way, or indeed, essentially, that it should *think,* and then act in conformity with its own thought?'

I said nothing; I went on looking at him with a heavy, sullen attentiveness. And then, all of a sudden, I felt that the Self-Taught Man, by dint of indoctrinating me, had in consequence turned me into a self-taught woman, if only in order that I might free myself from him. I said slowly, in a malevolent tone : 'You're right, it's marvellous, the machine regulates itself. But these are things that happen not only to machines but also to human beings. For instance, to me.'

He looked at me in astonishment, holding the glass in mid-air that he was raising to his lips: 'How do *you* come into it? We were speaking of boilers.'

'I do come into it – and how! Hasn't it ever occurred to you that I am a boiler in which your fuel-oil, that is, your intolerable love, has made the temperature rise to an excessive height? At this point – just think a moment, Mr Know-all – what do you suppose will happen?'

He was stupefied. More, perhaps, by the fact that I made use of his own science against him than by my hostile tone. I went on rubbing it in: '*I*'ll tell you what will happen, in fact what has already happened. Something that has the same function as the thermometer in your boiler will interrupt the flow of your love towards me. And you know what it's called, in plain language, this something? It's called hatred.'

This time, incredulous, he opened his eyes wide. 'You hate me?'

'Yes, I hate you because your passion gorges me, chokes me, very nearly makes me vomit – another type of retroaction, I suppose. I hate you and want you to go out of my life, for good. In this way – to continue with your speech-making – my temperature will go down to a tolerable level and I shall again be ready to welcome a new love.'

Frightened, he stammered: 'If you like, we won't see one another again for some time. I won't look for you, I won't appear at all. When your ... temperature has gone down, then we'll meet again. Are you willing for us to do this?'

In a fierce voice, I retorted: 'I don't trust you. Yes, I'll accept to be loved again, but not by you. You're too red-hot, my friend. Keep away!'

Clearly he was cudgelling his brains and his mind was bewildered: 'But only yesterday,' he said, 'you told me that you loved me, in fact that you adored me. You said so, you remember, at the restaurant, as soon as we sat down. You said, in a low voice: "I adore you." And now, on the other hand, all of a sudden ... What has happened to you, I beg of you, at least tell me what has happened to you?'

'Nothing has happened to me. Like your boiler, I have been self-regulated.'

Suddenly the Self-Taught Man prevailed, comically, over the lover. He objected : 'But one can speak of retroaction and self-regulation only if it's a question of machines, of automatic things. You're not a machine, nor are you automatic. You're a woman of flesh and blood, with affections, with passions.'

'No, it's not true,' I shouted. 'I'm a machine for making love. An automatic thing to go to bed with.'

'Automatic things don't love, they can't love. You understand love, until yesterday you loved me.'

'Certainly I loved you; but now I hate you : I am an automatic thing if only because, otherwise, it would not be possible to explain this change. Indeed I have no reason, no reason at all to find fault with you, except that you love me. And now, I'm sorry, but you must interrupt your meal and go away. Here's your coat. Clear off !'

He had taken off his jacket because it was hot. I held it out to him and made him put it on. Then he turned round and made as if to embrace me. I pushed him away, crying : 'Hands off ! If you touch me, I'll scream. If you persist, I'll call the police.'

He went away. But not without throwing me, hastily, from the doorway, a frightened look from those eyes which were now devoid of magnetism. I banged the door violently, then looked at myself in the glass. And now I understood his frightened look. With my hair standing on end, my face white, my eyes dilated and flashing, and my body, partly visible in my open dressing-gown, stiff and marble-like with anger, I struck fear even into myself.

I went back into the bedroom, threw myself on the bed with my face in the pillow and started sobbing. I realized now that I no longer knew why I had done what I had. And while I was crying, I was aware that my temperature – to adopt the Self-Taught Man's metaphor – was falling very rapidly. Suddenly I felt frozen from loneliness, icy from lack of love. Continuing to sob all the time, I put out my hand to the telephone, took up the receiver

D*

and, almost blindly, dialled the number of a certain student who had been repeating to me for some time that he loved me. Yes, indeed, I was a self-regulating machine. But, for making love, there must be two people.

# Mind and Body

∽∾

Even before she was thirteen years old my sister Alina had her first man, a blond, mellifluous youth with a face rather like a hyena, whom she used to go and see in the adjoining flat where he lived with two friends, students like himself. I was three years older than Alina and we were very affectionate towards one another; and so this was the first occasion when we realized that we were, so to speak, one single person, in which I, plain and pale and poorly developed but intelligent, represented Mind, and Alina, supple as a snake and shapely as a statue but with barely two finger-breadths of forehead above a face that was all eyes and mouth, Body.

The mind did not live on its own but by reflex action from the life of the body, to which, in exchange, it continually provided more or less ideal justifications for its appetites. Alina, that first time, tormented me with questions like these: 'What d'you think? He wanted me to go and see him, he promised me a present. I would go, but I'm afraid to; what d'you think?'

Enthusiastically I answered: 'Why, go on; what are you waiting for? Remember, you're not going to find a man, you're going to find love, the most beautiful thing in life.' So she went, and then she went again, and in the end she made love with the two students, his friends, as well, and then with numbers of other men, and every time I was always able to find good reasons for keeping her conscience quiet. The result of all this was that, five years later, Alina had had I don't know how many lovers and I myself none at all. In compensation, however, I had lived with her life, passionately, as if it had been my own.

The moment came when Alina no longer wished to stay with the family, partly because of the annoyance of having continually to lie to our parents, who looked upon her as a rather late-developing child with senses still unawakened. But she would never have had the courage to go away unless I, as usual, had now provided her with a good reason. Together we were studying at the art school; and I convinced her that she and I ought to become painters and, for this purpose, the first thing was that we should leave home and take a studio. Alina clapped her hands with joy at my contrivance and threw her arms round my neck, exclaiming: 'Without you, what should I do?' And so, after a brief but intense discussion with our parents, we got what we wanted and something else in addition : the help of the family.

Our father was a state official of some importance, and he agreed to give us a modest but sufficient monthly allowance; we rented an attic in the neighbourhood of Piazza Farnese, consisting of one small bedroom and one immense room as a studio. In the bedroom we put a big double bed, in the studio a large number of enormous cushions all round the walls and at the far end, near the windows, our painters' easels.

We began to lead the 'artist's life'. To painting we devoted the early hours of the afternoon. I, who believed always primarily in the justification of my ideas, painted with passion; Alina imitated me, but hesitantly, for she knew that her talent did not lie here. Towards evening we would stop painting, and then there would begin a coming and going of friends and friends' friends. Some would bring wine, others things to eat, others records or guitars, others again something in the way of drugs, but of a mild kind; and so with the music, discussion on art and politics, eating and drinking and smoking, lounging on the afore-mentioned cushions, we would continue till dawn.

We were very well known and very popular in the quarter; Alina as usual had many love affairs and myself none. From time to time, when there was no money left, Alina would go and see certain mysterious businessmen or shopkeepers, make love with them and get paid. Needless to say, I had provided her with an ex-cellent reason for these not disinterested services : 'These are men into whose life a breath of poetry has never entered. You bring it to them. They pay? I tell you that they ought not merely to pay but to kiss the ground where your feet have trodden.'

Then came the crisis, brought about by two apparently in-significant incidents. I tried to kill myself with barbiturates be-cause I had fallen in love with a young man and he did not want me; Alina, always promiscuous, caught a mild venereal disease. Everything came right for me with the use of a stomach-pump, and for Alina with treatment by antibiotics. But the charm was now broken; and it was Alina, as usual as brutal as she was un-decided, who put the question : 'What d'you think about it? I'm fed up with all these rags. I have somebody, a married man and not so very young, who is ready to guarantee me the com-fort which I feel is absolutely necessary for me. Of course this means a stop to all pretence; it means taking up the profession, without any fuss. What d'you think?'

Promptly and jubilantly, I answered : 'Why, certainly; we've had enough of painting, enough of objections, enough of rags. Don't say, however, that you've *pretended* to be a painter. You did it seriously as long as you felt you ought to do it. Now you feel that you ought to do something different. Well, you ought to know how to do it, without any false shame.' Note that I re-frained from naming the profession that Alina was now ready to take up and which, after all, to put it briefly, was that of a prostitute. But there is no need to believe that there was any hypocritical reticence on my part. At that moment, infatuated and participating, I would have been entirely incapable of calling 'prostitution' that which I considered, on the contrary, in good faith, as an experience of life similar to any other.

The proof of my good faith was to be seen, later, in the manner in which we organized our life when we had moved into our new abode, a flat in the Parioli district. The attic in Piazza Farnese had been open to all and was always filled with light owing to its bare windows through which the sun came in headlong and unopposed; the flat in the Parioli, on the other hand, was rendered discreet, silent and dim by quantities of curtains and hangings, rugs and fitted carpets, draperies and shutters; and it was not open to anyone except Alina's elderly protector. As for myself, in this new situation, I had decided to pass myself off as Alina's servant; and I lived, and allowed myself to be treated, as such. I had discovered that I had talent as a cook; while Alina, in the living-room, entertained her irritable, surly old lover (he was tall, thin, gaunt, with a big aquiline nose and two piercing eyes) I remained in the kitchen studying a cookery book; then, at dinner-time, in a maid's cap and apron, I would serve my dainty tit-bits at table. I liked this shadowed, humble, servile existence; I made it a point of honour to lower myself to the level of degradation, going on my knees to take off Alina's boots, while the old man, in shirtsleeves, his white head all rumpled, observed with his owl-like eyes; or, again, going into their bedroom in the morning to pull up the roller-blinds and place their breakfast tray on the bed. But this degradation was anyhow compensated for by the fact that Alina told me everything, asked my advice and was more subject than ever to my will.

Then there occurred another crisis, but different from the first: in life nothing repeats itself. Alina fell in love with a certain Danilo, a dishonest type who lived by means of successive expedients. Handsome he certainly was, with thick, honey-coloured hair, sky-blue eyes and a bitter mouth; and athletic, with a marvellous golden skin. Danilo took to coming to the house when the old man was not there; then Alina introduced him to the old man; and thereafter the three of them became inseparable. I do not know what happened during their frequent travels in Italy and abroad, in those expensive places so much beloved by Alina, because I was not there. I only know that in Kenya the three of them went off on a safari and only two returned: the old man was killed in mistake by a shot fired from the rifle either of Alina or of Danilo, it was never known which. The old man, after the inquest, was buried at Nairobi; Danilo and Alina came back to Italy and started living together.

This death, however, precipitated the third crisis in our life. Of money in the house there was now very little; one day Alina confided to me that Danilo had suggested to her that they should go by car to the East to acquire drugs there and then re-sell them in Europe. What, in my opinion, should she do? There was a lot of money to be made, it was true; but it was very dangerous and she was very frightened. Then I, with a last flash of my inventiveness, said: 'Why yes, that's a fine, splendid idea; I'm fed up, too, with this mole-like existence. Air, light, sunshine, wide horizons, happiness. Come on, let's go.'

Danilo, in reality, would not have wished to take me with them; and he tried every possible means to prevent my going. But he did not succeed because Alina, with strange, unexpected intelligence, said she could not get on without me, for I was her breath of life; and how was it possible, when going away, to leave one's soul at home?

So we started off in a caravan. We crossed Yugoslavia, Greece, Turkey, Iran. Air, light, sunshine – we had plenty of them; but happiness, which I had so lyrically promised, was, on the contrary, completely lacking. We were indeed, all three of us, bronzed and invigorated by this continuously open-air life; but at the same time, beneath this healthy sunburn, we were gloomy, confused and filled with hatred. I hated Danilo because I felt that he wished to remove Alina from my protection; Danilo did not conceal his firm intention of exploiting Alina to pay the expenses of the journey, and he hated me for preventing this; Alina, whose eyes had now been opened with regard to Danilo hated him in turn because she was afraid of him. Finally, at Ankara, one evening when Danilo had left us alone, Alina told me that it was certainly Danilo who had killed the old man; that she feared that during our journey he would sell her to some so-called merchant of human flesh; that, if we did not want to end up in some Oriental brothel, we ourselves must take the initiative and inflict on him the same end as that of the old man. But did I feel like approving her plan, supporting her, helping her? She spoke with the calm, desperate decision that comes not from feeling but from experience; and then I, who had always gone to fantastic lengths to invent justifications for what may be called minor transgressions against current morality, now that it was a matter of killing a man, immediately found the right reason: 'Why not? He's a worm, a despicable being, not worthy to live. Of course I'll help you. It is our duty to rid the world of such scum.'

And so, without any great fuss, both of us being overwhelmed with hatred, we decided to knock him out at the first opportunity. The chosen weapon should be his own pistol which he kept always ready with a bullet in the barrel, in the empty space of the dashboard.

Luckily chance spared us this final extreme proof of our old-established complicity. At a bend in the road, in Afghanistan, amongst bald yellow hills and under a sky of hard blue enamel, with a cold, blinding sun in the midst of the sky, two Europeans beside a stationary car were waving their arms. Danilo immediately braked, leant out of the window and asked the customary question: 'Any problem?' By way of reply, one of the two pulled out a pistol and fired three times at Danilo, first with two direct hits and then, from close up, quite calmly, in the temple – the *coup-de-grâce*. Danilo remained at the wheel, his head bent, a creeping trail of blood branching out all over his face.

Immediately afterwards there suddenly arrived a car with four Afghan policemen. But instead of pursuing the two murderers of Danilo, they arrested us and took us to the nearest village: it seemed that our passing had been reported not only to the rival drug-traffickers who had killed Danilo but also to the local police. They took us to a small white fortress with two little battlemented towers on top of a hill above the village. At the door was a big man with a moustache, in uniform, with two pistols, one on each hip. He interrogated us, me for two minutes, Alina for two hours. I do not know what happened between him and Alina and I do not wish to know. Next day they let us go; we went to Kabul and took the first plane for Rome.

Now we have gone back to live with our parents and Alina is pregnant, we do not know whether by Danilo or by the Afghan policeman. Meanwhile, as we wait for the birth of the baby, everything is in suspense : the Body does not act, the Mind does not justify. But after the birth, everything will begin again : the Body to act, the Mind to justify.

# A Rather Ordinary Woman

⚬⚬⚬

'Everything's coming to an end, everything's coming to an end, everything's coming to an end.' With this cry I awoke and abruptly sat up in bed, pressing my two hands against my temples and thrusting my fingers into my hair. This is the cry with which I welcome the new day; every morning, more or less, it is like this. My husband had already slipped away, some time before, without making any noise; I put out my hand to the part of the bed where he sleeps and seemed to be conscious of a surviving warmth under my fingers; and then I could not help being moved at the thought of his grief when I kill myself. This is because I know that, one of these days, I shall have to kill myself.

Feeling quite contented, I jumped out of bed and, humming under my breath, went through into the bathroom. I stood in front of a looking-glass and started making faces. I am young – twenty-three – I have a delicate, gentle face with very big dark eyes, a small transparent nose, a large, pouting mouth; goodness knows why it amuses me to disfigure myself with grimaces so as to look like a witch. I made my hair rain down over my face, ;ed my eyes in an ugly squint, I gnashed my teeth.

Then I exploded in a great burst of laughter, brought my face close up to the glass, gave myself a kiss and murmured : 'Who are you? I beseech you, tell me who you are.' It must be noted that, the whole time, I continued to feel desperate; but with a desperation – how shall I say? – lined with happiness. And now, the next thing was my bodily needs. At the very moment when I was asking myself, with genuine anguish : 'How shall I manage to go on living?', almost without realizing it I pulled up my chemise, sat down on the lavatory seat, gave vent to the minor need and felt happy. Then, while I was answering myself, twisting my hands in my lap and staring sadly into vacancy : 'No, it's not possible to go on living' – at that moment I rid myself of the larger need and once again happiness was mingled with despair and blackness turned rose-coloured.

What is the matter, anyhow? The matter is this : when I am desperate I am happy at being so; when I am happy, I am desperate at being so. Complicated, is it not? But, at this point, I should really like to know who and what is not complicated. At school, I remember, I learned that there are in nature certain organisms consisting of a single cell, called, in fact, unicellular. Well, I would swear that if those perfectly simple organisms were able to speak, they would surely cry out : 'We are complicated, extremely complicated, we are monsters of complication.'

It was twelve o'clock when, with my dog on a lead – he is a boxer endowed with enormous strength – I came out of the lift into the entrance hall of my block of flats. The porter, a good-looking dark man with the air of a suburban seducer, took off his cap as I went past, with a somehow allusive and artful emphasis; and then, all of a sudden, I had an impulse to say to him, quite simply : 'Nicola, tell me who I am; come on, let's go into the porter's lodge and you tell me who I am.' It so happened that, just as I started to open my mouth and the porter was looking at me in surprise, the dog, who has his own ideas on the subject of my morning walk, dragged me out of the building into the street. I let him do this, thinking that, after all, it was just as well to leave to chance the reply to the fundamental

question of my life. To chance; that is, to the dog which was
without doubt dragging me to some place where I should find
a precise and suitable indication to stimulate the mysterious
mechanisms of my unconscious. The dog, in fact, dragged me
from one street to another, from one house to another, along the
pavements of the avenue of plane-trees where I live. I should
have liked to linger, to walk in the cold but brilliant autumn
sunshine, amongst all those yellow and red dead leaves; but the
dog, irresistible and as it were knowledgeable, did not allow it.
He turned into a street of shops and went straight to the door of
a butcher's shop. How could *I* be concerned with a butcher's
shop? The dog dragged me along with all the strength of his
bull neck. I overcame my repugnance for blood and went in.

Immediately, as soon as I had entered, I understood everything. The counter rose up in front of me, all in shining grey
marble, so high that I could barely see the figure of the butcher,
who was looking at me with his arms folded across his chest. On
the left he had a big pair of brass scales, on his right an enormous
wooden chopping-block with the chopper on top of it. Behind
him, on the wall, hung a card giving the prices of the various
kinds of meat. The counter, the scales, the block, the chopper,
the prices – who could fail to see in this array the symbols of a
pitiless and irrevocable justice to which I surrender myself, urged
on by a mysterious feeling of guilt? Who could fail to feel that
the butcher's shop was in reality a tribunal and the butcher a
judge? But a judge, a tribunal to try what crime? Frightened
once again by the complexities I discover within myself on every
occasion, I asked in a faint voice for a couple of hectograms of
mince for the dog; then I paid, took the package and went out.

That same afternoon I put the problem to Dr Gargiulo, my
psycho-analyst, during my visit: why that sudden feeling of guilt
in the butcher's shop? Gargiulo, alas, was just the type of doctor
that did not suit me. He and I were too different: he was so very
sceptical, so accommodating, inclined to be undramatic; just as I
myself was imbued with a dramatic vision of life. Now if it is
true – as indeed it is true – that treatment depends to a very great

extent on the degree of collaboration between the doctor and the patient, I fear that Gargiulo and I, in one or even two years' time, will be at the same point as we are now, that is at no definite point at all. Anyhow, my visit was taken up with the examination of my sense of guilt in face of the butcher; but Gargiulo, as usual, tended to minimize everything, to treat me as a perfectly simple person; and in the end, as I got him with his back to the wall, he wandered off into long and entirely marginal considerations, so as to make the time pass and not to compromise himself too much, at least for that day. After my visit was over, as usual without any appreciable result, I went back home highly discontented, having decided to punish Gargiulo for his laziness and indifference by a prolonged delay in the payment of his fee. But then it occurred to me that he would be quick to interpret this delay as a manifestation of neurosis indicating that I was getting myself analysed not because I was suffering from being to that extent complicated; but because I might have fallen in love with him. Just imagine! A little stunted man with a shrunken face that looked like a small heap of crumpled rags in which there chanced to be two little pieces of blue glass — just the type of man I might become fond of! So I gave up the idea of punishing him; but privately I decided that as soon as possible I must find a pretext that was plausible and at the same time resistant to any sort of attempt at a psycho-analytic interpretation, in order to replace the evasive, antiquated Gargiulo with a doctor who was more energetic, more modern and, above all, who would take a real interest in me.

For, when all was said and done, the basis of the problem was this: I am complicated only with those who render themselves conscious of my complexity; with others, as, for instance, with Gargiulo, I feel myself becoming, all at once, simple, similar in every way to those organisms of which I have already spoken, which consist of a single irresponsible automatic cell. Of this consciousness (as I think I have already made clear) Gargiulo was absolutely incapable. On the other hand Cosimo, a slightly frivolous intellectual who for some time had been coming to see me in the late afternoon, in spite of the fact that he was not, like Gargiulo, a professional analyst but merely, as he himself likes to describe himself, a 'dilettante of the profound', Cosimo had this consciousness to such a degree that, after his exhausting incursions into my unconscious, I was very nearly consumed with longing for the evasive Gargiulo. Tall, elegant, thin and ascetic in his person, insinuating, inspired, stimulating in his manner, Cosimo needed only a confessional in which to sit, dressed in a cassock, behind a grill, to be a perfect priest, of the kind to whom you can relate any sort of enormity, in the certainty that they will not be scandalized but will, on the contrary, at once give their full attention to a thorough examination and dissection of everything, with a helpful and subtle indulgence. And indeed, even today, when I told him of my feeling of guilt in face of the butcher, he immediately threw himself upon it like a hungry dog on a bone. According to him, then, the idea that the butcher's shop was a tribunal and the butcher a judge originated from my sense of uncertainty in relation to my husband and my conjugal life. In reality I would have liked the butcher, from the top of his counter, to have enjoined me to abandon my husband or, at the very least, to take a lover as soon as possible. Perhaps at this point it may be thought that Cosimo was interpreting the affair of the butcher's shop with a secondary purpose in view, obviously that of getting me into bed. But it was not so. I was sure that, if I threw my arms round his neck, crying out that I loved him, he would be terribly frightened. He was not, in fact, one of those who progress from psychology to the divan; his passion for splitting hairs into four or eight or even sixteen parts was genuine; at most there existed in him the unconscious vocation of a disinterested but active destroyer of matrimonial bonds. And so, finally, after discussing his hypothesis with him for a long time, I sent him away with the excuse of a headache; and, once I was left alone, I realized with some bitterness that I was still all at sea. Gargiulo sees me as simple, Cosimo as complicated; but in reality neither of the two sees me as I truly am, in the sense of assuming a responsibility in my life, for my own sake and to my own relief. So, in the end, there is nobody left but my husband.

With him, I knew already in advance that I could not get my-self analysed as I could by the psycho-analyst, nor could I con-fide in him as I could in Cosimo. My husband is an intelligent man; but he places his intelligence entirely in his profession. He is an architect; but away from his office and his worksite he is a man like any other man, by which I mean that he is a rather ordinary man. How does a person like me, complicated as I am, behave with a rather ordinary man? The answer is simple : exactly like a woman who is, in turn, rather ordinary. And what, at present, does the rather ordinary woman do? Simple, again : she undresses in a great hurry, puts on a dressing-gown over her naked body, takes up her position at the window and impatiently watches the street. As soon as she sees her husband's car making its usual parking manoeuvre, the rather ordinary woman runs to turn the key in the door and then throws herself on the bed. After a few minutes there is a knock at the door. The rather ordinary woman does not reply; her husband's voice calls her by name, begs her to open the door, commands her, threatens her; she re-mains silent. Then her husband goes away, or rather, pretends to go away; then he comes back; and this time the door almost collapses beneath his furious blows. This does not cause the rather ordinary woman to yield; all she does is to tell her husband, in a voice at the same time both desperate and capricious, that she is not hungry, and that he must leave her in peace and eat his food by himself. Now the husband's voice speaks to her of love; and then the rather ordinary woman suddenly bursts into floods of tears, buries her face in the pillow and howls like a she-wolf. What, in reality, is happening to her? A short time before, as she waited at the window for her husband, she felt somehow pleased that he was coming; then she wanted to appear desperate to him, in order to stir his interest; and then, all of a sudden, she felt genuinely desperate. She repeated aloud, in order to be heard by him, that she had no more desire to live and that one of these days she would kill herself; and meanwhile she listened carefully and anxiously to his furious fumblings at the door handle. But the door did not yield; and so, still sobbing, the rather ordinary woman rose from the bed, slipped off her dressing-gown, letting it fall to the floor, and then, quite naked, went and opened the door and immediately afterwards turned her back and ran to throw herself on the bed again. There she lay on her back, covering her eyes with her arm. So what had to happen, happened; and now, between her and her husband, there is a sort of sexual ritual which is repeated every day at the moment of his return home in the evening. After making love, the rather ordinary woman feels happy and at the same time desperate at being so. But it would be interesting to know what is the point of being complicated if, in the end, one then behaves like a simple person.

# Time Does Not Exist

༚ཆ༝

When was it that I threw the telephone at the maid's head? Yesterday morning? *This* morning? A month ago? A few minutes ago? I do not know; and in any case it is not important for me to know because I know for certain that, on the contrary, any sort of reply would be incorrect. And this is because, after a great many efforts, I have at last succeeded in getting outside time; and so everything that is happening to me has either already happened or will happen; and words such as yesterday, today and tomorrow no longer have any meaning for me. It was time, in any case, it was high time – forgive the pun – that time ceased to obsess me with its dull, overcrowded, incessant clatter like a self-propelled old rusty machine, like the caterpillar tracks of tanks on the march or the belt of an assembly chain in sliding movement: a little more and I should have gone mad from having to listen to this clatter. But do you realize that one does a thing and then one does another and then a third and then again a fourth, a fifth and a sixth and so on, and all these things, instead of staying together all at the same time – like flowers in a flower-bed or pebbles in a river-bed – automatically line up like disciplined soldiers in some sort of absurd army, thus forming those interminable perspectives of cause and effect along which memory struggles in vain, like some old asthmatic general passing his troops in perpetual review? Now, as I said, all this is over: I have got outside time and no human force will be capable of making me re-enter it. But my triumph is recent; I still don't entirely believe in it, I need to feel the confirmation of it. And so, when the maid knocked and timidly poked her head between the two leaves of the door, I asked her, from my bed where I had just woken up, 'Gesuina, when was it that I threw the telephone at your head?'

'Signora, a few minutes ago.'

'A few minutes ago? Not yesterday?'

'Yesterday, Signora?'

'What I meant was: do you remember exactly the day, the month, the year in which I threw the telephone at your head?'

'But, Signora, the year is 1974, the month is May, the day the seventh of May, that is today.'

'And the time?'

'The time, Signora? Five minutes to eleven. I know for certain because you left word that you did not wish to be called before eleven and then the Signor telephoned from the engineering workshop and asked to speak to you and it was exactly five minutes to eleven and when I told him that I was not to wake you up he ordered me to do so with certain words I can't repeat and so I plucked up my courage and knocked at the door and you looked at the clock and saw that it was only five to eleven and so you threw the telephone at my head.'

'I looked at the clock? As a rule I do not look at clocks. And what were these words of my husband's that you can't repeat?'

'Rude words, Signora.'

'Anyhow, what did my husband want?'

'Nothing, he did not want anything. He only said that, instead of going away, as he had decided, and not coming back for a year or two . . .'

'He said that – a year or two?'

'Yes, Signora, a year or two: he would be back for lunch as usual.'

The door closed and I started to think. It was clear that I owed an explanation to my husband for what he saw yesterday evening (but was it indeed yesterday?); Goffredo and me embracing on the terrace, while he and the guests were playing cards in the living-room. To tell the truth there was nothing to explain: I have been betraying my husband, it can be said, from the very day we were married: this is a fact and about facts there is nothing to be said.

Nevertheless there is no doubt that there is something wrong between him and me, something that does not work, possibly from even before our marriage, from the time when he and so many others were paying court to me and I, all of a sudden, chose him on the grounds of the sensible and traditional criterion that he was the one I loved or anyhow thought I loved most. Whereas, in spite of that love, or perhaps actually because of it, on the very day before our marriage I was unfaithful to him with his best friend. According to my psycho-analyst, all this means that I want to punish myself for not having done something that I ought to have done, presumably in my infancy, by continually doing things I ought not to do and did not wish to do. Complicated, is it not? Unfortunately this complication, so comforting on the analyst's couch, does not cancel out the explanation which in a short time, to my great distress, I must give to my husband about the events of yesterday evening.

All of a sudden, like a bomb exploding in my head, came the affirmation, for me now an undisputed fact: time does not exist. Time, indeed, does not exist; and so, what becomes of the feeling of guilt, the guilt itself, punishment and all the other foolishnesses of my psycho-analyst who, when all is said and done, ought at least somehow to justify the high cost of his services? If time does not exist, as I am now quite certain, I can then deduce with some foundation that my relationship with Goffredo 'has not yet begun'. I also know, in any case, when it will begin and where: in three months' time, during a trip to Egypt by Goffredo, my husband and myself, and, to be precise, at Luxor, in the course of a visit to Tutankhamun's tomb. Here, while my husband, always in a hurry and not interested in matters of art, would have already gone out, Goffredo would assault me, seizing me round the neck and whispering to me between kisses: 'You know who I am? Tutankhamun. I've waited for you for thirty centuries and finally you have come and I have risen up specially for you and here I am.' A contrivance, if you like, and, given the place, also rather questionable; but yet still of great efficacy for a person like me, sensitive as I am on the subject of time. Thirty centuries? How can one resist someone who has been awaiting this moment for thirty centuries? Then, as if guessing my thought, Goffredo would add: 'Time does not exist; I am Tutankhamun; but I am also your Goffredo who is mad about you today as he was thirty centuries ago or in thirty centuries' time. In fact; always!' Fine, isn't it?

But I must now explain to my husband that I am innocent, entirely innocent, because nothing has yet happened with Goffredo; and if no guilt has been incurred, why then should one admit that one is guilty? But alas, I already know what his answer will be: the trip to Egypt, 'in reality', was made by us six months ago; consequently I am guilty and at least I ought to admit it; and a whole lot of other things of the same kind, all of them invidiously directed, on examination, towards the destruction of my wonderful discovery of the non-existence of time.

I was thinking of these things under the shower, the powerful jet of which, like so many pins hurled vigorously on to one's skull, stimulates my mind. Then, while I bent my fair-skinned, shapely body backward, inclining my smoothed-out, flattened breast to the hot flow of water that inundated and hardened and reddened it till it looked like a fine piece of rosy marble, it occurred to me that, seeing that time does not exist, I should tell my husband that 'at present' we are in Mexico (where, in fact, we did go at one time, on our honeymoon), at Oaxaca, and so, after all, I do not yet know Goffredo, and in fact we had only just come back, at that exact moment, from an exhausting visit to the pre-Colombian ruins and were standing together under the shower before going down to the hotel dining-room for lunch. The only difficulty was that my husband was not there beside me. But I was wrong; here he was.

I saw him appear in the steamy atmosphere of the bathroom, stark naked and gloomy in the face (odd, how ill humour does not fit in with nudity); then he climbed into the bath beside me and placed himself under the shower, taking care, however, not to touch my body with his. Then, with my wet hair sticking to my face, I said to him : 'Come on, don't look like that. Remember that we're on our honeymoon.' I saw him give me a furious glance and then get out of the bath and go away with a resentful, dignified expression on his face (dignity is another thing that does not sit well on a naked man). I called out after him : 'You're being ridiculous'; but he, without turning round, shrugged his shoulders and went off; and then suddenly, for some reason, my heart was horribly crushed with distress : it was true, I had always been unfaithful to him, but it was also true that I had married him for love and I could not bear to be treated by him with such coldness. I left the bathroom, dressed and went into the dining-room. My husband had almost finished eating; in front of him on the table stood a bowl full of strawberries. The maid served me with asparagus. I sucked the first asparagus stalk; suddenly I realized that my eyes were filled with tears. Trying to smile but without succeeding, I said : 'What a solemn husband I have ! Don't you know it's not right to be in a bad temper during one's honeymoon? These are such important days, the whole of life sometimes depends on these few days.'

Without raising his eyes from his plate, he muttered : 'We've already had our honeymoon, four years ago. And you know perfectly well why I don't want any jokes, today.'

'But I'm not joking at all. We're on our honeymoon. We've just come back from a visit to the ruins of Oaxaca and we took a shower together. Now we're at table in the hotel dining-room.'

'We're in Rome. I came home tired and dusty from the workshop. We're at table in our own home.'

'Yes, we're in Rome; but we're also at Oaxaca and, above all, we're on our honeymoon. And as for Goffredo — for it's Goffredo who is the trouble, isn't he? — as for Goffredo, don't worry: everything has still to happen.'

At these words of mine I saw his face brighten with hope. 'You don't really mean to tell me,' he said, 'that yesterday was the first time he'd kissed you?'

I was almost tempted to deceive him. But I could not, I had to be honest, fundamentally: 'I said "everything". And this everything will happen, it cannot *not* happen; and I can even tell you when and where: in six months' time, in Egypt, at Luxor, in Tutankhamun's tomb.'

I saw him stare at me as though transfixed by a sudden suspicion. Then he said slowly: 'But we've already had our trip to Egypt and, to be precise, six months ago, with Goffredo.'

'We've had it, we are having it, we shall have it.'

'We have had it. Now, at last, I understand. I myself went out, in that blinding sunshine. You two, on the contrary, stayed inside the tomb, for no apparent reason. Now I understand why.'

I cried in desperation: 'No, it's not like that; we haven't yet stayed behind in the tomb; we shall remain there in six months' time. Try, I beg you with clasped hands, try to understand me. Try to realize that between me and Goffredo everything is still to happen and that for this reason you have no fault, absolutely no fault, to find with me.'

Wham! Strawberries, bowl and plate fly through the air. A strawberry strikes me on my blouse, one of my best blouses: doesn't he know that strawberry stains never come out? Then the door was violently slammed, and I was left alone.

I rose and went mechanically to the window. We live on the Tiber Embankment; through the window-panes and the tears I saw the trees on the far shore, lined up like the years; and behind the trees, cars following each other swiftly, like the seconds and the minutes. But in transparency, behind the usual panorama, as in a photograph doubly exposed, I saw a very different scene. We are in Rome and time does not exist. Green, deserted hills slope down towards the river; coming from a hut, a shepherd dressed in skins drives his sheep down to drink the water of the Tiber. On the threshold of the hut stands a big, tall woman, draped in a kind of cloak, a spindle in her hand, spinning, and as she spins she follows the shepherd with her eyes. That woman is me.

# The Unhealthy Life

I made up my mind, pushed back the bed-covers, threw down my legs and rose to my feet; then, lazily, raising my nightdress and scratching my leg, I went through into the bathroom. Here the usual sight of a general awakening met my sleepy eyes: towels large and small thrown here and there; pools of water on the floor; liquefying pieces of soap in water-filled soap-dishes. The family had washed and then dispersed, leaving me asleep: the house, in fact, was empty; my father had gone to his lawyer's office, my mother to Mass, my two brothers to the University, the servant to the market. And I? When I came to think of it, I too had a fine job to do, a professional job, so to speak: at midday there would arrive the man who, theoretically (never was an adverb more appropriate), I was supposed to marry as soon as possible.

Why did I say 'professional'? Because, in effect, I had been brought up, educated – I might even say I had studied – to 'enmesh', at the right age, a husband of some kind. The right age should have been at about twenty; I am twenty-nine. What happened? What happened was that, by dint of hearing myself told that the object of my life was to get married and have a family, I overdid matters, that is, I went beyond the suggestions and incitements of those who brought me up, by which I mean my parents. I ought, according to them, to be a woman and nothing but a woman; that is, a person enclosed within the limits of her own physiology. I have overdone this; my physiology, so to speak, has gone to my head. What has followed is that men, seeing me so coquettish, so exhibitionist, so unrestrained in showing off my (alas) exceptional physical qualities, have imagined that I had an exuberant temperament whereas in reality I am rather cold and prudent; and so, following behind me as dogs do with bitches during their love-seasons, they have taken good care not to invite me as a wife. Such are the tricks of so-called traditional upbringing founded on the cult of the family.

I turned on the shower, pulled off my nightdress and went in under the jet of hot water. Then, as I twisted and turned, awkwardly, my shapely body, as the water flowed over me and I had the feeling of being an animal rather than a person, it occurred to me to wonder what, fundamentally, it means to be too much a woman. The usual prospect of having to spend a couple of hours in the bathroom before being ready suggested to me the idea that being too much a woman means being not so much an ordinary individual as a complex of feminine attributes, each of which, albeit co-existing in close agreement with the others, has its own conspicuous and arrogant autonomy. Which, among other things, involves an enormous waste of time – another womanly characteristic – as each one of these attributes demands separate treatment.

Yes, I concern myself with my physical appearance with the same attention and the same skill with which a soldier concerns himself with his weapons. Sometimes, for amusement, during the dedicated hours that I devote to my body, I try to calculate the time that I throw away in this manner. In twenty years, the length of time that a woman is at her best, between immature adolescence and ravaged maturity, how many hours, days, months shall I have devoted to my hair, to my mouth, to my eyes, my nails, my breast, my belly, my back, my legs? How many hours, days, months, alone in the house, and outside the house, with the various masseurs and beauty specialists? As a result of these calculations, however, I recognize that, in the last analysis, the fault is my own. Nobody, not even my parents who are so anxious to palm me off, would prevent me from behaving like so many young girls of the challenging type: a sweater, a pair of trousers, a washing of the face and hands and off they go. But where to? Inevitably, always in the direction of a husband.

At first slow and thoughtful, gradually, as time passed and midday drew near, my toilet took on a rapid, almost panic-like progress. Rushing from my bedroom to the bathroom and back again to the bedroom, I touched up my eyebrows and slipped on my tights, I brushed my teeth and fastened my brassière, corrected my lipstick and enclosed my hips in their elastic sheath. Finally, however, all the time gained by this frantic alacrity was lost by the slowness of my choice of a blouse and skirt answering to my idea of a blouse and skirt 'adapted' to the man who would shortly be ringing at my door. Irresolute, motionless, attired in my most intimate garments, I stood amongst a confusion of numbers of skirts and blouses spread out all over the room, like a warrior, still aggressive, amongst the corpses of a battlefield. Which should I choose? Unable to decide, I looked all around and meanwhile the time was passing.

Then, suddenly, the bell rang, discreetly yet peremptorily; and I, obeying my upbringing which taught me to be a temptress, rather than my real character which was stand-offish, went to open the door just as I was, half naked. I opened the door at once and found him there in front of me; I apologized, laughing, and invited him to precede me into the living-room, and I would come immediately. He was a good-looking dark boy, five years younger than me; but his surprise caused his face to twitch several times, and this for a moment made him look middle-aged or even old, with the sort of old age that is anxious and puzzled. He went into the living-room, muttering a protest of some kind.

I ran into my bedroom and finished dressing in a great hurry; then, serene, relaxed, smiling, I presented myself to him again. He had sat down beside a plant in a pot and, without realizing it, was picking off the leaves one by one. 'Leave my poor plant alone,' I said to him gently as I too sat down. 'You told me you wanted to describe to me what our life would be like after we're married. Well, here I am, I'm listening.'

He gave a start and immediately began stammering, for – I was forgetting – as well as being full of twitchings he was also a stutterer. Stumbling over the syllables he answered me rather mechanically, as though reciting a lesson he had learned by heart: 'We shall go and live in the country, in my villa, where my mother and my brother also live. We will lead a simple life, a healthy life. I shall be busy on the land, I shall administer my property, I shall sell my produce, my cattle, I shall go out shooting. You will stay at home with the children, looking after them and the household. A healthy, simple life, such as my father lived, and my grandfather and all my family, going back to the most distant generations.'

'But we shall have a house in town?'

'No, why should we? We shall be living in the country and if we wish to come to town we'll go to an hotel.'

'So then, we shall live in the country and I shall look after the household and the children. A word about the children. Are you sure you want to have children?'

'Absolutely sure. We're well off, we can afford as many children as we like and I want a lot of them.'

'How many?'

'Not less than six. Even eight or ten. I want a big family; if there are not a *lot* of children, what's the use of them?'

'I wonder about that, too. But have you ever reflected on the fact that it's I who will have to produce the children?'

He looked at me in surprise: for a moment he was a very handsome young man, with fine, sensitive features; then, all of a sudden, a twitch made him open his eyes wide and thrust his jaw forward; and out came a hideous sort of man, at the same time both brutal and feeble. 'But you've always told me,' he stammered, 'that you like children.'

'Yes, other people's children, seeing that I haven't any myself. But let's make a few calculations. I'm twenty-nine, almost thirty. Eight children spaced over ten years would mean, for me, that at the age of forty I should have eight children from one to nine years old. But children require the care of their mother, at least so they say, until the age of puberty. This means that when I am fifty I shall have to look after at any rate the youngest child, who will be barely ten. At this point I shall be more or less as your mother is today – an elderly lady, very refined, very distinguished, very aristocratic, with a noble face and grey hair. And you will be a middle-aged man; but you will have the land, the shooting, the administration. But I? I shall be like a bitch who has behaved admirably with regard to having her litters and, now that she is old, stays indoors more or less out of habit. Isn't that so?'

'No, it's not so. You're a human being, not a beast.'

'Rubbish. I've been brought up to be a kind of animal; it has nothing to do with you, but it is so. However, you think of it like those who brought me up, that is, my parents, and, with much logic but very little love, you would like me to do exactly what I have been brought up for. That's all very well, if it were not that the very fact that I am talking to you in this way proves that those who brought me up were wrong; they wanted me to become, as they say, an "agent", instead of which there emerged a human being who, for the precise reason that she is so, cannot accept the life that you propose for her. And now listen to me carefully.'

He interrupted me in an intransigent manner, but with the alarmed intransigence of someone who fears he will be overruled. 'I warn you,' he said, 'that our life will be as I said; otherwise it's not even worth the trouble of talking about it.'

'It's always worth the trouble of talking. I've noticed that several times you've used the expression "a healthy life". In the mouth of a person like you, this expression has a special significance.'

'What sort of person am I?'

'You're a neurotic of the first order. Don't say no : look at yourself in a glass, look at the way your face is contorted by all that twitching. Listen to yourself while you're speaking, take note of the stutterings that interrupt your conversation every three words. I don't know your mother or your brother; but, from your descriptions, I understand that they're even more neurotic than you are. And so, when you come and talk to me about the "healthy life", it seems to me that it's a matter of treatment to cure neuroses and nothing else. I myself, with my beauty, and life in the country, and the children one by one, and my future grey hair and all the rest of it – we shall be, for you, just so many pills that are swallowed without knowing what they contain, merely because the doctor has prescribed them for you, hoping blindly that they will do you good. But the doctor, whoever he may be, does not understand your illness. These pills called "healthy life" will not do you any good; you'll take them and continue more neurotic than before, in spite of the eight children and the wife who, to give you pleasure, has brought them into the world.'

I had perhaps said things to him that no one had ever said to him, and one could see this. He put on a gloomy face on which the twitches every now and then cast an anguished light, like flashes of lightning in a stormy sky. 'Well then,' he muttered, 'in your opinion, what would do me good?'

Calm and serene, I answered smiling : 'Listen, it may be that I am fond of you; in any case I have a sort of consideration for you. True neurotic as you are, you haven't behaved like other men, you knew at once how to by-pass my apparent quality of a woman who exhibits her body; you understood that I am different from what I seem and that, instead of paying so-called "court" to me, you would have to make some serious proposal to me. But what you call "the healthy life" is not a serious thing.'

'And what *is* a serious thing?'

I smiled and said to him gently : 'I wonder; perhaps the opposite, perhaps an *un*healthy life.'

'But what, in your opinion, does "unhealthy" mean?'

'First of all tell me what "healthy" means. But don't tell me that it means living in the country, going out shooting, having eight children and an elderly wife, because that isn't true. You must tell me the profound, ultimate meaning of the word "healthy" and then I'll tell you what "unhealthy" means.'

'But if we lead what you call an "unhealthy life", would you marry me then?'

'At once, at once, at once.'

# Contemporaries

I got into my car, a jewel of mechanical perfection, small and luxurious like me, and, as I put out my long, thin hand, its bony fingers laden with massive rings, towards the starting-key, I looked at myself, from ancient habit, in the mirror on the windscreen. I have a narrow, forward-sloping face, all artificial colours and tight-drawn skin, with green, mischievous eyes, a straight, slightly snub nose, a red, shrunken mouth turned downwards with a sensual, pouting expression. From my lean, flushed cheeks my black hair protrudes in two glossy, comma-shaped locks; but they leave uncovered my big, cartilaginous ears like those of a large, elderly ape. Then I smiled at myself, just to see what effect it had on me. An indecisive effect; my cynical, flattering smile was, without doubt, seductive; but my false teeth, too new and too white, were out of harmony in my brown, mature face. As I drove, I pulled back my head: stretched like violin strings, the tendons revealed the obvious loosenings in the skin of my neck. And then my figure: I lowered my eyes for a moment, looked at myself and once again verified the ambiguity of a thinness which might equally be that of a girl of fifteen or a woman of fifty, such as I am. My unbuttoned blouse gave a glimpse of two breasts, exiguous and distant from one another, which would not look out of place on the bosom of an adolescent girl; my narrow, clinging trousers concealed the fleshless rigidity of my legs and gave an impression of youthful agility and elegance. Ah yes, seen from a distance or from behind or in half-darkness, I might easily have been mistaken for a still partly undeveloped young girl. To such an extent that, every now and then, somebody in the street makes a mistake and pays me a heavy compliment, to be positively frightened when I turn round suddenly and tell them angrily: 'Idiot, I might be your mother.'

I came to the petrol pump. The attendant was a handsome young man with a head of fair, curly hair and the body of a swimmer, all rippling muscles and glinting with soft golden hairs. He was called Ruggero and he knew me because he was 'my' pump attendant, by which I mean that he was the one that I habitually made use of. He smiled at me; he enquired in a sing-song voice whether I wanted a complete fill-up; he saw to the pump with one eye while with the other he gave me an occasional glance of enigmatic attraction. Then, once the pump had been re-connected and the key of the petrol tank restored to me, he leant forward with his strong arm to polish the windscreen and, as he did so, smiled at me again. I responded with terror to these smiles, slightly curling up the corners of my lips in a distant, conventional manner; but at the same time I was assailed by acute despair; and when, in paying for my petrol, I realized that in spite of myself I had managed to touch the young man's hand with my fingers, I felt that I wished, that I truly wished that instead of me there had been an old woman, a really old woman, a venerable old woman, white-haired and tremulous, who had given up all idea of sex for at least twenty years.

Why this terror, this despair? I have no difficulty in confessing: for three months, that is, from the time when the young man was first employed at this pump, I have been thinking about him. I am not in the least in love; I am not even attracted; if anything, I am obsessed as it were by a fatal eventuality that might even not occur, that in fact certainly will not occur; but towards which it might be said that my whole life is tending. It will not happen; but, according to the so-called logic of things, it is bound to happen. This fatalistic foresight makes me suffer more than any kind of burning passion. Yes indeed, for passion would make me forget the question of age; whereas foresight reminds me of it.

I gave the attendant the usual slightly excessive tip, he gave me a last smile, I said to him: 'Au revoir, Ruggero' and started off again. I was driving now without thinking of anything. Partly because I had been thinking altogether too much, during the last few days, about the person I was going to see and the matter I had to discuss with her. I reached the steep, narrow, winding street; I came to the pleasant-looking villa in which the woman lived. Here, I could not help thinking, my son comes every day; here, if things go according to his desire, he will finally come to live in his wife's house. But why should I, personally, have to prevent him carrying out a plan which is fundamentally so reasonable and which, when all is said and done, did not, on examination, concern me in any way? I slipped into the lift, pressed the button, and then, as it went upwards, put my face close to the mirror and examined myself. Is it possible, I wondered, that for me it is really 'all over', as they say? And if it is not, I went on to think, what sort of ignominies would I have to undergo in order to 'continue'? Let us suppose, for instance, that, by seeing him constantly, I 'get off' with the garage attendant; what would happen then? Would an old working-class mother confront me, accusing me of ruining her son, exactly as I myself shall be doing in a short time with the woman I had come to see? Or, more probably, would it be he who would make me atone for the scanty joys of a selfish relationship with the prolonged torments of inevitable blackmail? Useless, in any case, to try and furnish any answer; partly because everything could be foreseen except the degree and the quality of the pain. The lift stopped and I got out.

One single door gave on to the small landing, and it was ajar.

E*

I hesitated a moment; then, instead of ringing the bell or asking in a loud voice whether there was anyone at home, I insinuated myself, like a thief, into the entrance. From there I could see, at the far end of a narrow passage, the bathroom, the door of which was open. I could distinguish a circular window of opaque glass, a wall of light-green tiles, a dark-green marble bath. For one moment the bath appeared empty; then a feminine arm, broad and white, was extended and its hand seized hold of a brass bar fixed into the wall. Beyond the arm was the profile of the head, with long, smooth, black hair lying in scattered, pointed locks on the massive white shoulders. The body remained still for a moment; then it rose up from the bath with a slow, gradual movement, revealing the plump back, the barely suggested waist and, as it finally rose to its feet, the powerful hips, curiously square in shape. It was the body of a woman of my own age; but, unlike mine, instead of being dried up, it had become heavy with the years. It was white, very white, but with a fat, opaque whiteness which, among all the greenness of the wall and of the bath, had itself a greenish tinge. The woman was now on the point of turning round. I thought I had looked at her long enough and had formed a sufficiently precise idea of her; promptly I enquired in a subdued voice : 'May I . . . ?'

Without turning round, she said : 'Is that you, Emilio?' And I, very naturally, informed her : 'No, I'm Emilio's mother.' At these words she twisted round with an abrupt movement that almost made her lose her balance; so then I had a front view, and I saw that her breast and belly were just as massive as her back. It was only a moment; then the door, pushed violently, was slammed in my face, and I heard her voice shouting : 'Go away, go away at once, there is no reason why I should see you. Anyhow I told you, on the telephone, that I did not wish to see you. How did you have the audacity to come into my house like this, by stealth?'

I stood in the doorway, leant my cheek against the door and shouted back : 'I came because I feel very deeply about my son's future.'

'*I* don't, in any way. Go away.'

'If my son is a person of indifference to you, why then do you accept this crazy idea of marriage?'

'It's he who wants it, he who torments me and won't leave me in peace. Go away.'

'A woman of your age ought to think twice before marrying a boy of eighteen. I'm your contemporary, and I can even understand it; but as to approving it, certainly not. Certain things, quite simply, are not done.'

'Ah, they're not done? Why shouldn't they be done? Or why can't they be done? But will you kindly go away?'

'You're still good-looking. But in a few years you'll be an old woman. Like me. We shall be two old women and . . .'

'Wait a moment, there's a difference. You will be an old woman with a family that does not care about you; I shall be an old woman with a young husband who will love me. Now, will you go away, yes or no?'

'How can you allow yourself to talk about my family? What do you know about my family?'

'Yes, your family does not care about you; and you're the terror of the house: as soon as you appear, everyone runs away. What d'you think? I know all about you. Emilio has told me everything. I know that your husband has a mistress with whom he spends his evenings. I know that your daughter, because she can't bear to be with you, goes out in the morning and comes home after midnight. I know that you have nothing to do all day long and so you invent maternal obligations, like for instance this absurd visit to me this morning. But no one wants to have anything to do with you, and so you, as happened a year ago, shut yourself up in the kitchen one day and turned on the gas-tap. They found you in time, took you off to a clinic and gave you the sleep treatment. Then you went home again and everything began again, as before. And now that I've proved ⟨ ⟩ that I know all about you, will you please have the goo⟨ ⟩ remove yourself.'

'You're a witch and a hag and a scoundrel.'

'The witch and the hag and the scoundrel is *you*. Go away; or I shall be forced to call the porter to chuck you out.'

I went away, I went away. Above all I felt the need to get my situation, too humiliating and negative as it was, into proper proportion. I went out of the flat in a great hurry; the lift was there, as I had left it; I entered it and pressed the button; it began to go down and I went to the mirror and looked at myself again, but this time with a very different feeling from what I had had shortly before, when I was going up. Shortly before I had examined myself with alarm and apprehension; now I observed my face with attention and calculation. Indeed, after all, I was not worse than a great many other women, perhaps some even younger than me; it was not yet 'all over' for me, and possibly it would 'never' be over. The lift stopped at the ground floor; I sprang out of it almost at a run; in a moment I was in my car, which went rolling speedily down the steep street, towards my goal.

On the far side of the sunlit asphalt desert, the yellow and red roof of the petrol station looked small and remote. The intense noonday light permeated it with a diffused glare in which colours and outlines trembled and dissolved. I attacked the open space of asphalt at the highest possible speed; and yet it seemed to me for a moment that the roof grew more distant as the car drew nearer. From the sun in the sky numbers of other suns seemed to detach themselves and to come slowly downwards to be scattered dazzlingly over the empty space. Then, all of a sudden, the light exploded like a soap bubble; and the roof with its petrol pumps stood out, hard, real, coloured, only a pace from me. The attendant was serving the first car; a second one was waiting with its engine running; docilely I took up my position in the queue, awaiting my turn.

# The Most Terrible Thing in Life

I am a woman who lives alone and who is very beautiful. This might seem an ideal situation, whereas it is not. The beauty which is a mere professional requisite in my job as an air hostess seems to change its character and function as soon as I descend from heaven to earth. On board it is an instrument of work – I was going to say a precision instrument – of which I make use as regulated by the rules of the company; on the ground, by some curious alchemy obscurely related to the fact that I am not married, it becomes a piece of goods that I cannot even put on sale, but which does not for that reason cease to be so, both for myself and for the men who approach me. In flight I am an angel in uniform; on earth, a walking show-case of female anatomy. Everything in me confirms this transformation : from the too-tight miniskirt of my uniform which, when I walk hastily from one end of the plane to the other, forces me to a swaying of the hips of which nobody takes any notice, but which, on the other hand, would be mistaken for a sexual allurement on the ground; to the gesture of my hands when I spread a rug over a passenger's legs or arrange a cushion at the back of his neck –

which, in the air, has no significance whereas on the ground it might invite interpretations.

But why this variation? Why, indeed – as soon as I arrive at the small, bare flat in the vicinity of the airport which I share with a colleague (but she is there when I am not there, and vice versa) – why is the first thing I do to go straight to the mirror in the bathroom, snatch off my cap, undo the bun into which my hair is fastened, and unbutton my tunic? I do not know. I only know that, immediately afterwards, I see in the glass my great blue eyes which, from having been glassy during the flight, now become cruelly languid; my bosom, as if by its own independent impetus, bursts forth from my tunic; my mouth, during the flight so prodigal with artificial smiles, assumes, naturally, a capricious, pouting expression; and my hair, slowly, as though gradually awakening, spreads out by itself across the whole width of my shoulders. Now it is done: the military angel has been transformed into an unchained, neurotic, frivolous girl, who does not know how she will spend the evening; but who has firmly decided not to spend it at home.

The second thing I do, in fact, after destroying the aircraft angel, is to go to the telephone and dial, one after another, with systematic cynicism, the many numbers of solitary men needing company who are lined up in my address book; that is, until I reach the right one, the one who would be available for the evening. Let no one think evil, however. The rigid regulations of the company have made me into a completely repressed woman. With the man who accompanies me there will be nothing, nothing intimate, not even affectionate. He will invite me in order to show himself off with a magnificent creature who will make him 'cut a fine figure', as they say; and I, in turn, will accept the fact of making him cut a fine figure in exchange for his company at a restaurant, at the cinema, at a night-club. That is the whole story. But then why does the suspicion of a subtle, chaste prostitution insinuate itself during the evening into all my gestures and my words? An erotic interpretation, abolished during flight, is now strongly imposed. In reality, in accepting the invitation, I have sold my presence neither more nor less than the peasant in the market who, by a handshake, ratifies the sale of a well-bred milch cow. Furthermore, that there has been a sale is proved, if for no other reason, by the fact that the man who is accompanying me, once we have arrived at the restaurant where we are dining, does not look so much at me as at the other tables round the room, to see what effect I am making. Well, I know what men are. Or rather, from the sadness which grips my heart at that moment, I understand that I am just now beginning to know them.

One night I decided to stay at home; to be an angel not only in the heavens but also on earth. Quite naked – for the heat was like that of a furnace and since the flat is on the ground floor I can't even open the windows – I sat down on a high-backed chair in front of the television. It was almost eight o'clock. In a short time there would be the news bulletin; then an old film of the 'fifties; then a documentary about animals; then a news bulletin again. All this alternates with little advertising scenes in which, for some reason, happiness appears to be connected with the use of some consumer product or other. So I shall watch the news bulletin and then the film. At that point I shall take advantage of the advertising quickly to eat my supper (a slice of roast beef and a tomato which I had put in the fridge the day before, at the moment of my last departure); then I shall turn back to the screen and watch the documentary and the second news bulletin, which is usually just like the first, but one never knows, some war or other disaster may always have cropped up at the last moment. By this time it will be eleven o'clock. Then, on tiptoe, in the funereal half-darkness of the deserted flat, I shall go from room to room, checking shutters and taps and locks. Finally I shall go to bed, for a light, restless sleep. I have a double bed but nobody has ever slept in it with me. In my sleep I anxiously change position; I get into bed from the right-hand side, I wake up on the left. The caprices of solitude.

This entirely unusual decision not to go out having been taken, everything proceeds more or less regularly until nine o'clock, that is until, on other evenings, contrary to today, I should 'go out'. I put this verb to 'go out' in inverted commas because going out in inverted commas, for me as for an infinite number of women, does not at all mean going out without inverted commas. In this latter case, one goes out to do shopping, to go for a walk, to pay visits; in the former, on the other hand, to go out means to live, so that this evening, by staying at home, in effect I forgo life or, at least, that one part of life that to me seems alive. Now, feeling myself more beautiful than ever, but with a beauty made spectral and dishevelled by solitude, I went into the kitchen, opened the fridge and discovered complete emptiness, contradicted only by the little dish of silvered cardboard in which the solitary pink and brown slice of roast beef usually lies side by side with a red and green tomato; all at once I couldn't bear it any more and ran back into the sitting-room. There, squatting on the floor, my breasts against my knees, like a starving wolf, I dialled as quickly as possible a number that I knew by heart. As soon as the masculine voice at the other end of the wire said 'Hello', I asked in a gentle, casual tone of voice : 'This is Lucilla. Doing anything nice this evening?'

Now you must know that this man to whom I was telephoning is perhaps the only one who makes me feel less of a prostitute when I go out at night with him. And this for an easily under-stood reason : he is the only one who is really in love with me. But here lies my misfortune. Alas, he is very poor; and so I hardly ever telephone him, in the first place because I do not love him and then because I know that he cannot afford to spend money; and I, frankly, would make the sacrifice of going to dinner in some cheap little restaurant only if I loved him. For, when all is said and done, I have finally to recognize that in me the impulse to sell my presence seems to be stronger than my re-pugnance, as though I were the owner of a magnificent fruit tree whose heart bleeds to see the fruit fall to the ground and decay among the grass.

Naturally, as soon as I suggested that we should dine together he agreed with enthusiasm. I do not know how he will manage.

He will spend a part of his salary, he will borrow money from a colleague: I don't know and I don't care. Moreover, in a cowardly way, I preclude the possible pretext of a modest restaurant by putting on a showy and eccentric nineteenth-century type American dress, which with its flounces that sweep the ground and its two plunging necklines, one to the small of the back and the other to the waist, demands an expensive restaurant. Yes, this is what is needed to make him 'cut a dash'; and in putting it on, I felt more than ever a prostitute, because I know that he has not got the money to take me around dressed like this.

At the repeated sound of the car horn I rushed out, holding up my long skirt with both hands above my splendid legs. But, when I reached the front door, I remained motionless and frightened. As in a sacred picture representing the Madonna between two saints, I found myself in the middle and two men standing beside me, one on the right and one on the left. On one side was my poor lover, a young man with an intellectual air (intellectual he is, he teaches philosophy), badly dressed and untidy, behind whom could be seen the modest little car in which he proposed to carry me off; on the other side, a comic character whom privately I have nicknamed 'the dwarf', for with his big red nose, his big soft backside and his big crooked legs he might easily be mistaken for one of Snow White's dwarfs. In my panic fear of staying at home alone I had, a week ago, given him an appointment for this evening; and of course, with all these daily flights, I had forgotten about it. Behind him, however, stood an enormous champagne-coloured car, a good match, as I had to recognize, for my appearance as a beautiful girl in an advertisement for some brand of cigarettes. A moment passed; and I just had time to consider (hypocrite!) that it was better to make a rich man spend a little small change than to empty the pockets of a poor man. Then, feeling justified now, I said to my lover who was coming forward with outstretched hand: 'Forgive me, I've made a mistake. But I must go with him because I made an appointment with him for this evening a week ago. Good-bye;

telephone me tomorrow morning.' Then I plunged into the big car beside the Snow White dwarf who, grasping the wheel with both hands and making an effort to perform the difficult manoeuvre of getting out of the street, asked me who that young man was. I answered him, I don't know why: 'The man of my life.' 'And you leave the man of your life to come with me?' 'Yes, he's the man of my life, but not of *this* kind of life.' Well, well, the most terrible thing in life is life itself.

# A Body of Bronze

❦

I awoke and immediately stretched out my hand behind me to feel for my husband. To tell the truth, I was married yesterday and I used habitually to make this movement in my bed at home, in which I slept with my sister Tina. So I put out my hand and, to my surprise but certainly not to my disappointment and even less to my sorrow, I found nothing but the untouched sheet, fresh and smooth, still with the folds where it had been ironed, just as it had come out of the drawer. What had happened? I could not manage to remember; I must have taken the sleeping-tablets for my head was heavy and inert, as if clamped down. Finally I made up my mind, thrust my legs out of the bed, rose to my feet and went, in the dark, walking with outstretched arms, to the window. Then, as I bent and straightened myself vigorously, impeded by my nightdress, in order to pull up the roller-blind, the consciousness of my body returned to me and with it the memory of what had happened last night. For I owe this marri-age of mine entirely to the very special appearance of my body. It was my body which, last summer, standing conspicuously on the pavement and making the gesture of 'thumbing a lift' – close

*141*

beside my sister's very different gesture – which brought my future husband's car to a halt with a prolonged screech of brakes. It was that body, again, which caused this casual companion to proceed from one telephone call a week to four or five a day; from an invitation to the cinema or to dinner every now and then, to continual presence at all hours. Finally it was my body which led the two of us to the altar. But perhaps, at this point, it would be as well for me to say what it is like, this body that is so important and so much desired.

It is a body of bronze. Do not smile: I merely wish to say that its very pronounced forms, without doubt highly provocative to a sensual man like my husband, appear to proclaim a temperament which, in reality, does not exist. It is perfectly true that every time, at the seaside or at a swimming-pool, I happen to show myself without clothes, the first idea that may occur to anyone looking at me is not that of beauty (even though my beauty is certainly noteworthy) but of solidity. That is to say, precisely what one thinks in front of a shapely bronze statue, cast and polished to perfection but at the same time cold, empty and hermetic. This is the impression, quite correctly described, that my body makes on a normal man. But my husband is not normal. It is exactly this solidity that most excites his desire. And in fact, during the brief period when we were engaged, he was always trying to take me by force, everywhere, in the car, in my flat, in his flat, even in his jeweller's shop behind the sales counter. Indifferent, rebellious, my body, almost in spite of myself, resisted him by means which were, in fact, of the body, that is to say kicks, punches, slaps, violent pushes and so on; but he comforted himself with the thought that, fundamentally, I was refusing him something to which he still had no right; and that without doubt everything would change after our marriage. I too thought so; or rather, I had allowed myself to be persuaded by my sister that it would be so. But what happened last night makes me see that we were all of us wrong.

Walking on tiptoe with my nightdress pulled up in front over my bosom, feeling more than ever bronze-like and hermetic, I went from the bedroom into the sitting-room. But I did not go into the room; I stopped in astonishment in the doorway, in order to look. It was as though there had been a furious battle between a murderer obstinately resolved to kill and a victim desperately decided to defend himself. The big white sofa in the corner had all its cushions disarranged and crushed. A picture above the sofa was hanging crooked. Overturned chairs here and there gave the impression of a furious chase. The table too was overturned; ashtray, vase of flowers, box of cigarettes, bottle, glasses – the whole lot had fallen on to the floor, scattering water, cigarette-ends, flowers, cigarettes, liquor. Lastly there was blood on one arm of the sofa; not mine, however, as I knew for certain, but my husband's.

I looked at this scene of violence and desolation; and then, no longer dulled by the effects of the sleeping-pills, I gradually recovered my memory of what had happened. On that sofa had taken place the savage struggle between my husband who, fortified by the nuptial contract, wanted, as they say, to 'possess' me, and my body, more than ever bronze-like, which, on the contrary, did not wish to have anything to do with him. As soon as we entered the flat, after the church ceremony and the lunch at a restaurant, this man, hitherto altogether too formal and solemn, was transformed all of a sudden into a kind of unrestrained hooligan, a rapist and almost a murderer. He turned the key in the door and then, with cat-like footsteps, came up behind me as I stood undecided in the middle of the sitting-room, looking round me, my bunch of lilies-of-the-valley in my hand; he seized hold of me by the arms, threw me violently face downwards on the sofa and tried to force me to make love in the way that animals do it. I repelled him with a movement like a horse kicking out with both hind legs, threw myself off the sofa, fled through the living-room, pursued by him, upsetting everything as I went. He caught me, seized hold of me by the hair, threw me down on my back on the cushions of the sofa, slapped me several times, then held my head back, thrusting it from below with his hand under my chin; meanwhile, with his other hand, he gradually tore off my blouse, brassière, suspender-belt and panties. I tried then to strike him, deliberately and with intent really to hurt him, with a blow from my knee in the testicles; he narrowly avoided it, threw himself upon me, squeezed my throat until I could scarcely breathe, as though he wished to strangle me, and at the same time seized me violently by my pubic hair. With a supreme and desperate effort I freed myself from him, lifted, with both hands, by its edge, the heavy steel and glass table and, turning it, brought it down on top of him. He gave a cry of pain, sat down, all ruffled and untidy, on the arm of the sofa, staining it with blood coming from a cut on his knee. Suddenly he calmed down and, still out of breath, told me he was going to the chemist's to buy what was needed to treat his wound; meanwhile I must go to bed and he would not be long in coming back. I listened to these quite normal instructions as I sat on the disordered sofa, naked, dishevelled, huddled up with my knees against my mouth and my hair over my face. Then he went away, I don't quite know how or when, and at this point my memory becomes confused. After staying for a long time squatting in this position, until I felt cold, I must have gone to bed almost without realizing it. Once in bed but still in this state of delirious stupefaction, I must have taken I don't know how many sleeping-pills, divided between the idea of sleep and that of suicide, and then I fell into a deep sleep and must have slept without interruption for twelve hours. And so here I am now, awake and without a husband.

What feeling does one have after such a wedding night as this? I will tell you at once; a feeling of irritation against the person who has given us advice. I went to the telephone table and dialled the number of my home, that is, the home of my parents. I was answered at once by the voice of my sister, who was still sleepy but already curious. She enquired greedily: 'How did it go?'

I replied: 'The fact is that he has already left me.'

'You don't tell me! What happened?'

'What happened was that I didn't do it. I wanted to; but then, at the last moment, it was too much for me and I rebelled.'

'And he . . . ?'

'He seized me by the hair and slapped me.'

'And you?'

'I kicked him, I threw the table at him, I hurt his knee. Then he went out, to go to the chemist's and get treated for it, saying he would be back at once; instead of which he never returned. Now I'm alone and I haven't even the money to go down to the bar and have a cup of coffee. It was a fine thing I did, following your advice.'

'How do I come into it, now?'

'It was you who advised me to marry him, saying he was just as good as anyone else, because I have no feelings and for me men don't exist.'

'It's the truth!'

'Yes, but there are men and men. This one's a maniac.'

'Come on, they're all the same. And what are you going to do now?'

'You ask me that? I'll get dressed and come over to you.'

'No, you can't do that. You went away so haughtily – what sort of a figure would you cut now? No, you must think of a different solution.'

'But what solution? I've thought about it and haven't found anything.'

'Listen, in your place I'd try thumbing a lift again. It's gone badly the first time; that's exactly why you should try again.'

'But you're crazy. Thumbing a lift! Better to go to Piazza Navona, or to Campo di Fiori and carry on for a few days with the usual young men.'

'A fine idea! And then what will you do? Now listen. Place yourself at a strategic point, at the beginning of the Via Aurelia, for example, and get yourself taken far up north, perhaps even as far as Genoa. Then, one thing leads to another.'

'Well, I'll think about it. And you – how are you, what are you doing?'

'Papa has already gone to the office. Mamma's still asleep. Since yesterday, nothing has happened here.'

'And the dog, how is the dog?'

'He's all right. He's here in the armchair at the foot of the bed.'

'What's he doing?'

'Sleeping.'

'Well, good-bye. I'll telephone you again.'

I put down the telephone and went back, somewhat reassured, into the bedroom. Yes indeed, thumbing a lift, perhaps even with a lorry. If only in order to see, beyond the radiator, the blue mountains on the horizon and, in the sky, the autumn clouds, dark and familiar, moving away in the wind that urges them on to discharge their rain in some distant place.

But my exaltation did not last long. While I was twisting and turning my bronze body under the shower, suddenly there was a vigorous knock at the front door. Wet and dripping, I went to the entrance and asked who it was; and then the voice of my husband requesting me to open the door made me understand the truth all at once : he had not left me, he had never thought of leaving me. It was I who had shut him out, the night before, without realizing it, after the struggle in the living-room. Now he had come back and wanted to be forgiven; I understood this from the suppliant, contrite tone of his voice. And so the marriage which I had thought to be already finished, was only beginning.

# The Voice of the Sea

My father hits me, especially at table, which is the place consecrated to family quarrels. He hits me not so much because I am hostile to him as because I am hostile to him with good reason, and he refuses to recognize it. My father is a widower and I am his only daughter. We live alone, without the moderating complications of a real family; and so we both abandon ourselves without restraint to our feelings, I myself to hatred and he to sensuality. My God, how sensual that man is! Never mind – provided he didn't show it. But not at all, he is sensual in an open, brazen manner. At past sixty he gets call-girls to come to the house (I spy on them as they arrive, through a crack in the door of my room, where I remain, for the most part, barricaded); he waylays the maids even to the point of getting his hands on them while they are waiting at table; he even tries to approach my girl friends, rushing to open the door to them when they come to see me. I have nothing against sex, of course; but I have a great deal against sex when it goes to the head. My father is intoxicated with sensuality as other people are with alcohol; and in fact he has a suggestion of the drunkard in his face, with a flushed look on his low forehead, on his fleshy cheekbones, on his bulbous nose and his ball-shaped chin.

This man who is so sensual is also a liar. He lies with incredible effrontery; if I contradict him, he does not then hesitate, as I have said, to hit me. With his red, thick-set, short-fingered hand, one finger adorned with a massive ring with a heavy setting and coat of arms (for he considers himself to be of noble blood, from some ridiculous, obscure provincial nobility), he deals me a particularly painful and humiliating blow, in which the diffused burning sensation of the blow itself mingles with the acute pain of the ring's impact. Not on this account, however, do I cry or go away. I bend my face over my plate and go on telling him what I am thinking, with perhaps even greater harshness. Then, sentimentalist as he is, he weeps a few tears and stammers that he loves me; and why in the world do I get so angry with him? He makes me pity him; but this pity merely serves to make me more pitiless. My answer is: 'I get angry with you because you're a swine and you disgust me.'

The chief result of this very unfortunate relationship with my father was that boys of my own age never meant anything to me and that I always liked mature or even positively elderly men. This is not one of those unconscious tendencies over which psycho-analysts are wont to labour: instead, it is a perfectly conscious inclination; I know quite well that I prefer men well on in years because I seek, in them, the father that I lack. It may be objected that there is no need to go to bed with the man who takes the place of a father: all that is needed is friendship. On the contrary, this is not so. For me, at least, the only relationship that can take the place of a blood relationship is a sex relationship. Friendship, however profound, is a different thing, above all infinitely more superficial than the relationship between father and daughter. And, in turn, the relationship between father and daughter is never truly friendly, as so many fathers and so many daughters profess to believe.

Well, after three or four infatuations for men who might have taken the place of fathers to me but whom I very soon discovered not to be capable of it; suddenly, in the end, I fell in love with one who seemed to correspond in every point to the idea that, through the years, I had formed for myself of what a father should be. He was a businessman, in other words, a stockbroker. He had a very bad reputation, being considered a pirate, a swindler and an unscrupulous gambler on the stock exchange. But, both in his physical appearance (he was tall, thin, with a long, hard face that looked as though carved out of a piece of old, seasoned wood) and in his morals, anyhow in his relations with me, one single word described him perfectly : ascetic. There are ascetics in religion; but, it seems, there are also ascetics in other activities of a less spiritual even if equally exclusive kind. He – however contradictory and even rather ridiculous it may seem when stated in this way – was an ascetic of finance.

I have never understood whether the absolute control that he had over his senses was due to age, or to experience, or again to the discipline he had imposed upon himself so as to devote himself more deeply to business. All three, perhaps. Certainly his love was a distant, objective, clear-sighted love. I don't know how to explain it : every time he looked at me I felt with absolute certainty that he saw me exactly as I was, without idealizing or beautifying me, as lovers usually do. This did not prevent his having a need for me to the extent that several times he suggested I should leave my father and go and live with him. But at the same time I was perfectly sure that, when I was not there, he did not turn his thoughts towards me even for one single moment of the day. In short, he certainly did love me; but his love was mingled with cynical, indifferent realism, like that of a man who has already done everything and who knows that he is re-living past experiences, even if with some variation.

Pirate, swindler, gambler, my lover took, it seems, one false step, losing his balance, so to speak, in some over-risky speculation. The fact remains that he went bankrupt; and, since he was very well known, I learned of it, even before I heard of it from him, from reading, by chance, the financial page of a newspaper. I rushed to his house and found him, as usual, distant, calm, cool, even though in a manner that, for the first time, did not seem to me altogether natural. He was packing his suitcases; for a moment I thought that he was going to run away, without me. But he reassured me : he was at a difficult moment; he counted on recovering himself as soon as possible; in the meantime he proposed that I should go travelling with him, so that he would have leisure to reflect and prepare for his recovery. I thought of some near-by place, somewhere quite near such as Capri or the Costa Azzurra. Then my eye fell on the airline tickets lying ready on the table and to my surprise I read : Tahiti.

So I said good-bye to my real father, my father by blood; and went away with my sham father, my father by sex. Sitting side by side in the plane, he with his fine head erect and alert, the head of a martyred saint of stock exchange speculation, I myself lying passionately close against him, we flew for many, many hours, together eating the aeroplane's meals, sleeping together wrapped in the aeroplane's blanket, together looking at the majestic layers of white clouds above which the aeroplane was rushing towards Tahiti. I loved him, I had never loved him so much as at that moment. And I was aware that one of the chief reasons for this increase in my love was precisely the fact that he remained so impassive in face of the disaster of his life. I had always dreamed of a father like this; now I had him.

We arrived at Tahiti in the morning and immediately, as soon as we came out of the airport, garlands of flowers were thrown round our necks by women who are always there watching the arrivals and departures. I clung to his arm and was happy, as though these women had prepared the flowers solely for us, although I knew perfectly well that they did this for all travellers. We stayed in an hotel on the sea-shore; it was entirely composed of a number of huts of imitation Polynesian type surrounded with the flowers and foliage of tropical thickets; and we started to lead a tranquil life altogether suitable to lovers. In the mornings we went to bathe in the lagoon that surrounds the island; in the afternoons we would make expeditions by car, stopping at the most picturesque spots. But what I liked best was to lie on the beach and listen to the remote, incessant roar caused by the waves of the ocean breaking continuously on the coral reef far away in the distance at the edges of the lagoon. It was a roar that seemed at first to be inarticulate and with a single voice, made up of one single hollow sound repeated indefinitely. But then, listening to it as I did all day long, I began to distinguish more sounds, alternating though always repeated, which, when combined, seemed to me to compose a word. What was this word? I puzzled over it for a long time and then finally seemed to realize that it was the word 'love'. Yes indeed, the ocean had been repeating, for ever, with its hollow, conclusive, authoritative voice, that one word. And I, perhaps, was the first person in the world to understand it.

All this I am relating principally in order to give an idea of how happy I was. I was so very happy that I surrendered myself completely to a feeling of confidence and told my companion, who as usual was sitting beside me without speaking, that in the roar of the ocean waves I could perceive a word, one single word; and I also told him what the word was. I saw him give a faint smile, in his own cool, indulgent way; then he said that he too would like to try listening to that distant roar to see if he in turn could distinguish a word in it. He put on an intent expression as of one listening and, in the end, told me that to him the waves were saying a different word from mine. What word? He shook his head and replied : 'Different'.

I again became absorbed in listening to the voice of the ocean which repeated, with a fierce, prehistoric monotony, the word 'love'. Then he rose to his feet, saying he was going to telephone to Papeete to order the car for the afternoon; and I myself fell asleep. I must have slept for about half an hour. Suddenly someone shook me by the arm and woke me up; one of the Tahitian waiters was bending over me and smiling as he said (they always smile, whatever they are saying) that my companion had killed himself : he had shot himself in the telephone booth and had fallen dead, down underneath the telephone.

After the funeral I returned to Italy and resumed my usual

life with my real father, my 'blood' father. I have become gentler and more understanding with him; I do not think I shall look for another father ever again : one cannot have more than one and the one I had found has remained far away in the Tahiti cemetery. Just possibly, indeed, I shall end by marrying some contemporary of mine who says he loves me. Loves me! The important thing is not to be loved but to love; and I shall be grateful all my life to my finance-ascetic for having made me love him without, perhaps, loving me. But I should like to know what word 'different' from mine he heard in the roar of the ocean waves. Or rather, I should both like to know and not like to know. I wonder; perhaps it was some terrible word, after which there was nothing left for him but to kill himself.

# The Other Face of the Moon

❦

I am two persons in one or, if you prefer, I am a double-fronted person, that is, with two faces, like the moon. And, like the moon, I have one face which is known to all and always the same, and one face which is unknown not merely to other people but even, in a sort of way, to myself. This entirely unknown second face might just as well not exist: things that are unknown – if you come to think of it – do not exist. But it is not like that. The other face of the moon, even if I do not know it or make it known, 'I 'feel' it. And this obscure feeling that the other face exists, invisible and different, behind my obvious face, on the back of my head, and looks out at the world behind my back, means that in everyday life I am always scrupulously, dutifully involved and, at the same time – how shall I say? – scatter-brained, 'unstuck'. Yes, unstuck; that is, detached from the things I am doing at the very moment when I am doing them. Have you ever seen a piece of antique furniture from which a piece that hitherto seemed an essential part of the whole had all at once become unstuck? You look at it and you see that, on the surface of the old, dry wood there is a faintly glistening veil, as it were, of the ancient glue. The piece was broken no one knows how many centuries ago; somebody, also dead centuries ago, glued it together; but one fine day the glue ceased to hold and the broken piece came unstuck. What is now needed is some new glue, as good as the first; but you must know which. Well, in everyday life, I am that morsel of a piece of furniture which seems to stick but which in reality is separate.

Unstuck and diligent, I am the perfect, young, beautiful wife of a middle-aged judge, every day from eight in the evening until six in the morning; the perfect stepmother of the two children of the judge's first marriage, from six in the afternoon until nine in the evening; the perfect bank employee, from half past eight until half past one. Why these time-tables? Because in my life no other time exists but that of the clock; all other times are excluded. Every day I rise at six, accomplish my toilet, dress, waken the children, help them with their toilet and their dressing, prepare breakfast for everybody. Then my husband goes out with the car; first he takes the children to the convent school where they are half-boarders, then he goes to the court. I go on foot to the bank which is a short distance from home. In the bank, serious and diligent to such a degree that my colleagues, as a joke, call me 'Miss Duty', I am occupied until half past one. Then I walk home again. The hourly maid will have already done my shopping according to a list that I make out for her each evening before going to bed; I go into the kitchen, open the parcels and packets, light the cooker and prepare a light lunch for myself and my husband. My husband arrives, we sit down at table; after we have eaten I wash up and make everything tidy; then we go through into the bedroom, for this is the moment for love-making; my husband likes to do it at this time because in the evening he feels tired. At four o'clock he goes out and shortly afterwards the children arrive. Without allowing myself a moment's pause, I prepare their light meal, watch the television with them, help them to do their homework, cook their supper, put them to bed. By now it is eight o'clock and my husband comes home. He settles down to read the newspapers; I hurry into the bedroom, put on a smart dress, see to my make-up and general adornment, and then we go out together to dine at a restaurant or at the house of friends, and then to the cinema. At this point, however, I give way because, for years, I have lacked at least two hours of sleep during my twenty-four hour day. So I doze off wherever I happen to be, at table at the restaurant, in my seat at the cinema, beside my husband as he is driving the car. Do I love my husband? Let us say that I am fond of him. In any case I haven't time to think of this sort of thing.

And yet, in spite of this life as 'Miss Duty', I do not cling to the things that I do; I feel all the time, as I have already said, 'unstuck'. Incidentally, I asserted that my other face of the moon was unknown not merely to other people but also to me. This is not altogether exact: if you know how to read it, this unknown face can nevertheless be divined in my physiognomy. I will describe myself and you can judge for yourselves. I am blonde, tall and thin, with a slightly Germanic countenance of the kind that looks out from niches in ancient Gothic churches. I have a triangular face, the broad part, that is, the forehead, hard and bony, the pointed part, that is, the chin, fleshy and soft. I have an aquiline nose and a thin mouth, both of noble design; but my ugly eyes, of a washed-out blue, contradict the aristocratic severity of my face with a frighteningly sinister look, with a shifty, furtive, cold expression, lying in wait, as it were, like the look of an animal that may bite at the first opportunity.

In the end the opportunity occurred, in the fourth year of my marriage. One November morning, as I was going to work in grey, stinging rain, I saw, at the wheel of a big, dark-coloured car parked in front of my bank, a man who was taking photographs. I saw him from some distance away: he put a minute camera up to his eye and took the photographs, three, four, five in quick sequence, with calm, expert haste. Then he hid his hand and for some moments gazed into space; then, all at once, he began taking photographs again. What was he photographing? There could be no doubt: the entrance to the bank. I walked on and then saw him better; he was a man of small stature, to

**155**

F

judge from his shoulders; he had a broad forehead, a hooked nose, a clear-cut mouth: he reminded one of the prints of a portrait of Napoleon as a young man. Then I passed close to him; he withdrew his hand and looked at me, as if waiting for me to disappear. And then, inexplicably, an instinct of some sort prompted me to wink at him. He saw me wink and nodded his head, as though to let me understand that he had noticed it. I crossed the avenue with a firm step, huddled in my flame-red waterproof, and joined the group of employees in front of the entrance to the bank. When I turned round the car was no longer there.

A fortnight passed. One morning I had left the bank to go home. As I walked, I became aware that I had no share at all in the relief and joy, like those of a Sunday, which were diffused in waves throughout the streets as offices and schools emptied themselves and those who hitherto had been shut up, forced to work or study, came out of them, liberated, and hurried off home. I was without any sense of relief or joy: I was already thinking of the meal I would be cooking, of the dishes I would be washing, of the love I would be making. Then suddenly I looked up and saw, quite close beside me, the photographer man who, at the wheel of his car, was following me step by step. Our eyes met; and then he questioned me with a brief remark, of unrepeatable obscenity. I did not hesitate. I nodded agreement; he stopped the car, opened the door and I got in.

We went no great distance and then stopped on a deserted part of the Tiber Embankment; and he, immediately, as though following out a prearranged plan, tried to kiss me. When he was stationary, as I have said, he looked like the young Napoleon; but as soon as his face became animated with any sort of expression, the vulgarity of a little suburban gangster was revealed, though not altogether without grace. I repulsed him and said: 'Hands off; there'll always be time for that. Tell me now what you want of me.'

He replied in an assured voice: 'I want you.'

'No, you don't only want *me*. If you only wanted me, it would mean that you're a fetishist.'

'Fetishist? What sort of a thing is that?'

'Somebody who, like you, doesn't only love a person but also the objects connected with that person. For instance, the door of the bank where I work.'

'But when do you mean?'

'When? Two weeks ago, at half past eight in the morning. How many photographs did you take? Twenty or so, at least, I should say.'

'One can't keep anything hidden from you. Who are you? The devil?'

That was the beginning of our history which, in the end, filled the headlines in the pages of the newspapers. There is no point in my relating here how the robbery was carried out; it was a 'classic' of its kind, according to the reporters; if you wish to know how it went, you can consult the crime news in the papers of that year. Nor do I wish to tell you of the part – no small part – that I played: it would be dangerous for me, because it remained unknown; and I am still, for my colleagues at the bank, the 'Miss Duty' that I always was. The only thing I would like to add is that the robbery happened in the early afternoon, when there were few employees there and the bank was closed to customers. It was about four o'clock and I had run away from home immediately after making love, as usual, with my husband, and I had barely an hour before the children came back from school. I had to wait, at the wheel of the traditional stolen car, in a quiet street, until my gangster and his companion should arrive, having completed the robbery. Well, would you believe it? Notwithstanding my fear, my usual tiredness had made me fall asleep at the wheel, with a sleep that was wonderful and unconquerable and blissful. In my sleep I was in my own way participating in the robbery. I dreamt I was shut up in the strong-room of the bank and then, all of a sudden, my gangster opened the strong-room and I, with a cry of joy, fell into his arms. But at that same moment, behold, I was awakened by him shaking me by the arm and blaspheming through clenched teeth. Immediately, like an automaton and without even looking round, I started the engine and we drove away.

After the robbery we didn't see one another for six months. He did not wish us to meet; he said that the police were certainly making enquiries into the life of every one of the bank's employees. We did agree, however, that at the end of these six months I should go and live with him, thus transforming myself from Miss Duty to My Lady Tommy-Gun or something of the kind, as no doubt my old working companions would nickname me, with detestable wit, as soon as they knew what had happened.

So I took up my usual life again, between home and the bank. Now one day I discovered that I had run out of eau de Cologne. That same afternoon I drove my husband to the airport; he was going to Cagliari for official reasons. On my way back I remembered the eau de Cologne, so I stopped the car in a suburban street in front of a perfumery shop which had on its sign the name of the Parisian perfumer who, in fact, produced what I wanted. The perfumer's shop, as soon as I went in, dazzled me with the glitter of the many bottles and flagons and flasks of toilet water and lotions that were ranged all round the walls in glass-fronted cupboards. Thus, for a moment, I did not see my gangster who, standing behind the counter, was serving a middle-aged lady customer who was in need of some sort of rare shade of lipstick. My gangster had various little tubes strewn about on the counter between his customer and himself; and as he removed the cap from one or the other he smeared it very lightly on the back of his hand, enlarged the spot with the tip of his finger and then showed it to his customer, talking to her meanwhile in a low voice, gently, lingeringly, patiently. But the customer looked and then shook her head : it was still not the right one, not the lipstick she was looking for.

My gangster had not told me that he possessed this magnificent shop; of him I knew merely that he lived with his old mother and two children and that his wife had left him and was in Milan with another man. But I realized that he had been a perfumer for some time, perhaps for years, because the discourse that he was holding with his customer was such as someone who was not in the trade could not invent. For me, the professional perfection of this discourse was like a flash of lightning in the night, when one sees a whole landscape even in its smallest details even if only for a single moment. I understood, indeed, that I had been wrong: I had mistaken him for a rapacious hawk, whereas he was a crafty mole. And then, in that moment of lightning thought, I made a calculation and realized that my husband was worth just as much as *he* was. He, too, had two children whom I should have to look after; he too would have expected me to slave away in the house. As for work, it was better to be a bank clerk than a perfumer's assistant, if only because I had to go to the bank in the mornings only. There was, it is true, the question of love; but I was conscious that now, after the discovery of the shop, I felt just as 'unstuck' in relation to him as in relation to my husband. So I did not wait for the customer to find the right kind of lipstick. I turned my back and went out. In the doorway, however, I turned round; he was looking at me now over his customer's shoulder, and I shook my head in refusal. He was not stupid and he must have understood, for he never sought me out again. Perhaps, who knows, he did not trust me as a perfumer's assistant. After all, between a shop and a bank there is no difference; and so he must have feared that I, incorrigible, might repeat the robbery, but this time with damage to himself and possibly even in league with a real gangster, one of those who attack banks with criminal intent and not in order to buy themselves a perfumery.

# Pooh!

✦

My friends tell me that my bad character is visible as soon as I am seen in profile. From in front I am reminiscent of a Pekinese dog: round, protruding eyes with a fixed malevolent look in them; squashed nose; big mouth with tortuous lips. But in profile, according to them, my face makes people think simply of a clenched fist, held out against somebody with the intention of hitting him on the nose. However, it must be said that, over and above a bad character with which one is born and about which one can do nothing, there is also the question of an obscure rage which came upon me at a certain age – at about fifteen, let us say – and has never left me since. This rage, like those watches which you do not wind because they wind themselves by the movement of your arm, rises up of itself without reason or provocation. Further, from this rage there comes upon me a continual desire for a quarrel. At this point I can already hear the usual Nosey Parker enquiring: 'But why this rage, why this desire to quarrel?' And I, as I always do with someone who wants to know too much and does not know, on the other hand, that there is nothing to know – I answer precisely like this: 'Pooh!'

## Pooh!

Above all in the morning, as soon as I awake, I find myself in such a fury that if the world was, as it were, a plate or a glass, I would not hesitate for a moment to hurl it on the floor and break it to pieces. Oh yes, I have the same urge to quarrel as the smoker has to smoke, the drinker to drink, the drug addict to drug himself. Unfortunately, however, at home I cannot give vent to my desire to quarrel. My parents, unsuccessful tradespeople (they have a perfumer's shop in a street in Prati in which there must be at least ten shops like theirs and better than theirs), are two elderly, senile angels who love one another as on the first day of their marriage. My sister, smaller than I, a student at a teachers' college, is also an angel of the studious, industrious, pedantic kind. My brother is an idler, perhaps even a bit of a delinquent; but for me, since I am fond of him, he too is an angel. And so, not being able to vent my wrath in this family of angels, I have discovered a system. In the morning I leave home and go and take up a position in some street or other, preferably near a set of traffic lights. Here I lean against a lamp-post, like the street-walkers whose attitudes I imitate, pulling back my chest and thrusting forward my belly, in such a way as to emphasize the prominence of my groin, distended and oblong like a cake of soap, and also my legs, my best feature, so perfect as to make people think they are not mine and that I have exchanged them for a pair of those that are to be seen in shops where they sell stockings. As soon as I see a car with a solitary man at the wheel, I raise my hand and thumb a lift. The driver looks at my hand, looks at my face, looks at my soap-shaped groin, looks at my splendid mannequin-like legs, and then his movement, though continuing as if by force of inertia, slows down, comes to a stop a little farther on with brakes applied. I catch up with him, jump in in furious haste, close the door. Without much ceremony I ask: 'Where are you going?'

The familiar *tu* makes them self-assured; they don't know that I make use of it to dogs and pigs. They answer without fail, in a kindly, accommodating manner: 'And you – where d'you want to go?' So then I make a brief mental calculation about the time required for a complete and well articulated quarrel; and then I reply – supposing that I am in my own quarter, that is, near Piazza Cavour : 'I have to go to Piazza Bologna.' Well, believe it or not, few of them refuse; most of them put the car into gear at once, hopefully; and then, as they drive along they begin asking the usual questions : 'Who are you, what are you called, what do you do, do you study, do you work, are you engaged, have you a boy friend, do you make love,' etc. etc. I answer briefly; then, without delay, I go over to the attack. Suppose that one of them answers my question about his profession : 'I'm a builder.' Immediately I fall upon him : 'What? What? A builder? You're a builder? Really a builder? That's fine, I've wanted for such a long time to meet with one of your kind to tell him all the bad things I think of him. Well, you know what I say? I say that you builders are disgusting. Yes, disgusting. You speculate on building sites; you buy at ten and re-sell at a hundred; there's no end to your black marketeering both in civic centres and in Vatican property; you work only for millionaires; you raise the price of flats so that poor people can't even hope to find themselves somewhere to live. And if they were at least good to look at, your houses! No, they're disgusting, they're like you, well dressed and respectable outside, ugly and rotten inside. And I say this because I know. A short time ago I looked at a lot of houses, I don't know how many, with a friend who is going to get married. And what sort of houses were they? The floors were uneven; the fixtures and the porcelain fittings were of the worst quality; pieces of plaster had fallen; you open a window and find yourself faced by a wall, you open another and look out into a courtyard that resembles a well. No trees, no green, no gardens. You bring people to starvation, except that, instead of hitting them in the stomach, you hit them in the places where they live, which are perhaps even more necessary than food,' etc. etc. And so, whatever may be the profession of my driver of the moment, I always find something to say, I am never left short of subjects.

But now comes what may be called the best part of it. Insulted and abused, the driver hardly ever does the foreseeable thing – that is, to open the door and ask me to get out. Whether he is hoping to get me to bed or, more probably, he is one of many masochists, he does not even argue but, bent and dejected beneath the hail of insults, he drives along, from one set of traffic lights to another, from one street to another, to the place where I have to get out. But then, when he stops, he does not by any means allow me to go like someone whom it is better to lose than to find. On the contrary, he will generally ask, humbly, insistently and – let it even be said – abjectly, for an appointment. But is it possible to know what men are like? Why do they so love to be treated badly? Pooh!

One day I left home thinking: 'My word, the first man I come across today, I'll eat him alive.' I went and took up my position at the traffic lights on the Tiber Embankment, my favourite place because there is space and motorists can draw aside and pick me up without difficulty. I was, as usual, in a miniskirt; I leant against the lamp-post with my legs crossed; my groin, like a piece of soap, stuck out with the maximum of visibility; as for my bosom, which is drooping and voluminous, I had pulled it up as much as I could until it almost touched my chin. At first I made the gesture of thumbing a lift in a feeble and careless manner, being sure of myself and my own fascination; then, seeing that it had no effect, with more energy: still nothing. Disconcerted, I then made a gesture to which I rarely resort – only when I begin to despair: I put my hand on my groin and scratched myself, pulling my miniskirt up a little, as though I had an itch. Immediately a big white car, of a rather old and yellowish whiteness, slowed down with a strident creaking of brakes and stopped a short distance away. I ran quickly forward, plunged into the car and said: 'I'm going to Corso Trieste; how about you?'

A loud, well-bred voice answered me: 'Corso Trieste? Very well.'

The lights changed, he turned on to the bridge, crossed it and started along Via Tomacelli. I settled myself down as well as I could and then looked at him. He had a strange head, flat at the back and with a bumpy forehead which made one think of that of an owl. His black hair was stuck down on his temples as though with sweat; his round eyes were deep-set in round sockets, beneath coal-black eyebrows; his nose was beak-like, so sharply curved that its point almost went into his mouth; his moustache was black and bristling; his chin turned upwards, with a dark dimple in the middle. His face was red, stiff-looking, the face of a peasant or a hunter, of someone, in fact, accustomed to the open air. I studied him closely, for there was something abnormal in his profile that puzzled me. Finally I said : 'I say, do be kind enough to turn towards me.'

He turned at once, saying boldly : 'There you are. What's the problem?'

Then I understood. Underneath the little black brush of his moustache, his mouth appeared to be pulled upwards as it were by a wound not yet healed, a wound of living flesh starting from his upper lip and ending inside his left nostril. 'Thank you,' I said. 'Now you can turn back again. I understand the whole matter.'

'What have you understood?'

'That you have a nauseating mouth, with a hare lip.'

For a short time he said nothing. Then he murmured gently : 'There are some who like it.'

'Not me.'

'Never mind.'

'To hell with never mind.'

I felt my temper rising, I was already wound up almost to the point where the key that worked the spring of this mysterious watch of my fury would turn no more except with an extreme effort. However I gave it a last twist with this thought : 'He has the soft R, a nasal voice, he must be a worldly man, a snob, a society man.' What I saw confirmed me in this opinion. He was wearing a dark-blue suit with a chalk stripe; a white shirt; a rather old-fashioned striped tie; and gold cuff-links. My eye travelled to the hands that grasped the steering wheel : thick, square, short, with sparse, straight hairs and glossy, flat, spatula-shaped, well-kept nails. He was evidently one of those who, at the hairdresser's, have a never-ending succession of warm cloths, cutting of the hairs in the nostrils and ears, frictions and cleansings; and in the meantime abandon their hands with languid complacency to a talkative manicurist perched uncomfortably on a tiny stool overlapped by her big thighs. In short, a first-rate 'dislikeable'. My glance travelled like a thoughtful fly over his hands, coming to rest for a moment on a ring that he wore on the middle finger of his right hand. The ring had a stone on which something, possibly a monogram, was engraved, but I could not distinguish it clearly. All of a sudden I asked : 'And what do you do?'

'How d'you mean, what do I do?'

'What trade, what profession?'

He did not reply at once; he seemed to be reflecting. Then he said : 'Export-import.'

'What sort of thing is that?'

With his characteristic, high-society, fundamentally insulting courtesy he explained : 'It means exportation and importation. Commercial exchange, in fact.'

A tradesman! Just like my parents! Like the people whom my parents knew and visited! Impetuously I cried at once, my head bent : 'Tradesman? You're a tradesman? I know all about tradesmen because I have them in my family. The worst class of people in the world, the laziest, the most useless, the most harmful! Yes, because it's entirely owing to the tradesmen that prices go up and everything costs more and more while the money for ordinary expenses gets less and less adequate. You know what you are, you tradesmen? You're just parasites, parasites of the real type like bugs and lice, which live by sucking blood and without being noticed, quite quiet, well hidden, well disguised, well camouflaged. Your great discovery, with which you have progressed for centuries to suck people's blood, is to rent a room, put a counter in it and a few shelves and then buy at ten wholesale in order to re-sell at twenty retail, while you sit idle behind the till with your bottoms on a chair and your arms crossed and your heads empty. Oh yes, I know all about you, everything, you don't take me in, I know all your tricks, your special offers, your sales, your windings-up, your novelties, your discounts, your reduced prices, your payment by instalments, your remainders, your cheap rates, your bankruptcies and so on . . .'

I stopped to get my breath; and he took advantage of this to say to me, without being in the least offended: 'That's all right. But I am not a shopkeeper, as it seems to me you have mistakenly understood. I haven't a shop. I have an office, I'm occupied with business.'

I felt uneasy. Partly because 'businessman' is a generic term which can mean all sorts of things and about which, for that reason, there is nothing to be said. Disconcerted, I enquired: 'Businessman? But what sort of business?'

'Business.'

I had to find something else. And at once. We were, in fact, already in the neighbourhood of Piazza Ungheria; Corso Trieste was not very far off. All of a sudden my glance, sharpened by necessity, perhaps, at last discovered what was engraved on the ring which he wore on his finger – a coat-of-arms. Indeed it was certainly a coat-of-arms, there was no doubt about it, with a coronet and the usual gadgets: balls, stripes, lions, lilies and other things too. With a sudden, angry change of voice I asked, pointing at the ring: 'What's that? A coat-of-arms?'

'Yes – at least until it is proved not to be.'

'Then you have a title?'

'So I'm told.'

'What are you? A count? A baron? A duke? A prince? A marquess?'

He thought it over and then, evasively, gallantly, answered: 'To you I'm Paolo; that's enough.'

Swelling with still unexpressed rage, I cried: 'I could have sworn you had a title. I could have sworn it because only a titled person could be as unpleasant as you are. I know you, you titled people; I had a boy friend who had a title; for a whole summer we went about in his grand car, from one seaside place to another, from one night-club to another, and he was a first-class idiot; he was called Uguccione. I know you and I say you ought to be shot, the whole lot of you – idle, ignorant, presump-tuous, feeble, degenerate as you are. What d'you think you're in the world for, eh? To carry your pride about with you? To give yourselves airs because you have a crest embroidered on your shirts, eh? To look down upon those who haven't any title, eh? And why, indeed? Because you have a family tree with all the little labels on which are written the names of your ancestors right back to the so-called founder of the family, eh? Because you know the names and surnames of your forefathers, eh? Be-cause you know or think you know who they were, eh? But you don't know anything. No, absolutely nothing. I'll tell you who the ancestors were that you're so proud of. They were all crooks, criminals, brigands, robbers, bandits – real, proper highwaymen. And so, from one insolence to another, from one robbery to another they accumulated all those riches that allow you, their descendants, to do nothing whatever in life, hanging around night-clubs at night and by day picking up girls who thumb a lift. Yes, your ancestors were bandits; and you, you're an idler, in spite of your import-export, and one finger-nail of a village young man is worth more than the whole of you, with your car and your blue suit, your cuff-links and your good education.'

What a relief! What satisfaction! I was unloading myself and I felt better – better and better the more I unloaded. I still went on for some time with my tirade against the nobility; and then I came out of it with this conclusion, a conclusion dictated by rage, unexpected and astonishing not only for him but also for myself: 'Now look, you'd better stop and let me get out. We're not at Corso Trieste yet, but it doesn't matter, I'll walk. I dislike you too much, you and your class. Shoo! Get away from me!'

But he did not stop; perhaps he understood that I did not really at all want to get out. All he did was to lick his hare lip with a piece of obscene red tongue, and then he said: 'Well done!'

'To hell with well done!'

He was not offended; on the contrary. He went on inflexibly : 'Yes, well done; because – even if with a little exaggeration – you said exactly what I myself think. Yes, our ancestors, the ancestors of us titled people, were bandits, brigands, highway robbers. In other words, they were genuine, complete men, still close to nature, with all the natural appetites still intact. Men of prey, indeed; and their predestined prey was the peaceful, the civilized, the sedentary people. Intrepid, strong and fierce, they devoured the weak and the cowardly. And I, and all the others like me, ought to try and resemble those pitiless ancestors, those bandits. If we don't want to disappear, we must take them as models.'

'Ah, that's fine,' I shouted, 'fine models, highway robbers; but do me the favour of having some sense of shame.'

He did not appear to have understood. He was silent for a moment, then he resumed in his characteristic tone, at the same time both didactic and 'social' : 'But people don't talk like you unless in some way – perhaps even without knowing it – they have ancestors of the same kind. What is your name?'

Did he mean this seriously or as a joke? He meant it seriously. I answered unwillingly : 'My name is Sebastiana.'

'Sebastiana *what*?'

It now seems impossible, but he had properly caught me out. I have in fact the name of a noble family even though I am not in the least aristocratic. A name which, especially at school, exposed me to facile sarcasms : 'What's your name? Colonna? Then you're a Princess Colonna.' 'No, Colonna, with a shop in Prati.' 'So you're not a princess, then, just any old shopkeeper.' Reluctantly I answered : 'Colonna.'

He gave an exclamation of joy, as though he had at last found the solution to a troublesome enigma. He cried jubilantly : 'Colonna! I could have sworn it. Good blood does not lie.'

Infuriated, I replied : 'Blood – what d'you mean by blood? I'm called Colonna just as I might be called anything – Rossi or Proietti. No one has a title in my home, thank God. We're poor, yes, but not noble. Besides, it's no use your trying to flatter me and fawn on me. I still dislike you, like everyone else of your class; and none of your flatteries serve any purpose at all. Your face is split in two, your real face because you have that cleft of your hare lip, and your metaphorical face because you're a turd and you stink of snobbery from a mile off.'

But you never know with madmen. He was not embarrassed; all he did was to shake his head, like a schoolmaster faced with a recalcitrant pupil. 'No, Sebastiana,' he said, 'there are no classes, only races, and there are only two races, that of the masters and that of the slaves. And you recognize the master from the fact that his morality consists in dominating. And you recognize the slave from the fact that his morality consists in obeying. But let it be quite clear : one is born a master, one does not become one. And it is the same with slaves. It is a question of race not of class. One can pass from one class to another; but, whatever one does, one cannot pass from one race to another. Now, Sebastiana, certain things in you make me think that you too, possibly even without knowing it, belong to the race of the masters.'

'What things?'

'For example, your capacity for indignation.'

Beside myself, I cried : 'You're wrong, you're always wide of the mark. What makes me indignant is you yourself, with your utterly filthy idea of being a "master". What kind of a master, indeed! You a master, with that face, with those cuff-links, with that suit! You make me laugh.'

He explained patiently : 'You understand the word as it is used in Rome – that is, as an elegant, rich man, liberal with his money. But, Sebastiana, that is only the current use. I've already told you : the word "master" to me means the beast of prey that throws itself upon weaker animals and devours them and has the right to do so precisely because he is the stronger.'

I started laughing hysterically : 'You've said it : beast. Yes, only a big beast can talk in this way. But please tell me – who do you think you can charm with these idiocies?'

He did not reply. He was driving carefully, calmly, absolutely calmly. Then he put his hand into his coat pocket and took something out. 'Does this charm you?' he asked.

Now you must know that I never have any money. I mean what I say : never. The shop, as I have said, goes badly; and my parents, even without saying so openly, make me understand that I ought to fend for myself. And in fact I do fend for myself. How do I do it? Here one comes to the greatest contradiction of my life. While on the one hand I have a need to quarrel, on the other I have need of money. Of course I could go to bed with the men from whom I thumb a lift, thus earning the money of which I have need; but I cannot do this, it is one of the many impossibilities of my life. Also I could give up making scenes and could display my difficulties in a whining, tearful, heart-rending manner : moved with compassion, the men who give me a lift would certainly help me. But this too is impossible for me; I have a need for scenes as for the air I breathe. And so, being both unable and unwilling to be either a whore or a beggar, I fall back on a contradiction : first I thoroughly insult the driver of the car; then, at the moment when I am getting out, I change my tone and ask in a timid, subdued manner : 'I say, could you make me a small loan?'

A contradiction, as I said. But it is clear that I am not as contradictory as I think I am; or rather, men love contradictions. For it is not at all uncommon for that same individual upon whose head I had just been heaping abundant insults to put his hand in his pocket and give me some money, when I have asked for a loan. In fact I have noticed that those who have been most insulted are often the most generous. Once again : masochism? And if not, what? Pooh!

And now, with this man Paolo, it actually happened that he gave me money before I had asked for it. I looked at the ten-thousand lire note that he had held out to me, with aristocratic negligence, between two fingers, and meanwhile the usual thing happened to me that always happens at the sight of money, perhaps just because I see so little of it : my mind clouded over, my rage subsided, a kind of stupor paralysed me, drained me of feeling. I was in a trance, hypnotized, magnetized, subdued. I

looked at the flesh-coloured note with the portrait of Michel-
angelo on one side and the white oval of the watermark on the
other; and my mind was a blank. In the end I articulated clearly:
'It's ten thousand lire.'

'It's for you.'

'Are you giving it me?'

'Yes.'

I seized the note and stuffed it into my bag. And then, suddenly, I was seized with a feeling of greed, this also as a consequence of the hypnosis into which the sight of the money had
plunged me. In a childish, imploring way I went on: 'Only ten?
Can't you give me twenty?'

What brazenness, it may be thought. But it was not that; it
was a kind of timidity, caused by poverty. I am so poor that the
same thing happens to me with money as happens with hunger
to someone who has had too much of it: after eating, his appetite remains and he wants to eat again. But this time Paolo did
not yield. 'Ten is enough,' he said. 'But if you come and see me
tomorrow in my office, I will give you as much again and possibly
even more.'

'But tomorrow is Sunday,' I stammered. 'Nobody's in their
offices tomorrow.'

'Exactly.'

Exactly what? This would have been an excellent pretext for
another scene, now at the moment when I was going away. But
I was 'unloaded'; and the money prevented me from 're-charg-
ing' myself, from taking in another consignment. Instead, in a
subdued voice, as though I did not wish to be heard by anyone
who might be listening, I said: 'All right, I'll come. But couldn't
you, in the meantime, give me a little something on account, for
instance five thousand? If I'm coming to see you, I do at the
very least need a decent pair of trousers.'

'It's not a party. There'll be nobody there but me. You're perfectly all right as you are now.'

He stopped the car and I looked round: to my despair, to my
horror I recognized Corso Trieste. A street like any other street,

at other times; now it was the street of my failure, of my defeat. Anxiously I asked : 'And at what time?'

'Come at five.'

'And the address?'

He put his hand in his pocket and for a moment I really hoped he would pull out another ten-thousand lire note. Not at all, it was a visiting card. Name, surname, address, export-import and, of course, also the nobleman's coronet, with a lot of rays, a lot of little balls, like an insect, above the name.

I placed the card in my bag and he opened the door for me. I said hurriedly : 'And thank you, of course'; and then, as I was on the point of getting out, like a real madwoman I suddenly bent my head over his hand and kissed it with abject gratitude. It is true that at the moment of touching it with my lips I was tempted to bite it; but this was only a temptation; and what is a temptation that is not given way to? Nothing, less than nothing. But then, why that kiss? Pooh! I got out of the car, then remained standing on the pavement, watching, in deathly fury, as it drove away.

On Sunday I found myself in a street of big new buildings. On other days it would have been a chaos of stationary, roaring cars, enveloped in clouds of fumes from impatient exhausts. But today being Sunday, it was a desert, so much so that I actually encountered a cat which at that moment was quite calmly crossing the asphalt in the opposite direction. Yes, a desert; but my appointment with Paolo made this otherwise pleasant desert rather sinister, vaguely menacing, certainly enigmatic. Paolo was not, in fact, the kind of young man whom one goes to see in his own home when his parents are away in the country or at the seaside for the week-end, to spend a quiet and relaxed Sunday afternoon with him on a basis of cigarettes, gramophone records, alcohol, sex and perhaps even an occasional whiff of drugs. Paolo ... is Paolo. In other words, a man whom I dislike, who is even repugnant to me and from whom nevertheless I accepted an invitation that was plainly equivocal and ill-intentioned. Of course there was the promise of another, or possibly even two or three more, ten-thousand lire notes. But as I have already said, money fascinates me if I see it in flesh and blood, so to speak, displayed under my nose; if remote and invisible, it ceases to hypnotize me and, for good or ill, I go back to being my ordinary self. But then, why was I here, why was I going there, why, in fact, did I allow myself to be enticed? A contradiction, as usual. So we go back to the point of departure : why do I contradict myself so often? Pooh!

Here, now, was the building I was seeking. I looked up at it and was dazzled by its façade, all glass and steel, clear and brilliant, with the cold, blue reflection of the sky in each of its windows. It was strange : all this glitter and brilliance, this purity of materials and lines; and then, hidden away in a room in one of the suites, Paolo with his hare lip, his moustache, his coal-black eyebrows, his owl-like eyes. I went up to the door, it was shut. I tried to look through the glass; but they were special panes, transparent only from inside, and I saw nothing. Near the main door, however, there was a row of name-plates and amongst the others, that of the export-import. I made up my mind and pressed the bell, which was in a brass circle as big as a soup-plate.

The door opened almost at once, as though my arrival had been spied through those panes of obscure glass by someone who was expecting me; and on the threshold appeared a young man with long hair. But not long in the fashion of the young men of today; long in the fashion of the young girls of yesterday. This hair fell on either side of a white, smooth and slightly chubby face which reminded one of the faces of the cherubim and seraphim with wings attached to their heads who flutter in the sky in church pictures. Angelic, too, were the rather languishing eyes which looked at me in an inspired, questioning way; the nose with its narrow nostrils; the heart-shaped mouth curled up at the corners. He was small, like a young boy, but well-proportioned, with hands and feet so tiny that they gave one a feeling of tenderness. I said to him gently : 'Are you the porter?'

Modestly he replied : 'No, his son. Dad's gone into the country.'

'Well, I have to go to the fifth floor, to the export-import.'

'To Signor Paolo? I'll take you there.'

He led me to the lift, entered it and I followed and he made as if to close the doors. Pointing to the buttons for the various floors, I said: 'There's no need for you to come with me. As for pressing a button, I can manage it myself.'

He looked at me without answering, then, coolly but not insolently, he stretched out his arm and pressed the button for the fifth floor. I insisted angrily: 'What are you doing, are you deaf? I said there was no need for you to come with me.'

He threw me an ambiguous glance and then announced: 'Superior orders.'

'Orders from whom?'

He did not reply. He was now staring at my chest, perhaps merely because it was at the level of his eyes. He had a curious, almost worried expression which I could not succeed in interpreting. He said hastily: 'Today's Sunday; this is an office building and there's no one here. You know we're alone in the building?'

'Who cares?' I answered roughly.

'Well then, give me a kiss.'

As he said this, he pressed the 'halt' button. The lift stopped.

Now I might even have given him a kiss if only because he was such a perfect altar-picture angel. I will go further and say: perhaps I should not have disliked it. But that 'well then' infuriated me. Why 'well then'? 'Well then' what? Obviously: 'Well then, give me a kiss, seeing that we're alone and you're just a feeble little woman and I can do what I like with you.' I stared him straight in the eyes, with a penetrating look. Then, emphasizing the words, I answered: 'Kiss *you*? You poor half-wit.'

Would you believe it? Suddenly the angel, with a resolute, concentrated expression, fell upon me, seized the edge of my blouse and, with one single tug, pulled off its only button. Then he got hold of my brassière and pulled it down on one side with force and determination. One breast burst forth; the angel, without hesitating, gave it a cruel squeeze. I groaned with pain; I replied with a blow of my knee to his stomach. He gave a leap, seized me by the hair and pulled my head down, trying to bring my mouth close to his. Wild with rage, blindly I scratched his face. He immediately let go of my hair; I straightened up, dishevelled and panting; and there he was, having retreated to the far side of the lift, looking at me, mortified, passing his hand over his scratched face. Then he said plaintively: 'After all, what did I ask you for? Just a kiss.'

Infuriated, and putting out my hand to press the button of the lift again, I replied: 'Look, you'd better keep your mouth shut.'

He implored me, in a voice of entreaty: 'At least promise me that you won't say anything to Signor Paolo.'

A good idea! The assault by the angel would be able to serve me as a pretext for a further scene with Paolo. And then, just because the angel, with his chubby face scored by scratches, gave me a feeling of tenderness, I wanted to show myself hard towards him. I shouted violently: 'I'm not making any promises.'

He looked at me with an expression that was not in the least frightened. If anything, it showed curiosity, as of someone watching, from behind glass, the convolutions of a fish in an aquarium. But I did not have time to examine this feeling. The lift stopped; I turned my back on the angel and hastily got out without turning round.

The door of the export-import was open; I pushed it and plunged with a rush into the anteroom and thence into a long corridor between two rows of doors. Grey fitted carpet, red doors, white ceiling. Where could Paolo be? I opened the doors one after another and found everywhere the usual spectacle of offices on holidays: typewriters covered, sheets of white paper and sheets of carbon paper scattered everywhere, as though by a gust of wind in a storm. At each door that I opened in vain, my fury increased. I was 'charging' myself, exactly as I do when I am going to thumb a lift. One phrase kept running in my head, like a spinning top: 'Now I'll settle him.'

I reached the end of the corridor and broke in. Paolo was sitting in a big, almost empty room, behind a glass and steel desk. He was wearing his usual dark-blue suit, the usual gold cuff-links, the usual striped tie – and I was almost going to say, the usual hare lip. I at once accosted him with unprecedented violence : 'The porter's son assaulted me in the lift. Look at my blouse, look at my hair. He tore my blouse, seized me by the hair, squeezed my breast. What sort of a place is this? Who do you think you are? You give yourself so many airs and then you allow people to be assaulted in lifts,' etc, etc.

I was shouting; but Paolo did not answer me, and did not interrupt me. He too looked at me in the same way as the angel, shortly before, in the lift – with an attentiveness full of curiosity, as it were through glass. Indeed I should have liked to know the reason why both of them peered at me in this way. 'What sort of behaviour is this?' I concluded. 'Who's going to pay for my blouse? But I shall report him, that hooligan, I shall certainly report him.'

Finally Paolo moved, but in a studied, as it were 'rehearsed', manner. He put out his arm to open a box on the table, took a cigarette and slipped it into the cleft of his hare lip. Perfectly easy and ordinary gestures, you will say, which anyone makes without effort and without intention, just as they happen. But Paolo, it seemed, was making these quite normal gestures on purpose to conceal something abnormal. And indeed he bungled them, like a nervous actor making his début : he put into his mouth the end of the cigarette without a tip, and did not notice it until he had lit the flame of his lighter. Then he put back the cigarette the right way round and applied the flame to it again. It was strange; his hand was trembling so violently that for a moment he could not manage to light the cigarette. Then suddenly I was frightened : it was clear that his hand was trembling because he had in his head a ready-made, premeditated plan for me, a plan which filled him with excitement, with shame, perhaps even with fear. I watched him, meanwhile, as he lowered his hand, replaced the lighter on the table and remained with downcast eyes, in silence, looking, it seemed, at his hand which was still trembling. Finally, in a strange tone of voice, he said : 'D'you want me to punish him?'

Impressed by the trembling of his hand and by the tone of his voice, I should now have liked to say no, that I did not wish it, that I had now forgiven him. But, as always, contradiction overcame me; and so curiosity prevailed over fear. Untruthfully I stammered : 'Of course I wish you to.'

Silence. Paolo was now looking at the table on which there was a sheet of paper. He was doodling with his pen and appeared to be reflecting. Finally he took up the internal telephone and pressed the button. An indistinct chirping sound could be heard; then, very clearly, the voice of the angel : 'Yes, Signor Paolo?'

'Come up at once.'

Impressed, I enquired : 'And what will you do with him now?'

He did not answer. He was absorbed in following with his eyes the doodles that he was drawing on the sheet of paper. Or rather, as I was aware, in contemplating the trembling of his own hand as he was making the doodles. I waited for him to answer me; and in the meantime I, too, for some reason or other, stared at the trembling hand, with fascinated curiosity. Then I heard his voice, curt, authoritative : 'Undress.'

I looked at him hesitatingly. Had he spoken or had I imagined it? 'Eh?' I said.

He repeated, this time in an emphatic manner : 'I said : undress!'

How strange is the human mind. Or my own, at any rate, so changeable, so full of contradictions. I have been unruly and rebellious and disobedient, it can be said, ever since I was born. And yet, an order given in the right voice and at the right moment was all that was now needed to make me as obedient and well-disciplined as a soldier in front of an officer. Or rather – as I said to myself as I started without hesitation, altogether too anxious and zealous, to pull off my clothes over my head – like an actor in front of a director. Yes indeed, a director, for Paolo had somehow or other imposed upon me a role of some kind in some kind of a comedy of his own; and I, inexplicably subjugated, so it seemed, had now agreed to act this role.

But what role was it, finally? Who, for example, once I had

slipped off my suit, made me go on tiptoe and place it on a chair? And then hurriedly to strip off my panties and brassière with a submissive fear, so it seemed, of not doing it in time before the angel, another actor in the comedy, made his entrance? By now I was naked; and since I was ashamed of my huge, sagging bosom, I folded one arm to support it, as one does with a baby whom one is suckling. Embarrassed, I went over to the table and asked shyly : 'Am I to remain standing or shall I sit down?'

'Remain standing.'

Then there was a knock at the door. Asked by Paolo, in his same strangled voice, to come in, the angel first peered in cautiously between the two leaves of the door, as if to make sure of the point which the performance had reached. Then, doubtless satisfied with what he saw (Paolo absorbed, with eyes lowered, in drawing on the sheet of paper; myself standing, naked but with my boots on, in front of the table), he came in, openly and deliberately, saying : 'Signor Paolo, you called me?'

'Yes, I called you. So you assault people who come to visit me, in the lift?'

There was a moment's silence. Then something happened which, by this time, I was expecting; and which confirmed me once and for all in the idea that we were, all three of us, acting a comedy. The angel, taking advantage of the fact that Paolo was still gazing at his trembling hand, turned towards me and, brazenly though still like an angel, winked at me, as much as to say : 'This is all a thing that has been agreed between myself and Signor Paolo. But we two are in agreement against him.' This was a matter of an instant. Then, in a contrite, obsequious, artificial voice, the angel explained : 'Signor Paolo, you are right. But the young lady was, so to speak, somewhat undressed, and so I lost my head ...'

I had barely time to reflect that the angel was an extremely bad actor when, all of a sudden, an inhuman scream burst forth : 'Silence, you slave.'

'But, Signor Paolo ...'

'Be quiet, you pariah.'

# Pooh!

At last! If the angel acts badly, Paolo, in compensation, acts extremely well; or rather, he is himself, truer than truth, so much himself as to be frightening. He leapt to his feet, banged his fist on the table and shouted: 'Slave, pariah, if you don't want me to tell your father you must kneel down now, yes, kneel down in front of Sebastiana and kiss her feet.'

Thus the comedy develops; and, as it develops, it involves me more and more, though without allowing me to guess at its further developments. A moment before I had been a poor call-girl undressing in front of her client; what was I now? Who knows, perhaps a kind of goddess. Almost incredulously, in fact, I saw the angel throw himself on all fours at my feet, with a comic gesture of prostrating himself; and then I saw that, with a lively, voluntary movement, he was stretching out his neck towards my boots. Paolo yelled, as though possessed: 'That's not enough. You must not only kiss her feet but lick them.'

Did the angel obey, or was he pretending? Difficult to say because, owing to the boots, I could not make out whether he was kissing or licking them. Paolo shouted: 'Both of them, both of them!' and the angel obediently moved his head from one foot to the other. Then I was startled and almost gave a leap. Paolo had come round the table and placed himself at my back, had seized me by the arms from behind with tremendous force, so as actually to hurt me. Meanwhile his head appeared on my shoulder and his voice, subdued, intense, frantic, was urging me, close to my ear: 'Now piss on his head. Yes, go on, urinate on to his head.'

What was happening to me? Simply that I was no longer the character in Paolo's comedy; I was myself again. And indeed, very naturally, instinctively, I replied: 'No, not that.'

'But why not?'

'Because I don't want to.'

'Why don't you want to? He's a pariah, a servant, a slave. Come on now, do it on his head. I'll give you all you want, but do it.'

It was clear, however, that in the agreement between the angel and Paolo this business of the urine had not been included. In fact the angel, after a moment's uncertainty and immobility, as of one who was not sure that he had heard properly, drew himself aside on the floor in disgust, staggered to his feet and said breathlessly: 'Signor Paolo, not that, after all.'

The matter seemed to be finished. It appeared now that the only thing left for myself and the angel to do – just like two actors who have finished their performance – was to make a fine bow and go away. But no; I felt with absolute certainty that the comedy was to have a further development. Nor was I wrong. Paolo walked round me and passed in front of me. 'Well then,' he cried, 'if you don't want to do it on *his* head, do it on mine. Yes, on mine.' And then he threw himself down on the floor, knelt and placed his head between my legs.

A picture! Myself with legs apart, one boot this side and one that, my arm bent to support my bosom, and leaning sideways against the table; the angel standing at some distance, still red from his efforts; this crazy Paolo on all fours in front of me, his arms raised to clasp my knees and his face turned upwards in hopeful expectation, as though beneath a shower that refuses to gush.

Now, however, you must know that everything which in some way has to do with the needs of the body arouses in me an irrepressible, hysterical hilarity. Why does this happen? Pooh, it's a fact like any other and that's all there is to it. I had already been tempted to laugh when Paolo told me to urinate on the angel's head; but, now that he was imploring me to do it to him, my laughter burst forth irresistibly. I laughed in spite of myself, like an idiot, like a lunatic, with a savage, stupid joy that I myself did not understand. Then Paolo insisted, from down on the floor where he was crouching: 'Come on, get on with it'; and I cried to him once more, writhing with laughter: 'No, no, I tell you no – ha, ha, ha, ha.'

'Come on!'

'No, I tell you. Ha, ha, ha.'

Then, as though beside himself, he suddenly started shaking

me by my ankles, in the way one does with a tree to shake down the fruit. I tottered, but went on laughing more than ever. However he gave me such a violent shake that I lost my balance and bumped my side against the table. The pain of it made me stop laughing. I cried out in exasperation : 'That's enough. Leave me alone now. Are you mad?'

Indeed he was really mad. He shook me again, and again I was on the point of falling. Then my eye lit upon a glass ashtray on the table. I seized hold of it, bent forward and dealt him a blow on the head, with furious violence. Immediately he let forth a yell, loosened his hold on me, put his hand to his head, turned over on his side and remained motionless, hunched up in the position – I could not help thinking – of the foetus in the mother's womb.

I bent down, started to raise his head, felt a sensation of wetness on my hand, looked at it and saw that it was stained with blood. A terrible fear came over me; but this fear not merely did not lessen but increased when I realized that he was not dead at all, as I had feared. In reality he was alive, altogether too much alive. He lay motionless, his cheek against the carpet, his hand on his head and those round, owl-like eyes wide open and staring, looking, it seemed, at something only he could see. It was precisely these staring eyes, which ought to have reassured me because they showed that I had not killed him, which finally terrified me. And so, in spite of myself and owing to this terror, I now did what I had not been willing to do previously of my own free will. I felt myself urinating, not normally, however, as in the lavatory; but in jets and spurts and gushes, little by little; and since I saw that the urine was falling on his hair, on his face and on those terrible staring eyes, I moved, so as not to soak him, in the direction of the chair on which I had placed my suit and my other garments. The urine continued to come from me in little involuntary jets, making a dark, wet streak on the light carpet and trickling over my boots. I seized my suit, my brassière and panties, turned towards the angel who was still standing there in astonishment, and said to him in a low voice, taking him by the hand : 'Come on, let's go.'

But we at once retreated, frightened and respectful. Paolo was rising and now he was on his feet. Possibly he did not see us, certainly did not look at us. He drew his hand over his face, then, staggering, crossed the room. However he did not go to the door by which I myself and the angel had entered. He passed in front of us, opened a small door which I had not noticed, and disappeared. Through the open door we heard the sound of running water. Paolo was washing himself. I turned towards the angel and said : 'Come on, let's get away.'

I knew that the building was empty and that it consisted entirely of offices and that it was Sunday. So I did not hesitate to rush down the stairs, naked as I was, breasts and hair flying, with nothing on but my boots, and my clothes over my arm. Holding hands, I dragging him and the angel letting himself be dragged, we twisted and turned from one flight of stairs to another for five floors, then reached the entrance hall. But we did not stop. The porter's box invited us; and a questioning glance from me was answered by the angel with an expressive look, as if to tell me that I had guessed rightly. I gave his hand a slight squeeze to confirm our understanding, and he did the same; then, still running, we hurled ourselves down a little narrow staircase, far down into the basement where the porter's living quarters were. In truth this was a continuation of our flight from Paolo; and as it continued it came to a conclusion in a foreseeable place : the big double bed of the angel's parents.

Later, we lay in silence, stretched out on our backs side by side on the gaudy-coloured silk coverlet. How I love basements, for making love and then resting and dozing after love-making. The room had a very low ceiling, and it was full of furniture and pieces of junk; and it had a smell of stuffiness and of cooking, like all porters' lodges. Behind the opaque glass of the two little round windows I saw, every now and then, the shadowy pairs of legs of passers-by. The looking-glass of the wardrobe, opposite the end of the bed, gave a foreshortened reflection of our two naked bodies, with feet which looked as though attached to our knees. My hand was clasping the angel's member, encircling it with two fingers like a ring; he placed his open hand flat on my groin. Finally the angel enquired: 'Why do you think Signor Paolo does those things?'

'Because he likes doing them.'

'And why does he like it?'

'Pooh!'

# The Electra Complex

The analyst by whom we have been treated for the last two years, my brother and I, says that with a pair of twins there is always one who is stronger and who acts as guide to the other, weaker one. This, at any rate in our case, is probably true. I am Sergio's succuba; the scientific coldness of his mind fascinates and subjugates me. It is true, we are both frail, insecure, inconsistent; but Sergio has at least managed to master the language of analysis, to fabricate for himself a mask of reassuring words; which I have not.

To make up for this, I have one superiority over Sergio, that of a strange consciousness – of the fact of having been together with him before we were born; of having lived with him through the experience of that absolute nothing which precedes life.

This allows me to have a – how shall I say? – biological intimacy with him, which no pair of normal brothers and sisters can ever know. The intimacy that comes from having been complementary to one another in our mother's womb. From having been one single person, even though formed of two bodies.

I thought of these things as I was going to see Sergio after

receiving, by telephone, a communication which by this time had
become commonplace and, in any case, foreseen and discounted
by us two, to the effect that our father had been kidnapped, that
he was in good health and that we, his children, must now wait
for a second telephone call in which the kidnappers would tell
us how much we must pay to have him back safe and sound.
Why do I say that the news was foreseen and discounted by us?
Not only because our father, a so-called businessman – and, let
me add, in very big business – had been for some reason expecting this for some time; but also and above all because we two
had been expecting it and almost, as will be seen, counting on
it. We had even gone so far as to make a bet on it: Sergio said
they would kidnap him early in the morning, when he was going
to the office; I on the other hand said that the kidnapping would
take place late at night, when he was going, as he was accustomed
to do every evening, to the house of a mistress of his by whom
he had had a child. Sergio insinuates that I had made a bet that
they would kidnap him at night because I hated that woman
who, after our mother's death, aimed at getting herself married
and thus becoming our stepmother. It may be so. Anyhow, Sergio
won the bet: our father was kidnapped early this morning,
probably at the moment when he was leaving the grounds of our
villa in his car.

I ran two steps at a time up the tortuous staircase of the
ancient palazzo at the top of which Sergio has his flat, arrived
out of breath and pressed the bell impatiently. I waited a long
time, then heard a sound of bustling confusion; the door was
opened; and at the very moment when I entered a naked, white
female body fled from the anteroom and disappeared into the
darkness of a corridor. I walked straight to Sergio's study and
went in. I found myself suddenly in the atmosphere, so reassuring to me, of my brother's false, childish, scientific-type impassiv-
ity. Through the window came the clear October sunshine to
light up the big glass and steel desk with papers stacked up at the
edges according to size, bunches of pencils and pens standing in
two leather holders, and an electric typewriter.

The bookshelves, of polished, shining chromium-plated metal, were cheerful-looking, with the books, all of them perfectly new, arranged apparently according to the colour of their bindings rather than their subjects. Nothing in the way of mechanical household apparatus was lacking: television, radio, record-player, cine-camera. I went to the window and looked out: far below, in the great courtyard of the building, a group of chauffeurs were chattering, amongst cars parked in a row under the arches of the arcade. Then I gave a start and turned quickly round as I heard Sergio's voice saying: 'Whatever are you doing over here? Has it happened, then?'

I looked at him and nodded without speaking. He was enveloped from his shoulders to his ankles in a green Turkish towel; from the triangular opening in this species of toga his blond head rose erect and aggressive. He had just got up; he came direct from the shower; and his long, white, bare feet left a wet imprint on the fitted carpet. He was very thin, from his elegant shins right up to his bony face; his blue eyes peered forth from sockets that were always rather tired and bruised-looking. He went and sat down at the desk, sideways, crossing his long, lanky legs outside the towel. He asked calmly: 'When did it happen?'

'At seven o'clock this morning, as he was leaving the drive, in the car. I had the telephone call half an hour ago. I said nothing to anybody and came here.'

'Then I've won the bet.'

'Yes, you've won it. And what do we do now?'

'We shall carry out the pre-established plan to the letter.'

So that was that. It was true; by common agreement we had decided, Sergio and I, on a certain plan of action, in the more and more probable event of our father being kidnapped. The plan was indeed very simple: we would reply to the blackmail of the kidnappers with a round 'no'. But now, all of a sudden, at Sergio's as it were military answer – like that of an officer who gives an order that is impossible even if long premeditated, to a soldier at attention – I was seized with great anguish. Bewildered, I stammered: 'The pre-established plan? Do you realize that this plan is practically equivalent to condemning our father to death?'

'Not at all. We're not condemning him to death. We're leaving the choice to the kidnappers. It's not a question of a sentence of death, but rather of a certain move in the game of poker. The kidnappers claim that among their cards they hold the joker of death. Well, by refusing to pay the ransom, we do two things: we get to see their cards to discover whether they are bluffing or not; and we face them with a choice which concerns them alone and frees us from any responsibility. If they are bluffing, our father will come home without a halfpenny being paid, and so much the better for him; if they are are not bluffing, well, we shall be freed for good from a man we detest.'

'But do we really detest him?'

'Yes, I should say so, don't we?'

'But why do we detest him?'

'This is a discussion we've already had a hundred times. To put it briefly: we detest him because he has deceived us.'

'Is deception enough to make one want a man's death?'

'It depends. If the deception is profound and, above all, if the man is one's father, I should say yes.'

'Has the deception been profound, in your opinion?'

'Well, discovering that one's own father is a swindler is a rather heavy deception, don't you think?'

I objected, desperately again: 'Let's suppose that the kidnappers restore him to us without a ransom. How shall we be able to justify our conduct? Won't he say that we wanted to cause his death?'

'He'll say so, of course. But isn't this perhaps what we've always been wanting?'

'What?'

'A conclusive explanation with our father. In reality we're cowards; hitherto the explanation has frightened us; now we shall be forced to it. Everything will be clear, at last.'

He was cold, utterly cold; but his coldness, for once, instead of reassuring me increased my anguish. Yes, it is the coldness of

G

science; but I know, and I know that he knows, that this pretence of science is only a pose like any other. With a deep sigh, I said: 'The fact is that in the past I loved him passionately. When I was a child – just fancy! – I thought he was perfect. I used to say in an almost frightened way: 'My father is perfect'."

Sergio accepted what I said with a nod of his head. 'An obvious Electra complex,' he said. 'Logically, with me, it's the Oedipus complex that is concerned. But since our mother is dead, the two complexes have changed places. For you, our father has become our mother, and so, like Electra, you desire his death so as to have me entirely to yourself, since I, in turn, have become, for you, your father. From my point of view, you have become, for me, my mother and for that reason I wish to have you entirely for myself, and consequently I desire the death of our father.'

Fascinating, it must be admitted; but my distress, instead of lessening, increased. 'Electra or not,' I said, 'I really considered him perfect, even to the point of mistaking his defects for good qualities. I recall that one day I said to a little girl who was a friend of mine: "Anyhow my father is lame whereas your father doesn't limp at all." The little girl was so struck with this boasting on my part that, on the spur of the moment, she could find nothing better than to object: "Yes, but *my* father is left-handed." '

He looked at me intently, coldly but benevolently and said nothing. I summoned up all my courage and proposed: 'What would you say if I suggested shelving our plan and paying the ransom?'

Without batting an eyelid, he answered: 'I should say that you are the usual sentimental idiot. But, on what we may call the experimental level, I should be pleased to find such a clear confirmation of certain anomalies of the Electra complex that I have been observing in you for some time.'

'In fact, you would give up the plan?'

'If you really wish it – yes.'

'Well, I do wish it.'

It was doubtful whether he now felt relief in face of my decision, which freed him from a terrible consistency. But now his ascendancy over me was at stake; he had to show himself, in all circumstances, impassible and superior; so the intentness of his expression betrayed nothing. 'All right,' he said; 'we'll pay. Meanwhile I'll telephone our solicitors.'

I got up at once, pleased, fundamentally, that he should again be the guiding, and I the guided one. Hastily I said: 'I'm going. I put the whole thing into your hands, you carry on. One thing I beg of you: no publicity in the papers about our great, heart-rending affection for our father. No filial love!'

'Don't worry, leave it to me.'

I left the room and started going very slowly downstairs. As I went down, I could not help imagining what would have happened if we had put our plan into effect. I imagined the 'second' telephone call: 'What have you decided, then?' 'We have decided not to pay.' 'But you know what will happen if you don't pay?' 'Of course we know, but all the same we shall not pay.' 'You haven't any family feeling, then?' 'It seems we haven't.' 'What, your father has worked for you all his life and you repay him like this?' 'Yes indeed, we repay him like this.' 'But what sort of children are you? Haven't you any fear of God?' 'We leave the fear of God to you – is that all right?' 'But what have you in place of a heart? A stone?' 'Yes, a great big stone. What d'you want us to do? We're not traditional people like you, we're a modern family, alas. Ever heard of Freud?' 'Who's he? A foreigner? Be careful, we don't want to get mixed up with foreigners.' 'Ever heard of the Oedipus complex?' 'Complex – how do complexes come into it? We're not in a public dance-hall. This is a question of your father's life.' 'Ever heard of Electra?' 'Electra? And who's Electra? Aren't you called Silvia, by any chance?' 'Alas, yes, you idiot, I'm called Silvia . . .'

# Physical Defects

I have an excessive sensitivity and thus feel a painful repugnance to this or that physical defect in the people I come across. It is in vain that I tell myself it is unjust as well as absurd to be hostile towards someone because of the shape of his nose; nevertheless I fall back into the same error every time and there is nothing to be done. For instance, this hypersensitivity of mine has recently been wrecking my marriage.

It began like this. Only a few days after we were married I was, as usual, painting at one end of the living-room where, for lack of a studio, I had set up my easel. Meanwhile, at the other end of the room, my husband, standing up, was telephoning to somebody who, from what I understood, was much older than him and, above all, more important. Then, while my husband was conducting a deferential, complimentary conversation interspersed with flattering allusions to a certain 'operation' which his interlocutor had completed with success, I happened, for some reason, to notice that my husband's jacket, being very tight and with vents at the back, was raised up by a prominent backside of which I had hitherto taken no notice. It was a backside that was in some way very expressive, with an air of delicacy and softness which suddenly filled me with an absurd, unjustified disgust. My husband still went on telephoning for a short time, quivering, so to speak, alternately with one buttock and then with the other, and in a curiously eager and servile manner; then he put down the receiver, came across to me and, taking me by the arm, improvised a little saraband of joy with me. Filled with merriment, he explained to me that our future depended upon the person to whom he had been speaking and whom he called – ironically perhaps – the 'chief', on account of a certain job abroad; and that he had for some time been paying court systematically to this personage, precisely in order to obtain this post which would allow us both to live better.

During the following days my husband's campaign for the job abroad progressed in a rational manner, like a real, genuine plan pre-arranged in every detail. Every two or three days he clung to the telephone and overwhelmed the so-called 'chief' with flattery. Intelligent, sophisticated flattery, all the more pleasing because it was cleverly disguised with objective, competent, disinterested opinions. Meanwhile I myself, though pretending to paint, listened to him, approved of what he said, admired him; but at the same time, for some reason or other, I could not help discovering in him, at each new telephone call, some other physical defect of which, inexplicably, I had hitherto been unaware. One time it was his shoulders, which suddenly appeared to me to be both fat and sagging; another time, the way in which his hair fell in pointed, greasy-looking locks on the back of his neck; yet another time a light, yellowish mole, never seen before, between his nose and his cheek. It was strange; as though each of the praises that my husband showered upon the 'chief' was immediately followed, on my side, by the discovery, in him, of some disagreeable, repugnant physical feature.

One evening he came home shouting: 'We've arrived! My plan has made an enormous step forward. He's invited us to dinner this evening, at an expensive restaurant. We're there! All is well.'

I immediately objected that I hadn't the right clothes for such an important invitation. Impetuously he cried: 'What d'you mean, clothes! Remember that you're only twenty and that you're very, very attractive. No question of an evening dress; come in there and I'll see about creating a personality for you.' He dragged me by the hand and there we were in the bedroom; he opened the wardrobe, pulled out a pair of faded and patched blue trousers, a discoloured and misshapen black sweater, a red handkerchief and a small black peaked cap. 'This is what's needed,' he said to me; 'the clothes you were wearing when I saw you for the first time. Now, slip on these trousers and this sweater. But first take off your brassière; you have a very beautiful bosom and it should stay free underneath the sweater so that it can breathe and move. And now pull a lock of your blonde hair over your forehead, cram down the peak of your cap over your violet eyes with their rather swollen, surly eyelids and put a little lipstick on your big, pouting mouth whose lower lip looks as if it had been stung by a wasp. Finally, tie this handkerchief round your neck. Now look at yourself in the glass and tell me whether you're not an irresistible little hooligan – who, I am sure, because I know his tastes in women, will at once make a hit with our Amphitryon.' I looked at myself and was compelled to recognize that he was right; if not exactly irresistible, I was very provoking with my look of a vicious and rather rascally adolescent. But why meanwhile did I discover, as usual for the first time, that the hands with which he arranged the hair on the back of my neck were sweaty?

The evening went well. The chief must have been a really important person, anyhow to judge from the deference and zeal of the waiters. He was not a bad-looking man, with the face of an astute old cat: a wide, curling mouth, a small nose, green eyes beneath thick black eyebrows. He was not alone, he had his wife beside him – an austere, lean woman who did not speak but whose whole cold, reserved bearing seemed to be saying that she was only sitting at table with us out of pure conjugal duty. The chief had a voice that recalled the purring of a cat: soft,

melodious, of what one might call infinite courtesy; one felt that
nothing, not even death, would be able to affect that extraordinary urbanity. I confess that I am very greedy; so I did not take
more than very slight notice of him but devoted myself entirely
to the food which was excellent and to the very strong wine which
went straight to my head. The chief found my greediness very
attractive; in the end he insisted on my taking a second helping
of the ice cream with hot chocolate sauce. After dinner we went
to their flat, a penthouse in the old quarter of Rome; my husband, as usual, embarked on his well-planned campaign of
adulation; and I, perhaps because I had eaten and drunk too
much, fell asleep. When it grew late, my husband woke me up
and took me home. In the bedroom, as he undressed, he repeated
exultantly that the dinner had been a great success; that I had
made a conquest with the chief: had I not noticed how he looked
at me when he was sure that his wife was not looking at him?
He was so pleased that he was determined I should dance the
usual ballet of joy with him. As he made me twist and turn about
the room, I reflected that I had a very good husband as far as
his career was concerned. Meanwhile, however, as he clasped
my naked body against his own, equally naked, I again discovered a new defect in him: a paunch. Not much of it, it is
true; but, like his backside, repugnant on account of a sort of
delicate softness.

During the following days my conquest of the chief continued
to make progress. After each telephone conversation my husband
repeated that he was decidedly interested in me and that without doubt I had made a great impression upon him. He was now
asking about me every time my husband telephoned to him; he
actually went so far as to ask questions about my painting. My
husband told me that he possessed a fine collection of modern
pictures. After a moment's reflection he added: 'Wouldn't you
like him to buy one of your pictures, one of these days?'

Now if there is one thing that is certain, for me, it is that I
have no talent and that my pictures are worth nothing. An ad-
venturous adolescence spent in night-clubs and painters' studios

has left me with a slightly haunting desire to paint; but I paint for myself, more or less in order to have something to do. And so, when my husband told me that one of these days the chief might buy a picture from me, all I did was to shrug my shoulders. But at the same time I gave him a furtive look and then ... didn't I notice, as usual for the first time, that his legs are crooked, in the sense that his calves are turned outwards and his knees inwards?

Then, unexpectedly, my husband became nervous, gloomy, irritable, melancholy. One day, as he was on the point of going out, he explained the reason for his change of humour: things were not going so well with regard to the foreign job; there were difficulties; what was needed was another little stimulus. What stimulus? He repeated: 'Stimulus', and went out.

Left alone, I started to think. As I have already said, I had had a lot of experience, from the age of fourteen (I had my first man at that age) to the age of twenty. The fact of going to bed with a man seemed to me neither important nor difficult. Besides, in this case, was not my husband's future at stake? And so?

I did not think about it for very long. I telephoned to the chief. I told him I had heard he was interested in my painting. I told him I was alone in the house. I told him that, if he wished, he might even come and look at my pictures at once. He agreed, as though taking the pretext seriously, without surprise and without irony; whereas for some reason I expected that he would say something intimate and conspiratorial such as, for instance: 'But isn't there a chance that your husband might come in at the critical moment?' Thenceforth everything happened in the manner foreseen, except that at what I may call the supreme moment I started laughing at seeing him so courteous and distant all the time; and I said to him: 'Even when you're making love, don't you forget how well-bred you are?' Later, however, when he said good-bye to me, I could not help reminding him, with loyal frankness, of the foreign post for my husband. He gave me a brusque look, just like a cat that appears to be asleep and yet, at some noise or other, opens its eyes wide. This was a matter of a moment; then he smiled at me, gave me a little tap on the cheek and went away.

When my husband came home I wondered whether I ought to tell him what had happened; and I decided not to. After all, he had not asked me in any way to do what I had done : it had been on my own initiative. Besides, if I told him, there was a risk that, out of pride, he might refuse the job; and then all the effort I had made that afternoon would be rendered useless. So I said nothing to him. He gave me a kiss on the forehead and then went straight to the telephone : he wanted to speak to the chief, as he did every day. My heart was now beating fast because I thought that the other man would announce that the post had been assigned to him; and I was afraid that, at the news, he would burst out into one of his usual intolerable joy-dances.

Luckily the chief was not there. After almost a month my husband announced to me that, at last, he had got the job he had so much wanted. Once again I recognized the perfect good breeding of the chief; he was paying me but with some delay, in such a way that he allowed me to deceive myself into thinking, if I so wished, that I had not been paid.

Now I am here in London, in a flat that is fairly large but old, and with the special feature of having no connecting passage. Thus, to go from one room to another, one has to pass through other rooms : there is no other way. This arrangement of rooms, which prevents one ever being isolated, has recently given rise to a strange relationship with my husband. He comes and goes and cannot help passing through the room in which I happen to be; consequently I make incredible efforts not to look at him because, absurdly, he is now repulsive to me – the whole of him, from head to foot. Either I become absorbed in the book I am reading, or in my painting, or in the food I am cooking. If I can, I run away the moment he comes in. On one occasion I actually shut myself up in a wardrobe; another time I hid under a sofa. Of course we do not make love any longer : I have told him I am

G*

expecting a baby. But what will happen when he discovers that I am not pregnant? How, in fact, can I manage to overcome this absurd repugnance that I feel for his physical defects for which he, obviously, is not to blame?

# The Black Swan

಄

I like exhausting, strenuous sports which demand vigour, endurance and effort. I like an open-air life, with burning sun and numbing frost. I like nature and her seasons, all of them beautiful, and the passing of the seasons which is felt in the blood even before it is visible in outward things. Crowded city streets, so extrovert and communicative, to me say nothing; I prefer the dumb, insignificant solitude of the countryside, where things live on their own account, introverted and silent, from dawn to sunset, asking for nothing, not even to be looked at. Have you ever noticed that, whereas in the city everything – lights, traffic, passers-by – constitutes an appeal, a spectacle, publicity; in the country, on the other hand, a cyclamen plant, growing in the depths of a grey hedge of brambles, is not to be seen, in spite of the vivid colour of its flowers, unless one looks closely or actually throws oneself on one's knees in the dust of the pathway?

With regard to this open-air life my father, a rich, widowed lawyer whose only and deeply loved daughter I am, falling in with my taste for nature, recently bought for me a hunting lodge, formerly the property of a Roman prince, situated in the most rustic region of Latium, a short distance from a coal-black village whose houses climb up the sides of a great tufa rock. After signing the deed of purchase my father, giving me the keys of the lodge, gave me a pat on the cheek and said to me: 'The best investment of one's money is in something that serves to satisfy personal taste, to broaden individual character, to give expression to the most intimate inclinations. I have been fortunate in that your tastes and your character and your inclinations are all to be encouraged and promoted. You're a good girl, beautiful and, above all, healthy. D'you know what your aunt Giovanna said to me the other day? "Marta? When I see her with her clean face, her square shoulders, her long, strong legs, I feel quite comforted and once again I hope for a better world." '

My good Papa certainly could not have given me a more welcome present than this so-called hunting lodge which in any case is a two-storey villa with a dignified façade and a portico with columns. Here I devote myself passionately to 'doing things': cooking, cleaning, gardening, looking after chickens and dogs and horses. Françoise, a Swiss friend, keeps me company and helps me; she is a little too clinging and romantic for my taste, but is trustworthy and faithful. For instance we are now occupied in shoeing a horse. Françoise holds it by the bit; I have pulled up its foot and examine the hoof. All this happens on the gravelled open space in front of the villa. The horseshoes and the new nails, the hammer, the pincers and the other tools are spread out on the ground, black against the white gravel. The weather is grey, the cloudy sky threatening rain, a deliciously autumnal kind of weather. Françoise and I are both in riding-breeches with rough leather boots, I with a black sweater, she with a pink one. After having very carefully examined the hoof, I put out my hand to take up the pincers when I suddenly caught sight of the elderly manservant whom we have inherited from the former owners of the villa, as he appeared at the front door. 'Excellency, you're wanted on the telephone.'

I was cheerful, as always when I am in the country; I said to the manservant: 'Don't call me Excellency; I'm not a Roman princess, I'm just an ordinary person,' and I ran at once across the open space towards the door. I rushed into the ground-floor drawing-room. It was almost in darkness, in spite of its four big windows; there was not a single piece of furniture there; in the half-darkness one could just see the black lines of the beams in the ceiling and the brown chequer pattern of the earthenware tiles on the floor. The telephone was there, on the stone shelf of the mantelpiece. I took up the receiver and, at the sound of the voice that spoke to me, I remained for a moment breathless, like an idiot, my heart in a tumult. Finally I managed to overcome my confusion and said : 'Very well, I'll come at once'; I put back the receiver and ran out again on to the gravel.

Françoise was still there, her blonde head half hidden by the horse's neck, and looking at me with her anxious grey eyes. I announced to her in a falsely offhand manner : 'Look, I've got to go to the village. I'll be out for a couple of hours. We'll shoe the horse tomorrow.'

There it was; and Françoise was on the point of making the usual sentimental-moralistic scene; I guessed it from the sorrowful perplexity that suddenly filled her lofty white brow with furrows of anxiety. 'It's that man ?' she said.

'Yes, it's him.'

'Don't go.'

'Why shouldn't I go ?'

'You're a criminal and an idiot.'

I listened to her insults, mentally approving them : this was exactly what I thought of myself. 'You're right,' I said, 'but I'm going just the same.'

'You're aware of what you're doing, you realize the whole position; you know what you're doing and in spite of that you do it. So what's the point of being conscious of it ?'

'I ask myself that, too. Probably it's too strong for me.'

This was a commonplace, I know; but it was the truth. 'And so,' said Françoise, 'in order to stop you, I should have to be stronger than the thing that's too strong for you.'

'Put it like that, then.'

She looked at me, from behind the horse, with eyes that were suddenly dilated with an expression of challenge. 'I *will* be stronger,' she said. 'Look here : if you go, I'll kill myself.'

Bored, I answered : 'Possibly you don't realize that you often talk like a character in a comic-strip cartoon. You know perfectly well that you won't do it. Besides, why raise a relationship like ours, one of pure friendship, on to such a passionate plane? We're friends; but if you interpret friendship in this way, it would be better for you to pack your bags and go away.'

My words, and above all my tone of voice, petrified her. She stayed motionless, her hand on the horse's bit, looking at me. I added, sharply : 'I'm going now. Please take the horse back to the stable.'

I turned my back on her, went to the garage, at the far end of the open space, where I keep a small utility car and a big motor-bicycle. I hesitated; to go over rough roads, the motor-bicycle was more suitable than the car; however, on the other hand, to let myself be seen in the village with the motor-bicycle and, into the bargain, with a man on the pillion, was imprudent. So I got into the car, backed out and turned and went off down the drive. I saw Françoise walking in a melancholy way, leading the horse by the bridle. Greeting her cheerfully, I passed her and went out on to the main road.

A few minutes later I was below the rock-perched village, on the by-pass road, in front of the petrol pump, at the place appointed. Athletic, and, in his rustic way, elegant, he was standing at a short distance from the car, with folded arms and eyes elsewhere, and he did not move. I had to open the door and call to him : 'Why, what are you doing? Come on, get in, what's the matter with you?' Then he made up his mind, walked slowly towards the car, got in and said, in a tone of sulky reproach : 'You've kept me waiting.'

It was not true, I had been punctual; but this was one of his ways of making himself felt, of getting over his intense inferiority complex. I said nothing; driving with one hand only, with the other I extracted from the dashboard a packet done up in white tissue-paper and held together by two elastic bands. It was very heavy; I threw it on to his knees. He seized hold of it greedily, took off the elastic bands, undid the tissue-paper with his big, fumbling peasant's fingers. A black, flat pistol appeared, by no means very small and with a long, massive butt. 'It's an unusual calibre, it seems; I had great trouble in finding it. Besides, it was expensive; if I had known, I wouldn't have promised it to you. And anyhow, what use is it to you?'

He was doing up the packet again; then he put it in the pocket of his corduroy jacket and said sententiously: 'It'll do.'

'But be kind enough to tell me what use it can be to you, since you're just a common countrified thief, robbing uninhabited villas at night.'

For want of arguments, he observed: 'Now, as usual, you're insulting me.'

'I'm telling the simple truth. Aren't you just an ordinary stealer of chickens?'

'If you think so, why d'you go with me?'

'Because I like to.'

'And why d'you like to?'

'Ugh! Because I do. Well, tell me how it went yesterday evening.'

'I went with Augusto to that American couple's villa. But we found almost nothing. Augusto took an old saddle, I took a big box of cigarettes.'

'You're a couple of idiots. I told you not to go to the Americans. You ought to go to that family from the Parioli neighbourhood – what are they called? – who have the villa a short distance from the Americans. There you'd find some stuff. Idiots, that's what you are!'

'But what have you got against the Parioli people? What have they done to you?'

'Ah, that's just it, what have they done to me?'

He was stupid, thick-headed, massive, with centuries of peasant life behind him; but perhaps it was just because of that that I felt myself attracted to him. We reached the usual narrow lane.

I turned so sharply that he fell on top of me; then I moved forward amongst the branches of the shrubs which knocked against my windscreen. How long did we stay in the bushes? An hour, perhaps. When we came out, as usual I was furiously angry with myself and avoided looking at him as I drove. Then, on the main road, he put out his hand and tried timidly to stroke my cheek. At once I snarled at him : 'Hands off !'

'Why, what's the matter?'

'The matter is that you disgust me, d'you see?'

'Now you're insulting me again.'

'You see we're at the fork in the road, it's only a kilometre to the village. Get out here.'

'But I . . .'

'Get out; otherwise I'll go to the village and deposit you with the police. Like that, they won't have the trouble of going and arresting you at home.'

The threat had its effect; he got out, still grumbling that I insulted him. Impetuously I made a half-turn on the road and went back at full speed to the villa. The fear now occurred to me that Françoise had really tried to commit suicide : with a comic-strip mentality one can never tell what may happen. But it was not so. When I went into my room, I found her lying on my bed, flat on her back with her hands clasped at the back of her neck. Sitting down on the bed, I said to her : 'By the way, weren't you going to kill yourself?'

Instead of answering me, she took my hand. Once again, spitefully, I said : 'Hands off !'

She withdrew her hand, stared at me with pathetic grey eyes and then declaimed, in a subdued fashion : 'Do you remember when we met, in Geneva? You were walking by yourself along beside the lake; you stopped, leant against the parapet and looked at the swans. There was a group of white swans and one single black one. Then I went up to you and said in a low voice : "You are like that black swan. You are the different one, the only one, the unique one." '

Intolerable comic-strip sentimentality! I did not answer her.

## The Black Swan

Mechanically I raised my eyes to the window and then suddenly I felt relieved as if by something true and genuine amongst so much falseness. It was, in fact, raining – at last! Violent, pale, the rain streaked the window-panes which were now darkened by the autumn twilight.

# Psycho-Analysis Square

༄

I do not wish to tell you where I live; you will very soon see why. I can, however, indicate the quarter, in fact I must, otherwise certain details of my story will not be intelligible. Well then, I live in the EUR district, in the most spacious and deserted part of that deserted and spacious quarter. My house, constructed entirely of cement, glass and metal, looks out upon a vast square of smooth, grey, desolate asphalt. The streets and squares in the area all have very suggestive names: Literature Avenue, Avenue of Art, Avenue of Humanism, Sculpture Avenue, Avenue of Roman Civilization, Poetry Square. Let us suppose that I live in Psycho-Analysis Square. I say, let us suppose; for there is no question that a square of that name exists; the EUR is, in fact, a quarter that was built under Fascism and it is well known that Fascism, both repressed and repressive, did not love psycho-analysis. Nevertheless it would give me pleasure to live in a square of that name, if only because I have a doctor's degree in psycho-analysis and I receive every day at fixed times, as you can read on the brass name-plate on the door.

It was to psycho-analysis that I clung during the longest vigil of my life. I was sitting at my desk in front of the typewriter; the pistol which I had grasped shortly before with such force that it had left its imprint in my palm, lay beside the ashtray full of cigarette butts; and I was struggling to finish an essay on which I had been working for nearly a year. The essay was centred round the following idea: 'Sigmund Freud has projected the light of reason into interior life. Where before there was darkness, he has erected a well-lit stage on which the same play is always acted, always by the same actors: the Id, the Ego and the Super-ego. But round this stage, clear and visible as it is, the darkness is thicker than ever.' I wrote with an effort but with desperate determination, tapping on the keys with two fingers only. Every now and then I would rise, go to the window and look down into the square; and I saw that the body was still there, lying face downwards, the arms above the head. I went to the window at half past two, at three, at half past three, at four. Cars must certainly have gone past, even though it was night; but no one had stopped, everyone thinking of a fatal accident and fearing it might be attributed to him. At five o'clock the body was still in the middle of the square, and my essay was not finished. Then I got up from the desk and lay down on the couch upon which my patients usually place themselves. I should have liked to sleep. Instead of which I began reconstructing, almost mechanically, the story of my relationship with Giacinto, the man lying dead down there in the square. Why did I do this? Certainly not from nostalgia, nor yet from horror. For I did not understand it and I wanted to get to understand it.

In the beginning there was the scornful smile. In Giacinto's broad, flat face with its slightly oblique eyes, this mocking, disgusted sneer, as it were of perpetual nausea, was striking because it did not seem an essential part of him: Giacinto, in fact, was not disgusted by anything and the mocking smile was there even when he was asleep. But why did this sneering look attract me? This is where one enters into the incomprehensible: it was because, for me at any rate, it stood to indicate the kind of person who commonly goes under the name of scoundrel. I might have said 'criminal' but then I should not have been able to proceed from Giacinto to myself. Giacinto was a scoundrel; and I, consciously even if incomprehensibly, had wished, by making him my lover, to become nothing less than a scoundrel myself.

There is no need to tell how and where I met Giacinto. Let us suppose it was in a bar and that he, after an understanding glance, came out after me and got into my car and sat down beside me at the moment when I was starting the engine. After that first time, I took to seeing him in my own home, always late at night. He used to remain with certain companions, or rather accomplices, of his until midnight or later, in some café or restaurant; then he would come and see me, after telephoning. I would wait for him standing by the window; he would leave his car, with careful precaution, in a street not far off and would come on foot across the deserted, dimly lit square in the direction of my home. As soon as I saw him I held myself ready to press the button of the entrance door. What feeling did I have when I distinguished him at the far side of the square, recognizable by his small stature and the disproportionate width of his shoulders? A profound excitement which made me hold my breath, and at the same time a hatred of myself.

Afterwards, everything went forward in a habitual and almost ritual manner, at the same time with impatience and a fury of the senses. Giacinto, in reality, was a very boring scoundrel. He always did and said the same things; he was sententious, full of good sense, logical and down-to-earth. If it had not been for that mocking smile which had fascinated me, I could have believed I was making love with any ordinary lower-middle-class man, commonplace and normal in every possible way. But this normality on his part, instead of reassuring me, frightened me. As I looked at him lying on the bed with his bare chest outside the covers, smoking and talking, I reflected that, to create a scoundrel of that kind, so quiet, so solid, in fact so like his opposite, centuries and centuries of criminal life must be needed, criminal life of what may be called a positive sort, indissolubly bound, that is, to the so-called eternal values of the family. A far cry, indeed, from psycho-analysis! Psycho-analysing Giacinto, the living champion of archaic immorality, would have been like psycho-analysing the sculptured married couples on Etruscan tombs or the callipygous statuettes of Malta. And I, with my Viennese science, faced with his Mediterranean refractoriness, felt myself as powerless as a workman armed with a small scalpel and faced with a block of concrete.

Talking of this and that, as they say, but preferably about shops (he actually had two of them, one, of motor accessories, managed by his brother, and one of hosiery, run by his wife), smoking exactly three cigarettes and drinking, from time to time, lemonade with sugar, Giacinto would stay with me for a couple of hours, then leave me to go to his 'other' woman. For he 'protected', as it is called, a prostitute of the name of Valeria who 'worked' for him every night in an avenue of the suburbs. Was Valeria the only one who passed on her hard-won gains to him, or were there others? I wouldn't know; in any case he had spoken to me only of Valeria, perhaps just because she sought to be something more to him than a mere object – in fact, she rebelled, giving him, according to his own expression, continual 'displeasures', so that some time or other, he concluded thoughtfully, he would be forced to 'teach her a lesson'. I would listen to him, stupefied as I listened, trying to understand why I went on seeing him and always running up against the same obscure, obtuse incomprehension. Then he would stub out the third cigarette, dress himself and go off to pick up Valeria. I would place myself at the window again and watch him in astonishment as he crossed the wide deserted square with hurried steps. Then, without a thought of any kind, satisfied in body and empty in mind, I would go and sleep.

One day I got into my car and drove quickly to the suburban avenue where I knew that Valeria was in action every night. Arrived there, I slowed down, looking at the women standing there, each one in front of her own small fire, against the background of the huge trunks of the plane-trees. I recognized Valeria at once: a small blonde, with a tall mass of hair on her forehead, blue eyes, a square face, a highly developed bosom and very narrow hips. I stopped, signed to her with my hand and she replied to me with a gesture of denial: she thought I was a lesbian. I persisted, pronouncing her name; then she moved, majestically, in spite of her small stature, on account of that crest of hair and also of a kind of haughtiness in her bearing. She put her head in at the window and asked me how in the world I knew her name. I did not know what to say; I had come to that street on an impulse which, like everything that concerned Giacinto, was obscure and incomprehensible; I mumbled that I was a sociologist and was making an enquiry into prostitution, and wouldn't she come to my house? I would pay her, she would not be wasting her time. She stared at me for a long time with her deep-set, penetrating eyes; then she said she consented, we agreed on the fee and the day, and then I went away.

The appointment was for Saturday, the presumed day of her monthly disorder, during which she would not be working. On Friday I opened the newspaper and in the local news read a headline that aroused my curiosity: I looked down and saw a picture of Valeria. Then I read the item of news. She had been found in the boot of a car, dead, tied up in such a way that she had very slowly strangled herself. I hurried to see the details, but of Giacinto there was not a shadow. However it was to be supposed that Valeria had tried to rebel and had been killed in that cruel manner as a warning to any other woman who might seek to follow her example.

What I did after that morning was perhaps the least comprehensible thing about this incomprehensible story. I went on seeing Giacinto and meanwhile got him to explain the working of the pistol that he always carried in an inside pocket of his jacket. I told him that I was frightened at night in those streets that were so wide and deserted and that I wanted to apply for a licence to carry arms. He approved of this without hesitation: it was true, there were groups of hooligans going about who attacked solitary women; I would do well to be armed, in fact he took it upon himself to give me a pistol, not the one he had which was too big for me but a smaller one, a lady's pistol. So, a few days later, he brought me a pistol, explained its mechanism to me and himself undertook the slipping of a bullet into the breech. Someone perhaps may wonder whether Giacinto commented in any way on Valeria's horrifying end. Yes, he did comment. He said, sententiously as usual : 'She was a strange girl. She was bound to end like that.'

One night he telephoned to me that he was coming; so I placed myself at the window, grasping the pistol in my fist with spasmodic violence. Then he appeared at the far side of the square and made his way, small and broad-shouldered, towards my house. All at once, from a rectangle of black shadow projected on to the asphalt by a completely black and unlighted building, there suddenly issued, with lightning speed, a dark car which rushed at Giacinto and rammed him in the back. I saw Giacinto make a leap into the air with his arms stretched forward like a diver throwing himself into the water from the bank; then the car passed over him, went off, and Giacinto's body was lying face downwards, motionless, with the arms stretched above the head. Meanwhile the car had reached the far end of the square. But there it was now, coming back, still at the same violent speed; again it passed over Giacinto's body, then it turned the corner and disappeared. All this lasted only a moment but was imprinted for ever on my memory, owing to its bewildering intensity like that of a film scene glimpsed for one single intense instant by the stroboscopic method.

So that was that. At this point in my recalling of the incident, I looked at the clock and saw that it was half past eight. I got off the couch, went to the window, slowly pulled up the roller-blind. Brilliant sunshine, darting its rays from a tangle of dark, ragged clouds, dazzled me. I looked down to the square; there was a certain coming and going of employees on the way to their offices; the body was no longer there. I thought I saw a police van down there, in the very place from which the homicidal car had started. Then, involuntarily, I reflected that, amongst the many disadvantages of city life, there was, nevertheless, the advantage of the services: any sort of object that obstructed the traffic or in any way disturbed order, was promptly removed. Then I closed the windows and went to bed.

# The Discovery of Discoveries

❦

I was eighteen, and was studying for my school-leaving exams;
I was the daughter of a poor minor civil servant and was so
serious and well conducted that I did not even know I was
beautiful. In the street men would turn round to look at me; and
I would turn round too, not to look at the men, however, but at
the women's clothes, comparing them with my own, studying
the colour, the design, the cut, calculating the cost. The fact of
not having it in my power to dress as I should have liked, had
finally aroused in me a kind of mythological obsession based on
the wardrobe, by which a jacket or a pair of trousers ceased to
be mere articles of clothing and became symbols of freedom and
happiness, rather like the blue of the sky to a prisoner who sees
it between prison bars.

One day I stopped in front of the window of a fashion shop
in which a certain skirt that I had noticed and admired for some
time was displayed. Then in turn a man stopped behind me and
started looking at me with the same fascinated longing with
which I was looking at the skirt. Then his desire for me came into
contact with my desire for the skirt and caused an explosive short

circuit, so to speak, of a sudden twinge of consciousness. To my surprise I all at once found myself thinking: 'I want the skirt and he wants me. Therefore, he ought to buy me in order that I may then be able to buy the skirt.'

No sooner had I had this thought than the man came up to me and, speaking in a normal voice so that a couple of people nearby heard him and turned to look at us, said: 'A lovely skirt, isn't it? If you like it, we'll go in and I'll make you a present of it.' I twisted round a little and saw a young man, slightly corpulent, with a crafty, free-and-easy look, and, almost without thinking, I answered in a voice loud enough for the people who were listening to hear: 'Agreed! Let's go in.' So we went into the shop, I indicated the skirt to the assistant, and the man, as soon as the parcel was ready, went, like a good father or a kind husband, to the cash-desk and paid.

His office was only a short distance from the shop; in the lift and then in his flat he continued to behave like a rather heedless and casual old friend. I put down the parcel with the skirt in it on the desk and began, without hurrying, to undress; he meanwhile was coming and going, doing various things in his natural, evasive way. Finally he threw a red-and-green checked tartan rug on the mattressed leather sofa, and we made love. Immediately afterwards there was an insistent ringing of the telephone in an adjoining room; he went out, stark naked, in great haste, and I was left alone.

Then suddenly I had a feeling of elation which was at the same time one of astonishment and almost of incredulity, the feeling of someone who has made an important discovery. Do not smile, do not laugh at me: at eighteen, without ever having thought of it before, in the midst of a life spent between school and my family, in complete innocence, I had made the discovery of that extremely ancient, extremely well-known and extremely ordinary thing known as prostitution. Indeed I had discovered that I possessed something which cost me nothing and for which men, on the other hand, were ready to pay a correct price. But above all I had discovered that the whole operation of, so to

speak, sale and purchase could take place on a serenely con-
tractual plane, owing to which I could put it in action with
absolute tranquillity. This thought filled me with joy. Dressed
only in my tights, I started to dance in the middle of the room,
repeating like a refrain : 'Is that all? Is that all? But is it really
true? Is that all?' My purchaser (of the skirt? of me? of both?)
at this moment came back into the room and was astonished by
this joyful outburst which he did not know to what to attribute.
I explained to him that it was an explosion of physical well-being
and he believed it; I finished dressing, we exchanged an affectionate kiss, just like two old friends, and I went away.

Do not enquire how I behaved after my first initiation into the
oldest profession in the world. All you need to know is that, in
one way or another, either directly like the first time, or through
mediations that were not disinterested, I managed, over a couple
of years, to buy myself all the clothes which, as time went on, I
desired. Please note that I did it only for clothes; otherwise I
went on leading my usual life, between the university where I
studied zealously and profitably and the home in which I lived
with my parents and three brothers. Incidentally, I had also
become engaged, to a boy who was studying the same subject as
I. I loved him and he loved me; but I still went on, all the time,
acquiring clothes in my usual way. Certainly I would have
stopped prostituting myself if fashion had no longer fascinated
me so much. However it continued to be an obsession with me,
in a profound, obscure manner, as though before me there had
been entire generations of women in my family who for centuries
had been forced to wear rags.

The 'Is that all?' worked, as I have said, for a couple of years;
then, unexpectedly, I discovered that I was pregnant. So my
fiancé and I decided to bring forward the marriage which, previously, we had put off till the day when he would have achieved
what is called a 'position'. And then, as the day of the wedding
approached, I developed a fixation upon a certain knitted jacket
of unbleached wool with big pockets and metal buttons which
had been for some time in the window of a shop in the town

centre. It was an ordinary sort of garment; but, as usual, since I was not in a position to acquire it, it had become a symbol and a fetish. I thought of it by day, I dreamed of it by night; all of a sudden I actually feared that, if I did not buy it, the baby would be born with a birthmark of unbleached wool in some part of its body or even, perhaps, with the entire jacket imprinted in miniature on its cheek. And so, not seeing any other way of procuring it for myself, I decided to have recourse to my usual practice of prostitution.

However, at this juncture there arose one of those questions which, on account of their ambiguity and subtlety, have come to be called 'nice' points. This is how it was: I should earn the money for the jacket *before* the wedding; but the jacket itself I would not inaugurate until *after* the wedding, during the trip that I should be making with my husband to the southern province where he had been born. Now I had solemnly sworn to myself that, once I was married, I would cease to prostitute myself. Why this oath? Fundamentally, for no reason at all. Perhaps because I thought that, with a husband, a child and a house to occupy me, clothes would cease, once and for all, to occupy my mind. But in the meantime the 'nice' point persisted. Would the jacket cause me to violate my oath or would it not?

One day I went to a goldsmith's shop to buy the two wedding rings that my husband and I would exchange in church. It was a small shop, evidently one that was managed by a single family; there was an elderly woman, and there was a girl of about my age who greatly resembled her and who must have been her daughter. The latter, at that moment, was displaying to a customer, with a strange look of endurance, a tray of black velvet laden with rings adorned with real precious stones, such as sapphires, rubies, emeralds and diamonds. I asked the mother to show me some wedding rings and meanwhile was looking idly at the tray of rings, and then it came into my mind that just one of those rings, even sold off below cost, would suffice to solve the problem of my so-called 'nice' point and perhaps even some minor questions of the same kind. What was happening to me? Suddenly I had the same feeling of exaltation and astonishment at trespassing into the new and unknown that had been aroused in me, two years before, by the unforeseen discovery of the quite obvious and hackneyed act of prostitution. Again this time I discovered something extremely ancient, extremely well-known, extremely ordinary which nevertheless had, for me, the freshness and light of absolute novelty : theft. How was it that I had not thought of it before? Is it really true then that the most hidden things are the most visible, the things which, so to speak, are right under our noses?

Now the customer went away without buying anything and the daughter accompanied her to the door. At the same moment the mother turned her back on me in order to open some drawer or other. I promptly took a ruby ring from the tray and put in its place a small valueless ring of my own which I had just taken off in order to try on the wedding ring. I slipped the valuable ring on to my finger and started to put on my glove again. Then I said I had not found what I was looking for and went out.

Once I was in the street I went into a doorway, took the ring from my finger and slid it down between my tights and my skin : it slipped down, pulled by its own weight, and came to a stop below my belly, just where my baby will emerge when he is born. Sure, now, that I had got away with it, I started feverishly repeating as I walked : 'Is that all? Is that all? But is it really true? It that all?'—when suddenly, I felt myself seized by the elbow. I turned; it was the elderly woman from the shop, her grey hair flying loose, her face distorted as she said to me, breathlessly : 'The ring, there's a ring missing, the ring with the ruby.'

Without letting my agitation be seen, I went back with her to the shop. We went in, and I protested in a forceful tone of voice, showing my hands devoid of rings, turning my bag upside down on the counter. The mother, distressed and persistent, went on repeating : 'I don't know anything, I only know that this ring here – you took it off to try on the genuine one. I noticed it because it is a cheap ring with an imitation stone, which I had never seen before. I noticed it, I say, and now the ring is here in place of mine.' The daughter, for her part, said nothing; she looked at me fixedly, in a curious penetrating fashion and was silent. Then finally she came to a decision and suggested to her mother : 'I would like to say something to the signorina, alone. Would you mind coming in here with me?' So saying, she made a sign to me and I followed her into the back room.

She closed the door, then said to me gently : 'I saw you take the ring. I showed the customer to the door, then turned and saw you. But I didn't tell my mother. I wouldn't have told her in any case; it was she who noticed it.'

I was astonished, and asked her : 'Why wouldn't you have told her in any case?'

She smiled and replied : 'Let us say that I don't get on well with my mother. Let us say that I act as assistant here in the shop because I have to. Let us say, finally, that I've discovered that what counts in life is not ruby rings.'

'You've discovered that?'

'Yes, I've discovered that; what is there strange about it? At our age it happens that we make such discoveries, don't you think so? But now, give me back the ring. Take it out from where you put it and give it back to me. I'll find some excuse for my mother.'

I no longer persisted. I slipped in my hand under my tights and fished out the ring from below my belly which was already a little swollen with motherhood. She took it, opened the door, made a movement as if to stoop and pick up something and exclaimed : 'Why look, Mother, it was here on the floor.' I took advantage of the mother's delight to slip away out of the shop.

In the street, I again had the feeling of having made a discovery. But this time the discovery was concerned with the fact of making discoveries. I had made a discovery, the girl in the shop had made another quite different one, even though it was of a thing just as well-known, as ancient and as ordinary. But what a lot of discoveries in one single day!